SMOKE

AND

KEY

KELSEY SUTTON

Entangled Publishing, LLC
2614 South Timberline Road
Suite 105
Fort Collins, CO 80525
rights@entangledpublishing.com

Entangled Teen is an imprint of Entangled Publishing, LLC.

Visit our website at www.entangledpublishing.com.

Edited by Stacy Abrams and Judi Lauren
Cover design by Stefanie Saw and Bree Archer
Cover images by saemilee/Getty Images and kuschelirmel.deviantart.com
Interior design by Heather Howland

Print ISBN 978-1-640636-002
Ebook ISBN 978-1-640636-019

Manufactured in the United States of America

First Edition April 2019

10 9 8 7 6 5 4 3 2 1

an imprint of Entangled Publishing LLC

*At long last, I dedicate a book to my partner,
Jordan. Through life and death, I will love you.*

CHAPTER ONE

A voice penetrates the silence.

At first, it's just a string of syllables without meaning. I float in the unending darkness, disoriented and drowsy. The voice calls to me again. Frowning, I try to concentrate. When it comes a third time, I finally understand some of what it's saying. *Wake up.*

My eyes fly open.

Darkness surrounds me. The voice reaches out a fourth time, still muffled but easier to comprehend now. *Please wake up*, it's pleading. At last I try to answer; the only sound that emerges from my throat is an odd grunt. The beginnings of hysteria stir within me. *All right,* I think. *Be logical. Find out where you are.*

Slowly, I work out that I'm lying down. Whatever is against my back and shoulders is plush and foul smelling. I lift my hands, blinking, and touch a smooth ceiling. What is this place? How did I come to be here?

I strain to hear the voice, but it's gone. Now confusion

gives way to fear and my hands become fists. I shove at the ceiling—it doesn't move. A frenzy overtakes me as I begin hitting it. The grunt has progressed to a hoarse shout. Wherever I am is so quiet, so still that I know I'm alone. Panic burns through my veins and I attempt to roll over in the tiny space, kicking and clawing. Then someone screams, *"Let me out!"*

It takes a moment to recognize that it's my own voice, weak and rough. Suddenly a new sound vibrates through the stillness, a thundering *crack*.

Then I'm falling.

Air rushes past me. Acting on instinct, I spread my limbs out in a wild attempt to save myself, but there's nothing to latch onto. Faint lights shine below. I blink, too shocked to scream again. The ground—or whatever awaits at the bottom—approaches rapidly. I glance backward and see long hair and a skirt flapping like a sheet in the wind.

There's no time to notice anything else; I'm seconds away from the ground. Somehow I think through the panic and curl up into a ball to brace for impact. I do so just in time, and as I crash down, the entire world trembles. Earth billows up around me, and a shock goes through my limbs. There's not as much pain as there should be, though, only a slight disturbance on the skin and bones I landed on.

Trembling, I open one eye and watch the dust settle. A thousand questions churn in my mind as I uncurl and look around.

"Hello? Is s-someone there?" I manage to whisper. The words shake so badly even I can hardly understand them. I'm sitting in what appears to be a narrow alley. Everything is dirt, even the walls on either side. Lit torches appear sporadically, giving this frightening place an orange tint. The small flames sputter every few seconds, and it's the only sound I detect around me. A faint musty smell fills my nose. I push myself up on unsteady legs and turn in a circle, searching for anything familiar or living. I cup my elbows to protect myself from terror rather than cold.

"Hello?" I call again, louder this time.

There's movement out of the corner of my eye and I spin toward it. A face peers around the edge of the doorway. One of the torches is directly above it, casting flickering shadows over the little girl's face. I recoil instinctively, gasping, and the girl vanishes back into the house-like structure made entirely of earth.

But it's too late. I saw her. I saw the way her eye dangled from its socket and how her skin was half withered away.

I retreat until my back hits the wall behind me. *This is a dream,* I think faintly. So I squeeze my eyes shut and will myself to wake up. Nothing changes, though. Intending to run from this place and the appalling girl, I slide away from the wall and into the path.

"She won't hurt you. Doll's afraid of her own shadow," a voice drones.

I let out a small cry and stagger back yet again. This time my heel catches on something and I land hard on my bottom. I frantically search for the speaker. The words came from another doorway, one opposite where I spotted the young girl. No one else appears, though, and it takes several attempts to speak again. "Who's there?" I squeak.

Seconds pass. Then the same voice answers, "No one."

His tone is so reasonable, so indifferent, that I'm able to gather my thoughts. Perhaps this person can help me? Swallowing, I strain to see in the gloom. "If n-no one's there, then how are you talking to me?" I challenge, finding a bit of courage.

"Perhaps you're talking to yourself."

Instead of responding, I get to my feet. I dare to step closer, and when nothing leaps out or attacks, I take another. There *is* someone beyond the threshold—the light is just enough that I can make out the details of his appearance. It's a boy.

He sits in a wooden chair, bent forward, wrists dangling atop his knees. Between two of his fingers is a single, unlit cigar. The holder containing it is lovely, shining white like a pearl, the edges adorned with carvings. As for the boy himself, his features are hidden, but I can see a shock of blue-black hair against the back of his neck and curling over his ear. His profile is lithe and... sad, somehow.

"Who are you?" I whisper, stopping again.

The boy doesn't react. "Weren't you listening?" he asks without glancing up, as though he's carrying on a conversation with the dirt. His accent is distinctly American. "I'm no one. We're all no one."

"I'm someone," I say without thinking. It doesn't make any sense, because of course I am, but suddenly I need to prove it's true.

An odd sound escapes him, something that is more

bark than laugh. The edges of it are sharp and mocking. "Oh, really? Then what's your name?" Now his head tilts slightly in my direction, though not completely.

Curious, in spite of the alarming strangeness all around me, I fiddle with my skirts and resist the temptation to move even closer. "It's…" I begin, then trail off. This shouldn't be a difficult question. Yet I don't remember. It's a sensation similar to fumbling in the dark, reaching for an item that should've been there, and finding empty air. How can I not know my own name? Everything has a name. I can tell him what the oceans and continents of the world are called, so why can't I recall that one word that defines the entirety of my being?

The boy lets me struggle for a few seconds. "See?" He doesn't sound smug, just resigned. He still doesn't turn. I want him to *see* me, to say that this is a terrible nightmare. There's a bleak feeling spreading through my chest, a sinking sensation, because there can't possibly be any good answers to the question I'm about to ask.

"Where are we?"

The torch closest to us is dying. It makes a pathetic sound, and I'm so distracted by the dwindling flames that I almost don't hear the boy. "…one of those, are you? Need to have everything said out loud." I wait for him to go on, refusing to rise to the bait, and he sighs. He puts the cigar to his nose and takes a long inhale. "You're dead, darlin'. This isn't hell, but it's the next best thing."

"You're lying," I manage, frozen despite everything inside me urging me to *run*.

His shoulders lift in a careless shrug. "Wish I was."

"I think I would remember dying."

"Not in this place, you wouldn't. No one remembers anything here. Also, why don't you try finding a heartbeat? Go on. I'll wait."

My hands rise of their own volition. The skin they flatten against is cold. *Too cold*, I think numbly. I stand there, waiting, praying to sense that steady *thump, thump, thump*.

Nothing.

It feels like my lungs are swelling, horror trapping all the air and protests. In that instant, I realize I'm not breathing. The corset; it must be too tight. Disregarding rules of propriety, I reach behind me to undo the strings. The dress hinders every effort, but I stubbornly keep at it. When the stillness lingers too long, the boy finally looks at me. "You don't need to breathe…" he starts to say, impatience coloring the words. Our gazes clash.

Every thought I have vanishes. I nearly bolt again. The boy is pale…too pale for someone living. His eyes are a too-light shade of blue and his lips are nearly white. His shirt is buttoned up the front but open at the collar, revealing the raised tissue across his throat and the line of stitches closing it up.

No one would survive a wound like that.

A sound of terror escapes me as I retreat. The boy studies my face, and now there's obvious interest in his expression.

"Wait—" he starts.

I flee.

He says something else, but his words are overpowered by the roaring in my ears. There's no sign of the little girl as I burst out of the alleyway and into another. There are more doorways, more torches, more moving things in the darkness. It's a maze.

Mindless with terror, I sob and stumble along. "Help! Please, help! Anybody—"

My face slams into a wall.

No, not a wall. "What we 'ave 'ere?" a new, deep voice rumbles above my head. The brogue of someone who works in fields and has calluses on his hands. Fingers catch hold of me, huge and rough, and I scream as I try to yank free. The grip on my arms tightens as though I'm no stronger than a child. The man pins me with one hand and explores my face with his other—I'm so shocked that the next scream catches in my throat. An acrid smell assails every sense. Before I can look up or demand release, he continues. "Aye, dis is a new bake. Boys, come greet our latest arrival! Gracious, you're a juicy lassie."

Indignation shines through the terror fogging my mind. "Let *go* of me!" I finally snap, flattening my fists against the man's chest to put distance between us. I kick at his shins, and he chuckles. Torches approach from every side, held aloft by hands of all shapes and sizes. My gaze flicks over the people surrounding us, and colored spots mar my vision when I see the various states of decay they're in. Exposed tissue and gaping teeth and flapping skin.

I shriek yet again, a high and piercing sound. Then I happen to catch a glimpse of my captor's face, and I go mute with horror.

He might have been a man, once. But what I see now is purely a monster. His skin is charred and peeling, his scalp red and shining. The tips of his fingers and ears and nose are missing, and he has no eyes. Empty sockets leer down at me.

I open my mouth to scream again.

"Let her go, Splinter."

Through my terror, I recognize that voice—it's the boy with the unlit cigar. Several moments go by as I search for him in the crowd. Eventually I see his silhouette leaning against one of the dirt buildings close by, hands shoved in his pockets. That cigar dangles from his lips.

"An' if I don't?" the hideous Irishman snaps. Seconds tick by, thick with tension. The boy doesn't say a word; he just stares. Slowly, the steel grip around my middle relents. The man spits on the ground next to my foot. Or, at least, he tries to—nothing leaves his mouth. "Was just a bit o' fun. Not much else to do round 'ere." He stomps off.

Some of the creatures still eye me with curiosity. So much pale skin. So many dark eyes. My stomach quakes when I realize there's nowhere to run.

After another moment, the boy shoves off the wall, pocketing his cigar. The moment he approaches, the crowd begins to disperse, taking their torches with them. Like black iron, they meld with the darkness. One of them hesitates, though, and glances back at me. A man in rags who's less rotten than the others. The hair at his temples is a distinguished gray and there's a slight limp to his step. Our gazes meet for an instant, and then he's gone.

The boy reaches my side and touches my elbow. "Are you all right?"

It's too soon after being assaulted by that monster. I jerk away. "Don't touch me!"

He eases back and puts some distance between us.

"Are you all right?" he repeats carefully.

I push my hair out of my face, shaking so badly that there's no way to hide it. "Yes, I'm fine. Just fine." No matter how many times I say the words, they don't become true. He waits, giving me a chance to regain my composure. Eventually I can think again, and the need for answers intensifies. "You said this is hell?" I whisper, keeping my focus on the direction the creatures disappeared.

Now I believe it.

I can feel the boy looking at me as he answers. "Well, we call it Under."

At this, I frown. "Why—"

"Look up."

Obeying, I arch my neck back. Instead of sky, there's a ceiling, of sorts. More dirt and what appear to be tree roots. Scattered among these roots are splotches of shadow, though it's too far away to tell their purpose or origin. "What are those?"

"Those are the holes each of us fell through. Our graves are right over them."

The word *graves* jars something within me, and suddenly everything makes sense. Opening my eyes in that dark, soft space. The closeness of those smooth walls, the muffled noises above. Something cracking beneath me. Then soaring through open air and hitting the ground.

It was a grave. *My* grave.

He's telling the truth.

If I had any food in my stomach, it would be surging up right now.

Tearing away from the sight of those holes, I face the boy. I know I should thank him for saving me from

Splinter, but there are too many questions to ask. "So this is it? This is the afterlife?" My voice is faint. I want him to lie to me. I want him to tell me there's something more, something better. Whoever I was in life must have spent time in a church, because I find the thought of wooden pews and stained-glass windows comforting.

But he only shrugs again. "For some, I suppose. Judging from the size of the graveyard and the number of holes above us, there are many who don't fall."

"If that's true, why did we?"

"Who knows? Maybe it's unfinished business. Or it only takes a particularly loud noise. Or we're just too stupid to stay dead." He begins to walk, and after a brief hesitation, I hurry to follow. Splinter might come back, or some other creature from a nightmare, and this boy has proven to be an excellent protector. His long-legged strides make me break into a run to keep up. The space is so narrow that our arms brush.

Neither of us attempts conversation, and I realize this place isn't as quiet as it seemed in the beginning. There are sounds echoing through the giant cavern. A laugh, a hiss, a whisper. A reminder there are monsters here. How can I know that this boy isn't one of them? *He did save you,* a tiny voice reminds me.

Glancing at him sidelong, I find his profile is appealing. His eyelashes are long and dark. He has a generous mouth. Upon our first meeting, I remember with some shame, I'd been too horrified by the wound across his throat to notice anything else. "What's your name?" I blurt. He raises a thick brow at me, and I bite my lip. "I mean, what do they call you here?"

After a long moment, he murmurs, "Smoke."

I'm about to reply when I recognize where we are. We've reached the location where I fell; the indent my body made is in the dirt. There are the doorways where Doll peered out and I first encountered Smoke.

Now that I'm not running from something, there's more time to absorb this place. In every direction, there are crude houses of dirt with no spaces between them, as if the occupants were trying to create a city. There are no cobblestones or carriages, no trees or signs. Just passages that end in darkness and these earthen homes. But if I squint just so, it's easy to imagine a sky beyond the line of roofs, the faint colors of dawn.

Eventually I realize not all of the structures are the same—some of them have square openings next to the doorways, crude imitations of windows. Of course there's no glass, though. There must be torches inside a few of the dwellings, because shadows dance on the ground, cast by gentle flickers from within. In a way, it's almost comforting.

While I examine our surroundings, my eyes feeling so huge they might as well swallow the rest of my face, Smoke watches me. "You'll have to pick one of your own, you know," he says. "A name, I mean. Usually we just use whatever we fell into Under with. Splinter, Smoke, Doll."

Something we fell into Under with? Unconsciously, I run my hands over my stomach and sides and thighs, searching for any kind of pocket. His eyes track the movements, an odd tightness to his mouth. My hands halt and I wonder if it's possible for the dead to blush. But now I know there's nothing else on my person besides the dress.

No, wait.

For the first time, I notice a weight against my skin, near the center of my chest. I reach for it…and my fingers collide with something curved and hard. It hangs from a chain around my neck and glints gold in the firelight.

Smoke smiles, a ghost of what a smile should be. "Nice to meet you, Key. Welcome to Under."

CHAPTER TWO

I toss and turn, waiting for sleep to come. It doesn't. The silence is too alien; there should be crickets, owls, wind. Anything but this ringing in my ears. The ground is also miserable without a blanket and pillow.

Smoke left me in the alley hours ago, leaving no instructions besides, "You might as well choose one of these holes for yourself. That's what they're for. Just make sure no one else already has."

I was too timid to ask if he would accompany me, and he didn't offer. Even after he disappeared, I lingered outside his doorway, but eventually I went in search of a place to claim as my own. It was a frightening process, whispering into the shadows and hoping nothing whispered back. In one of the houses a voice rasped, "Take one step closer an' I'll rip yer 'ead off." I clumsily backed away, almost tripping over my own feet.

It was at that moment I spotted Doll in one of the passageways. She sat in a doorway, holding a lump of rags that wore a tiny dress and had buttons for eyes. She moved it this way and that, as though the doll were shopping for a hat—I envied her ability to pretend so easily. Guilt pricked my heart when I remembered recoiling upon our first meeting.

The child must've heard me approach, but she didn't acknowledge it. I knelt beside her, heedless of getting dirt on my dress. "I'm sorry for being scared before," I said softly, so as not to spook her. She didn't lift her head or respond, and I watched her play for a moment or two. Her movements were surprisingly graceful. "Smoke said your name is Doll? But then what do you call her?"

There was teasing in my voice—now she glanced up. Her single eye was brown and shone with intelligence. Someone had attempted to braid her hair, but the silky strands were coming loose. She looked badly in need of a mother or a friend.

Well, now she had one. I knew nothing about being a mother, even if I'd been one in life, but a person didn't need memories to know about friendship.

"All right, I'm off to find an empty house. Wish me luck." I resisted the urge to touch the top of her head as I stood. I walked away and felt her watch me go. Hopefully our conversation was a balm on whatever wounds my foolish reaction had caused the child.

Within minutes of this encounter, I did find an empty home. It was three doors down from Smoke's. With the silence still the only sound in my ears, clenching the key in a desperate fist, I pressed against the wall and slid down. For what felt like days, I sat there and tried to find a scrap of memory from a life before this. Frustration flooded me, threatening to drown everything, so I sought anything else to occupy my thoughts. Following some instinct, I used my free hand to explore every part of my body again. This time I discovered a bump on my temple and a wound on my back, clear indications of my demise.

My death had not been peaceful or natural.

Sensation suddenly radiated through my other palm, and I realized that I was once again gripping the key around my neck so tightly that the ridges were digging into my palm. The key. Why was this the single thing that accompanied me into the ground? Did it have any sort of meaning?

When I still came up with no answers, I gritted my teeth and tried to fall asleep. Unconsciousness, no matter how brief, would provide an escape from all this. I tried to ignore the fact that there were no stars above me—that it could very well be morning, for all I knew.

The only thing that does come is a girl. She peers into the dim at me. "Are you there?" she asks. Her voice is kind, instantly soothing. It feels as if I've been drowning and someone has clasped my hand to haul me out of the water.

"I'm here," I say, sitting upright. The words taste false on my tongue. *Am I here? Is any of this real?*

She takes a torch down and carries it inside, illuminating both her face and my new home. The single room is empty and cold—just like me.

I glance up at the girl. Despite the fact that she's dead, she's lovely. Her hair is dark and long, her skin pale and smooth. She wears what once was a fine gown, as blue as the sky neither of us will ever see again. While I stare, the girl kneels beside me. "Tintype told me there was a new arrival," she explains. A scent drifts past, a combination of death and…something else I can't name. Something pleasant.

The girl watches me fuss with my dress, which is wrinkled from lying down. "Oh, were you trying to sleep, dear?" she asks. "We can't, I'm afraid. Apparently our bodies no longer need rest. I'm surprised no one told you. That's why I'm here, actually—I thought you might have some questions. Many of us aren't exactly forthcoming in Under."

After what happened with Splinter, I'm wary of trusting any other person in this place, no matter how harmless they seem. Perhaps the girl senses my hesitation, because she smiles and says, "I'm Ribbon. Have you found a name yet?"

For what feels like the hundredth time, I wrap my hand around the chain against my chest. "Key."

"Key," she repeats, an odd note in the way she says it. Her gaze drops to my hand and an emotion flits across her lovely face. Sorrow?

Strangely protective of the single thing in my possession, I hold it tighter. Once more, Ribbon's gaze flicks down to take note of the movement. Swiftly she asks, "*Do* you have any questions?"

Questions. Yes, I have so many. Here in the darkness, I've had some time to think, and my confusion has only increased. One concern burns hotter than the rest. With a tentative waver in the words, I venture, "Is there any way to…return? To our graves, I mean?"

To heaven? I add silently.

Pursing her lips, the girl adjusts her hold on the

torch. "You want to be truly dead." She says it like a statement, not a question. I don't respond. I couldn't even if I wanted to because of the ball of shame and hope and fear expanding in my throat, and after a moment, she shakes her head. "No, there is no return. Once you've fallen, you must remain here. You can't move on and you can't go back." There is pity and regret in her voice now. Maybe I'm not the only one who doesn't want this existence.

"It's not all bad, though," she adds, abruptly belying this last thought. "All of us have something to do down here. Collarino does his weekly sermons. Eye Patch and a few others are always digging out new houses. Spoon is trying to make a garden. A real challenge, mind you, since we don't get any sun. You just need to find something, see?"

I'm finally grasping the looming reality of it all. For the rest of eternity I will be trapped among these terrifying creatures and surrounded by dirt. Overwhelmed, I bury my face in my knees and wish I could cry. My voice is muffled when I demand, "Then what is the purpose of this? Why are we here? Did I commit a sin that made me unworthy?"

The flame crackles. "That is an answer every single person in Under searches for," Ribbon says. Without warning, she gathers her skirts and stands. I lift my head and watch her move to the doorway. "Come. I think you should meet someone."

I blink. "Who?"

She takes the light with her into the alley. When I don't move, Ribbon gestures encouragingly. In the open like that, more of her is illuminated. A blue piece of silk is woven through her hair. Longing for the warmth of the flame again, I get up and go to her.

Farther down the alley, someone ducks out of sight. Doll?

As we leave my house behind, Ribbon talks. About the others here, about the trick someone played on Collarino recently, about the new chapel they're digging out. Walking past the gaping doorways feels safer with her at my side. She leads the way with such assurance, never pausing once to determine which path to take. How does she know where to go? Everything looks the same down here.

Suddenly a tearing sound disrupts the stillness. Ribbon stumbles and utters a low oath; she's stepped on the hem of her skirt. She bends over, holding the light close to the ground, and peers at the damage with a critical eye. "Do you mind if we stop at my room?" she asks me, straightening. "I've a needle and thread for these sorts of occasions. One of the other girls lent it to me."

I muster a polite smile. "Not at all."

We change direction, and once again, Ribbon fills the silence with mindless chatter. After so much time alone, surrounded by just my thoughts, it's comforting. She doesn't seem to expect any response or input, for which I'm also grateful.

We meet others along the way. Ribbon greets every single one, her voice so warm, it's almost possible to forget the chill in the air. Most glance toward me with open curiosity, and fear fills my throat, trapping any words or hope of belonging. Though Ribbon makes courteous introductions, she keeps them brief, often taking my elbow to pull me along. It's as though she senses how unsteady I am.

Minutes later, she stops again and ducks inside one of the doorways. A warm light beckons within, and I hurry to follow, not wanting to be alone in the passageway.

Before I've entered the room completely, Ribbon has already begun repairing her skirt. I stand at the bottom of the steps, taking everything in. It's like something from a memory. On the left side of her home is a fireplace. A small flame crackles and flickers—close to dying—feeding on what looks like roots and bits of paper. It gives the space a cozy feel. Shelves have been dug into the earthen walls. There are a few books, but they're mostly full of various objects. If I squint just so, it would be entirely easy to forget that we're deep inside the earth.

I can't help but think she's brought me here on purpose.

"How long have you been here? In Under, I mean?" I ask, approaching the fire. Either its flames are too far gone or the dead can't feel much, because the warmth is barely more than a whisper against my skin. I try not to frown as I turn away.

Ribbon sits on a neatly-made bed. A stab of envy pierces me; where did she get a blanket? Oblivious, Ribbon moves a needle through the torn hem with such skill that I speculate whether she was a seamstress in life. "Oh, I stopped counting long ago," she replies. "Or trying to, that is. It's not exactly easy when there are no sunrises or sunsets."

She bites the end of the thread. I continue along the edges of the room and pause in front of the shelves. In the dim lighting, I spot a wooden box with surprisingly intricate carvings. "Were these things in your grave?"

"Gracious, no. There would've hardly been any room left for me!" Ribbon laughs. She finishes securing the new thread, puts the needle aside, and stands. Her feet make hardly a sound against the ground as she joins me. Her bright eyes peer at the items as though seeing them for the first time. "No, most of these things were gifts. From Doll, Boots, Handkerchief…"

There are so many. How has one girl inspired such adoration?

Rather than voice the question, I murmur something polite in response. We stand there for a few seconds in silence. Shadows flicker over the strange collection of gifts. After another moment, Ribbon hesitates. I'm not looking at her, but I feel it. "I could be your friend, too," she ventures.

My first reaction is relief. To have an ally, a rope in the darkness, would make Under a bit less terrifying. Then…suspicion. Though I know it's rude, I can't help but say, "Why would you want to be? You hardly know me. *I* hardly know me."

"Well, I have an instinct for this sort of thing." Ribbon pauses again. Out in the passageway, someone laughs. The earth swallows the sound whole. "And truth be told, I also wish someone had made the same offer after I fell."

Now I turn fully toward her. Ribbon's face is wistful, almost ethereal in the firelight. Guilt tugs at the cold thing lying in my chest. Here is another girl, like me, who's found herself in strange and frightening circumstances. If she can be brave enough to offer friendship, and strong enough to choose life, why can't I? "I'd like that," I say. My voice is soft, but in the stillness, it feels like another burst of noise.

Ribbon's smile is instant and radiant. She moves closer to link our arms—I'm so startled that I jump, but she pretends not to notice. "Very good. It's official, then. Shall we continue on our journey?"

"After you," I say, smiling back. We leave the shelves behind and make for the doorway. The stairs are too narrow for both of us to climb at the same time, so Ribbon releases me. I follow her outside, and she takes my arm once more, as though we truly are bosom friends. This time, I partake in the conversation as we walk. But part of my attention still goes to the twists and turns of our route.

I'm so preoccupied with trying to find a pattern in them that it takes me a few moments to realize Ribbon has stopped. A shadow falls over us, intricately shaped and larger than anything I have yet encountered. Following my new friend's gaze, I look up. The tower is made mostly of tree roots, with some boards nailed in here and there. Someone must live at the top, because brightness shines through the makeshift walls. Like a finger pointing toward the heavens.

"What is this place?" I breathe, awed by the unusual beauty of it.

Without answering, Ribbon leads me to an opening at the structure's base. The torchlight reveals a flight of winding stairs. How is this possible? Intrigued, I don't hesitate to trail after her when she begins to climb. It crosses my mind that if Ribbon isn't careful, the dry roots around us could catch fire. She doesn't seem worried, however, as we wind through the tower.

Eventually we come to a doorway. It opens into a wondrous room, larger than I thought it would be, full of items that I believed lost to me forever. Books and chairs and tables and trinkets and instruments. There is even a small painting hanging on the far wall. *Perhaps my future here isn't so bleak*, I think.

The owner of this tower—at least I assume he is, considering there's no one else around—has his back to us. He must hear us cross the threshold, because he throws some papers down in a fit of impatience. "I'm busy!" he shouts without looking in our direction, then bends and rummages through a different pile on the floor. Four torches hiss and spit from perches on the walls, and I'm relieved they are a safe distance from the kindling that would make this place an inferno.

Unperturbed, Ribbon loops her arm through mine and tugs me forward. "Key, I would like you to meet Journal."

"Damn it, Ribbon, I said I'm—" The words fade the moment he lifts his head and sees me.

He is a thin boy, a bit on the short side. His clothing is stained and worn, but not so old it's unraveling. Gray trousers hug his slim hips, which his shirt and waistcoat match. The collar and cravat beneath these are yellowed with age. Cuffs loosely circle his wrists. Dull shoes thud against the uneven floor and I spot an abandoned jacket nearby. His hair is neatly tied back and his eyes—as rich as tree bark after a rainstorm—pierce mine. His features are not handsome, but they're refined. If I had to make an assumption about Journal's previous life, it would be that he came from a family who dined on fine china and had servants to do their bidding.

The most notable detail about Journal, however, is the peculiar tint of color to his skin. It's a sorrowful blue-gray. At the moment of his death, he must have been ill.

When Ribbon makes the introduction between us, an instinct consumes my arms and legs to curtsy. But then our eyes meet, and I forget all about it. Something unexplained passes between us, this boy and me.

"How do y-you do?" I shift uncomfortably from the intensity of his attention.

At the sound of my voice, the boy gathers his composure. "Another one?" he asks, as if nothing happened. But he continues to drink in every detail of my appearance, tucking a stray strand of hair behind his ear. The simple movement is surprisingly graceful. "Extraordinary. And you are remarkably well preserved. You said your name is Key? Well, Key, would you mind helping me with a study I'm conducting? All you need to do is answer the following questions as best you can, and—"

"Journal, she only just got here," Ribbon interjects. "Let the poor girl be."

"Of course." He doesn't sound happy about it, though. "What can I do for you, ladies?" He begins to pick up the papers he scattered at our arrival.

"Key has some questions of her own, actually." Ribbon nudges me, her expression urging me to speak freely. I blink.

Something snags Journal's attention and he plops into the rickety chair by a table. This, too, is made out of roots. "Go on, go on," he says distractedly. I open my mouth to ask him where he found all these things, but one of the shadows shifts. Journal is still tinkering with something in front of him, but he sees how I go rigid. He twists around to look at the boy standing beside a stack of books. "Oh, don't worry about him. That's only Handkerchief. He hardly speaks, and he has no interests beyond myself and his ever-mysterious thoughts."

His words aren't reassuring; something about the other boy doesn't seem right. He's doughy in appearance, his expression devoid of emotion. His clothing is nondescript and colorless. So I'm not sure what it is that sounds alarms in my head.

I angle my body in such a way that I can see both him and Journal. What had I been about to ask? "No one remembers anything about their lives before?" I say, unable to recall but needing to fill the silence.

"Not a thing." Journal shoves away from the table and faces me. "I have a theory about that."

"He has a theory about everything," Ribbon whispers conspiratorially.

Ignoring this, Journal's countenance brightens with enthusiasm. He moves his hands as he continues. "Essentially, we are dead. Our bodies do not function as they once did, thus eliminating the need for nutrition or rest. The fact that you're blinking right now? You only do it because it feels natural, not because there's a need to. Our physical sensation is nearly nonexistent and we have no recollection of a time before Under. Yet we are moving, we are speaking, we are reacting. Our decomposition halts once we fall from the grave, though it takes some longer than others to wake up. Consequently, they are prone to more…gruesome deterioration.

"But that's not the point. I believe that, though there is no blood flow and no oxygen reaching the brain, a part of it is still active somehow. Just not the part that allows us to tap into our memories."

"Magic," Ribbon says.

The boy rolls his eyes. "Yes, to put it in blunt terms. A combination of magic and science. The fact that the ground and the casket give way only supports this idea."

My brow lowers as a contradiction in his explanation occurs to me. "Wait. If it's as simple as part of our brain operating, then how is it I know of the world but not the details of my own life? Aren't they all considered memories?"

A scowl twists Journal's features. "Every theory has its holes," he mutters. "We seem to come back with basic knowledge, though I'm not sure how our personal memories have been excluded. What I would do to get my hands on literature about the occult—" Before he can go on, he's interrupted by a bellow in the distance. The earth absorbs the sound but not the urgency of it. The boy gives Ribbon an expectant look.

"I suppose I had better go back." She sighs, turning to the stairs. Her skirt brushes against the wall. "They're probably ripping one another apart."

"That reminds me, Lint was looking for you. He needs his ear sewn back on again."

Ribbon cringes. "Bother. Would you like to accompany me, Key, or stay here and ask your questions?" She pauses with a hand on the edge of the doorway.

If I had a heartbeat, it would pound harder and faster

at the thought of being left alone with these strangers. But there's so much to learn about Under. "I…" When I see that Journal has all but forgotten me again, my anxiety lessens. I clear my throat. "I'll be fine here, thank you."

My new friend is either in too much of a hurry to hear the wobble in my voice or chooses to overlook it. "Very good. I'll find you once I've straightened those fools out."

With that, she leaves us. Her steps echo, and after she has exited the tower, silence hovers like a fog. I shift from foot to foot, trying not to look at Handkerchief or stare at Journal. He doesn't offer me a seat or attempt to start a conversation. It's obvious I am not welcome to stay. Even so, I'm reluctant to depart. What do I have to go back to, after all?

Smoke's face flits through my mind.

Journal has returned to his papers. I clear my throat to get his attention and to distract myself, as well. "If I may ask, how did you come by these things? The books and furniture?"

His reply is distant. He doesn't look up. "Tintype finds them. He brings whatever he thinks I'll have a use for."

"I see." *Perhaps I could ask Tintype for some things of my own*, I think. I may as well begin the process of getting settled and finding my place in Under. After all, if there were a way out, it would've been discovered by now. There seem to be no other alternatives.

Seconds tick past, and Journal seems wholly immersed in his work. I cast a wistful glance toward the books around his feet. The notion of returning to that dark hovel with no company besides my thoughts is nearly enough to break me. Taking a breath, I force myself to ask,

"Would it be possible... That is, would you mind terribly if I borrowed one of your books?"

Journal goes still. Once again I have his undivided attention, and as the moment stretches and thins, I realize his eyes are not simply brown; they also have flecks of green in them. "You can read?" he says finally.

I tilt my head, considering. "Yes." I have not turned a single page since waking in my grave, but I can see the words in my head. I understand them.

"Very few in Under have the ability. If you are willing, I would enjoy discussing the book with you once you've finished." Without waiting for my response, Journal squats to survey his titles. As the silence embraces us a second time, he caresses the spines. Finally he selects one and holds it out, a book bound with a beautiful indigo cover, like the deepest part of the sea. I smile with genuine pleasure.

As I take the book from Journal, our fingers brush. It's fleeting, almost inconsequential, yet he jerks away so abruptly that he bumps into the table. Items clink and clatter onto the floor.

"I'm s-sorry," I stammer, disarmed by his reaction. I backtrack hastily toward the doorway, and Journal stares at me with wide eyes.

Just then a sound comes from the doorway, a heel scraping against the floor. I turn, and something inside me stirs at the sight of Smoke. My grip on the book tightens. He barely spares me a glance, and in this light he's even paler than before, the wound across his throat starker.

Journal seems to recover; he rakes his hair away from his face and pulls at the bottom of his waistcoat. His voice is stiff as he says, "Smoke. It's been a long time since you've graced my tower with your presence. To what do we owe the honor?"

Smoke delivers the news flatly, as if he's talking about the weather. "There's been a murder."

CHAPTER THREE

Handkerchief leads the way, followed closely by the rest of us. As we weave through the passages, my mind buzzes with questions. Didn't Ribbon say death was impossible? How was the murder accomplished? Are the rest of us in danger?

I gather an unnecessary breath several times, about to put voice to my confusion, but it feels as though talking isn't allowed. The only sounds we make are our shoes shuffling through the dirt. Then suddenly, another sound reaches my ears: a high hum. The closer we get, the louder it becomes, until I realize that it's not a hum at all but a chorus of voices. We round a corner, and the narrow alley falls away into an open area full of the dead.

"We call this the town square," Journal informs me in a clipped tone; his eyes are on what's happening before us. Their square isn't much, just an open space surrounded by more dirt houses. It's the size of a small field and ablaze with torches, which cast eerie flickers over the faces in the crowd.

I long to press close to Smoke. Despite his detached manner, I'm drawn to him like stars to sky. Drawn to the safe feeling he gives me. Instead I squash the urge and cast my gaze in all directions, searching for Splinter. None of the faces are familiar until I spot Doll, sitting in the dirt and playing with her toy again. The girl is so small that I worry someone will trample her. Just as I'm about to approach, a man steps onto something that brings him a head higher than the crowd, and everyone turns in his direction. The din becomes a hush.

"I'm sure you're very frightened," he begins, the words calm and measured. He's impeccably dressed. His hair is white and half his face sags. I can see the man's teeth through his rotted skin, and an involuntary shiver goes down my spine. I remind myself that his appearance should have nothing to do with how he's perceived. "An incident like this has never happened in Under before. But I want to assure you that—"

"'Incident'?" a voice repeats from the throng. "You mean murder. His tongue was ripped out, for goodness' sake."

"It isn't murder if the person is already dead," someone else protests.

Now another man steps up, fierce-looking with his eye patch. Even before he opens his mouth, I know he was the one who first spoke out. "I refuse to waste time on logistics," he snarls. "Something must be done. Immediately. We can't twiddle our thumbs and allow a killer to walk through our midst, cookin' us like sides of beef."

"What is 'logistics'?" a person in front of me whispers. But the words don't sink in; my mind is lingering on what the man just said. Trying to understand. *Cookin' us.* What does that mean, exactly?

"What do ye suggest we do, then?" another yells.

It's chaos. The shouts begin anew, and this time the man with the white hair is unable to maintain order. Some clamor for a culprit while others insist it is God's will that we should succumb to death once again. A fight breaks out in the center, but there's so much happening around it that I can't see anything. Where is Doll? I move to look for her, but a hand seizes my arm, stopping me. I look up and find Smoke's fathomless eyes burning into mine. "It's not safe here," he says, his lips touching my ear. The skin there suddenly feels hot. "Go."

Without watching to see if I obey, he plunges into the fray. One man gets a glimpse of Smoke's face. It must be fearsome, because the man quickly withdraws from the fight.

Tempting as it is, my conscience won't allow me to hide. Doll is just a child. So in spite of the fear churning in my stomach, I move into an empty alley and try to locate her. Eventually I spot both the girl and Ribbon—they stand on the sidelines next to a large woman, pressing their backs to one of the houses. Their expressions are tight and anxious. Keeping to the outskirts of the madness, I ease my way toward them.

I haven't taken two steps when a woman with red hair goes flying past and crashes into a wall. Dust billows and dirt crumbles. She snarls, pushes herself up, and dives back into the fight. Terror makes my stomach heave as I hurry on, and Ribbon catches sight of me. "I can't believe they brought you here!" she hisses, wrapping a protective arm around my shoulders. Unafraid, Doll peers up at me with her dirty face. I manage to wink at her before turning my attention back to the fray. "This is not what Under is normally like, Key. You've just arrived at the most inopportune time possible."

It's difficult to hear Ribbon's words, even if I weren't already distracted by Smoke. Every line of his body is elegant, and my fear is overpowered by admiration. He stands in the middle of the bedlam, feet firmly planted, movements certain as he ducks and swings.

He makes me think of lightning, a sight to behold and striking where he wishes.

Though Smoke doesn't have the advantage of bulk or width on these people, anyone he hits finds their senses and abandons the fight. He is regarded with wariness and begrudging respect, and soon there aren't many left in the square.

"We think he may have been a boxer when he was alive," Ribbon murmurs to me. She, too, is enraptured. I notice that Doll is gone.

The one-eyed man who demanded justice lingers. "You think you're stronger than me, boy?" he spits at Smoke. He raises his beefy fists, and if it had been me facing his formidable size, I surely would have cowered. But Smoke is unflinching and silent. He waits. This seems to enrage the man even more, and he runs at Smoke with a shout. In the space of a blink, Smoke is somewhere else, a taunting smile curving his lips. The man tries to check himself but stumbles. Like a bull, he turns, rumbling and hulking.

It happens so fast that I almost miss it. One moment the man is thundering toward Smoke and the next the boy sidesteps him and lashes out. The man's flesh and bone must be soft from his time in the grave — or Smoke is stronger than he looks — because he rips his opponent's arm off as easily as one might tear the wings off a fly. The man loses balance, swinging the arm he has left in a wild attempt to remain upright. Moments later he crashes to the ground.

There is no pain in his countenance, only more rage. "Damn you! Damn you!" he screams, clutching the stump. Old blood stains his fingers.

"I will not hesitate to take the other one," Smoke says lightly.

Onlookers shift uneasily and whisper to one another. It's obvious from the man's flaring nostrils that he's considering another round. Whatever he sees in Smoke's face, though, ends this train of thought. Wordlessly, he fetches his arm and slinks into the darkness. And at last Smoke is the only one remaining.

"Anyone else want to have a go?" he asks, his muscles tense and coiled like a snake's. He looks more alive than anyone else here.

Beside me, Ribbon mutters under her breath. I catch snippets like *fool* and *reckless*. The woman on her left snickers.

A moment later, the white-haired man emerges from the shadows. His expression is indignant. "We may be dead, but we are not barbarians, sir," he sputters. "The aim was to have a civilized discourse!"

Smoke's eyes gleam. "Do you consider burning

someone to a crisp civilized?"

"Of course not!"

"Then I suggest you adjust your way of thinking, Pocket Watch, or you won't survive much longer here. Something tells me this is only the beginning." Smoke ignores whatever Pocket Watch says next and walks away, silent as my pulse and swift as my fall into Under. As he passes, our gazes meet. A frown pulls the corners of his generous mouth down, and it feels as though my heart stumbles. He couldn't possibly think I'm responsible for this murder, could he?

Just before Smoke disappears completely, I watch him produce that now-familiar cigar. He glances back, and our gazes meet once more in an instant of heat and uncertainty. Then he steps into the darkness and disappears.

I glance around again and see that nearly everyone is gone. Neither Journal nor Handkerchief stayed.

"This must be the new arrival," a deep voice observes. Expecting a man, I raise my gaze and can't hide my surprise when I see it's the heavyset woman who's spoken. I didn't get a chance to look at her before, but now I see that she's dressed in a greasy apron and homespun gown. Peering at me from the pocket of that apron is a short wooden spoon. A cap adorns her head, yellowed with age, and it does little to contain the hair that's coming undone. There's a gap between her two front teeth.

This woman must have died of some sort of sickness, as well, because there is a tint to her skin similar to Journal's. The revelation makes me wonder. Did everyone in Under die within days of one another? Though we seem to fall from our graves at various dates, the clothing and the way we carry ourselves marks everyone as being of a certain time. But the causes of death are so different…

"Spoon, this is Key," Ribbon says, gesturing between the two of us.

I force a smile. "It's a pleasure."

In response, the woman laughs and slaps her thigh. "Oh, would you listen to that, now? Talking prettier than a princess, I would say. Did she fall with a crown and some diamonds, as well?"

"Stop your teasing; can't you see she's terrified?" Ribbon chides.

I'm not, though. Not anymore. Watching Smoke awoke something within me. It feels like there's a thought or image hovering at the back of my mind, just out of reach, like a feather riding a wisp of air. I stand there, frowning, trying again and again to grasp it.

In a misguided attempt to comfort, Ribbon clasps my hand; the touch startles me back into the present. She and Spoon are talking about the murder. There's a mixture of worry and excitement in the way they recount how one of the others discovered the remains. I suppose in a place such as this, where hardly anything happens, a grisly occurrence like murder would be thrilling. But as Spoon goes on to describe the condition of the corpse in excruciating detail, I long for a distraction.

"Good thing we don't feel much pain, because Eye Patch was right—poor soul looked like a chicken that stayed too long in the oven," the woman says in a hushed tone.

Feeling eyes on me, I scan the crowd. My gaze clashes with that of the man from earlier, who was slower than the others to leave when Smoke rescued me from Splinter. This time I notice the uniform he's wearing. He was a soldier? For an instant, I entertain the idea of going up to him and demanding why he stares so. But it's as if the man hears my thoughts, because—despite the limp—he hurriedly turns and vanishes into an alleyway. It seems he has no interest in talking to anyone. Still, something about him nudges at my mind, like a forgotten task or an old song.

"Who was that?" I ask Ribbon, interrupting. "The man in the uniform?"

Ribbon opens her mouth to answer, and Spoon murmurs something in her ear before moving away. The large woman squats next to Doll, who has returned and discovered a finger in the dirt.

"He's called Tintype," Ribbon says once we're alone. "He's the only one of us who was buried with a picture. He showed Doll once. It was a woman; I think she must have been his wife." She lowers her voice. "He also has an unusual talent for finding things. He procured half of the effects in Journal's tower. No one knows how he does it. Maybe he digs through the dirt somehow? He barely shows his face, though, let alone answer us when we ask him questions."

It's not much more than Journal said. But there's another pressing matter that's been weighing on me from almost the moment Smoke first mentioned the murder. Steeling myself, I clutch the key around my neck. The solid coolness of it is strangely comforting. "Ribbon... you told me there was no way to die. Truly die, I mean."

To my surprise, she shows no shame. Instead, the

girl just shrugs as if it's nothing. "I lied. We can endure anything up to being chopped to pieces, but we can't survive fire. A man committed suicide that way, once. His name was Undertaker. He was quite mad, I think. I didn't want to tell you because the notion of you taking a torch to yourself was unacceptable. No matter how distressing you find our situation."

She speaks so matter-of-factly that I find it difficult to argue. I decide not to pursue the matter. Now I ask, curious in spite of myself, "Who was killed today?"

"See for yourself," Spoon says. She nods at something over my shoulder.

Frowning, I turn. There, across the square and resting in the shadow of a house, is a black lump. There's a sensation within me like my heart dropping, too far and too fast. The body has been reduced to bones and ashes, probably unrecognizable even to those who knew him best. Only the sheer size of it gives him away.

Splinter.

Ribbon is called away again. I barely hear her murmur an excuse, hardly register the sound of her footsteps padding away into the darkness. I stay where I am, gaping at the remains of the creature who took so much enjoyment in frightening me when I first arrived. Was he killed because of that incident? But who would care enough to go to such trouble? Thoughts and theories and questions are a whirlwind in my mind, scattering everything so none of it connects or makes sense. Above all, however, is one realization, ringing like a high, pure bell.

I don't want to die.

Because Splinter, however terrible he was, is truly dead. He will never speak again, never open his eyes again, never walk the passages again. Whatever I am is different from that thing lying on the ground.

From a vast distance, I hear Spoon speaking. Grateful to have something else to focus on, I find my voice. "Why didn't he call for help?" I ask her faintly. Splinter may have terrorized me, but no one deserves to perish like that.

"Didn't you hear us talking about it earlier? Someone cut out his tongue just before they killed him; we found it in the dirt. Only part of him that wasn't burned." The old cook watches me shudder. "Yes, I suppose it's a bit ghastly. You need a distraction, you do. Let's find Ribbon."

"Where is she?" I allow her to take hold of my elbow and pull me along.

"I've an inkling. Are you ready for your true initiation into Under, girl?"

Uncertain how to answer, I follow her ample form through the labyrinth. Once again the noise grows, and a doorway appears on our left with light pouring out of it. Without pausing, Spoon ducks inside, and I hurry to follow.

Just past the threshold, I falter in surprise. The room is a sort of…tavern. Crude chairs and tables have been constructed out of the same materials as Journal's tower. There's a long, counter-like object at the far end, complete with stools and cups.

Spoon is waiting for a reaction and grins at my questioning look. "When it rains aboveground, some of the water drips down. We have cups set up everywhere to catch it. Can't digest anything, of course, but it's nice to feel something sloshing around in your gut."

I shake my head. "I don't understand. Why do you bother, if you can't—"

"Because we do what we can to feel alive, silly thing. You'll do the same once you've been here a while." She pats my shoulder and leaves my side to join a group sitting in the corner. Opposite the bar is an area free of furniture, with a lit torch on the wall behind it that gives the impression of a stage. Also supporting this assumption is the fact that a man with a fiddle stands in the center, adjusting some rusty-looking strings. His beard is full of maggots.

Averting my eyes to hide a sudden wave of queasiness, I spot Ribbon talking to a girl at one of the tables. Other than Spoon, she's the only one I know. I walk over to them, smoothing a wrinkle in my skirt.

"Key!" Ribbon chirps in greeting, glancing up. "Have you met Shilling?"

There are already so many faces and names crowding my memory, but I resolve to remember this one, too. The girl must have fallen shortly after she was buried, because there is hardly any decomposition in her features. Her hair is dark and her body slender but subtly muscled. She is wearing a simple, faded gown of brown cotton and her looks are plain but not unbecoming. Murmuring a polite response, I seat myself when no invitation is forthcoming.

As I study Shilling, the fiddler lifts his instrument

and begins to play. While everyone watches him, I sweep my gaze over the listening crowd, noting their wistful expressions. It's strange to think that only minutes ago they were an incensed swarm. "Isn't anything going to be done about the murder?" I ask Ribbon.

Spoon—playing the part of barmaid, apparently—hears me as she passes by and mutters, "Hush. Listen to Fiddle, girl."

Frowning, I twist in my seat. Fiddle closes his eyes as he draws the bow over the strings. It has a slightly off-tune sound, and I'd guess it's because of the crack running through the wood. It must have happened when he fell.

My attention returns to the other people sitting in their chairs. A group of men is playing a game of cards. One of them tosses his head back and laughs. A woman wears an expression of contentment as she mends a shirt. Two children toss a ball between them, calling out jokes and taunts. It all seems so…ordinary. If they can find happiness, if they can have a place here, why can't I?

A jolt goes through me; I realize suddenly that Smoke and I are staring at each other across the room. In the dimness, his blue eyes are darker, even more closed off. But that doesn't change the fact that he's looking back at me. *Maybe there's one more thing to stay for*, a voice whispers.

Smoke looks away first, wearing a troubled expression. I drop my gaze, too, feeling as though I've been rejected somehow. "I'm going back to my room," I say to Ribbon quietly as I push my chair back. The legs screech along the floor, drawing attention to us. If I can't find an escape in sleep, perhaps I can do it within the pages of a novel.

She nods and starts to rise, as well. "No one should

wander the pathways alone. Let me just—"

A shadow falls over the table. "I'll walk her back, Ribbon. I'm heading that direction anyhow." Smoke offers his arm. Surprised—and perhaps a little pleased—I take it with a tremulous smile. We go to the door, and Ribbon watches us leave with an expression I can't discern. Worry? Curiosity?

A moment later we step into the open, and it seems as though there should be a change in light or temperature. But there's only more dirt and flames. Smoke guides me down one of the alleyways and into another, his strides casual and confident.

I'm painfully aware of where my hand rests on his sleeve, the contact sending a strange and restless feeling through me. Pulling free, I clasp my hands and clear my throat. The only sound in the stillness is the rustling of my skirt. "I never thanked you, by the way. For helping me upon my arrival when Splinter…"

"Don't mention it." He shoves his hands in his pockets and quickens his pace. "Is it to your liking? Under, that is."

"I'm not sure," I answer honestly, struggling to keep up. "I like the people. Ribbon, Spoon, Doll."

"Are they the only ones you like?"

If there'd been any moving blood in my veins, I would've blushed. The corners of Smoke's eyes crinkle with amusement. Seeing that, something mischievous steals over me. "No, of course not," I say. "I also think Pocket Watch is perfectly pleasant."

Smoke makes a coughing sound that's partly surprise, partly laughter. "I shall try to be more pleasant in the future, then," he manages. As I construct a response, there's movement out of the corner of my eye, a small flash, and I glance downward. Smoke is twirling the cigar between his fingers. His expression hasn't changed, and I don't think he's even aware he took it out of his pocket.

"Why don't you light it?" I ask impulsively.

Smoke's brow lowers. He follows my gaze and understanding flits across his face. He shoves the cigar back into his trousers. "Not sure, really," he answers with a shrug. "I suppose I've been waiting for the right moment."

I tilt my head. "What constitutes the 'right moment'?"

"Well, I'll know when it happens, won't I?" he counters. There's a playful glint in his eye as he says it, though, and my stomach flutters in response.

"And why aren't you called Cigar?" I ask next, genuinely curious.

Smoke snorts. "Because I said if anyone called me that, I'd send them back to the grave."

We walk in silence for a bit, and now there's an amiable feeling to it. I know it won't last, though; there's another question I must ask. Another question that has haunted me since the moment I first realized whose body lay in the town square. I wait until we reach the doorway of my darkened house. Then, taking a breath I don't need, I plunge in. "Smoke, did you kill Splinter?"

I don't know what I expected. Indignation, perhaps, or guilt. Instead his lips curve into a smile. "Couldn't I ask the same?" Smoke counters, a glint in his eye. So he *had* been wondering if I was responsible. While I fumble over a response—no words or denial will emerge, and all I can manage is an odd sort of croak—he plucks one of the torches free of its perch and presents it to me with a mocking bow.

"Thank you," I manage, taking it. Our fingers brush for the first time. Just as Journal did in his tower, Smoke reacts strangely. He stiffens and the light in his eyes goes out. "Smoke?"

He doesn't respond or react. I say his name again and, when he still doesn't speak, I hesitantly reach out and touch his arm. This seems to jolt Smoke back to the present. He blinks rapidly and focuses on me. If possible, he seems paler. His eyes are so wide I can see the white around those blue irises. Before I can ask anything further, Smoke turns his back and hurries to his own place down the alley.

Sighing, I bring the torch inside with me. I tilt it close to the dirt wall, searching for something to place the handle in.

The light illuminates all the rocks and crevices, drawing my attention to the strange shadows on that uneven surface. No, not shadows. The instant I realize what I'm seeing, I cry out and nearly drop the flame in my hand.

A few moments pass, then I swallow and force myself to move toward it again. The handwriting is nearly illegible—as if the writer was either ill-educated or in a hurry—but the message is still clear. I read it over and over, wondering what it means. If it's true.

I remember you.

CHAPTER FOUR

I sit with my back to the wall, ignoring the dying flame of the torch, and stare at those words so hard my eyes should hurt. As if there is something I am not seeing, as if there is more to those etchings in the dirt than what appears. *I remember you.*

There aren't many who could've left this message; Journal mentioned that most in Under don't know how to write. But why wouldn't the messenger speak to me directly? Why the secrecy?

Soon enough, Ribbon stops by and urges me to come out. She hovers in the doorway, angled in such a way that the words are not within her line of sight. "It'll do you good to spend time with others, don't you think?" she asks.

My grip tightens on my knees. I meet the girl's gaze reluctantly. "You're so kind. I just can't right now, Ribbon. I need to think."

"Think about what?"

For a moment, I consider not telling her. A lie would

be simpler. Easier. But Ribbon has done nothing to deserve my mistrust. "I'm trying to remember something. From before," I say.

Pity swells in Ribbon's eyes. "That's impossible, Key."

You're wrong, I think. Apparently it *is* possible, if someone else has done it. But I don't want to say this out loud, and eventually, the other girl drifts away. The instant she's gone, I refocus on the message. My insides feel loose. Twitchy. Hours pass in the dim and the sensation doesn't subside.

"What is this?" someone asks. I startle at the sound of Smoke's voice and jerk toward it. My latest visitor stands in the doorway—no, somehow he's already leaning against it—looking at me with something like disappointment in his eyes.

I bristle at that look. "I beg your pardon?"

"Are you waiting for death to claim you?" he clarifies, tilting his head. The movement makes his hair glint in the faint light. "Hate to remind you, darlin', but that's already been taken care of."

It's a strange feeling, wishing someone would go away and wanting them to stay all at once. "No, I'm not," I tell him curtly. Smoke doesn't question me further; he pushes away from the wall, shoves his hands into his pockets, and saunters inside without invitation. Dirt shifts beneath his shoes. He stands in the middle of the room and studies the walls and the ground. I haven't done anything to make it my own, so there's nothing to see. A moment later, Smoke fixes his piercing gaze on me. Something inside me shivers.

For an instant, we just stare at each other. I don't know

what to say, but his presence is a welcome distraction. I'm about to open my mouth and blurt something, anything, when Smoke draws nearer and lowers himself to the ground. He stretches one long leg along my right side and brings the other to his chest. His foot nearly touches my hip, and I pretend to be unaffected by the sudden proximity. "Would you like to see some magic?" he asks. Now the torch illuminates only one half of his face, the other cast into darkness.

I'm so preoccupied with the planes and angles of Smoke's face that his question takes an extra moment to reach me. Though I know it's impossible, my face feels hot. "M-magic?"

In response, Smoke runs his hand along the ground and gathers a fistful of dirt. I try not to stare at the way his eyelashes cast intricate shadows over his skin. When Smoke meets my gaze again, his expression is so grave that a flutter of apprehension goes through me. "I shall make this dirt completely disappear," he says. "Prepare yourself. Many a lady has fainted from the shock of this feat."

The apprehension evaporates. I don't know whether to roll my eyes or nod. Instead, a faint snort escapes me. Smoke ignores me and holds his other hand out. He touches the side of his fist to the open palm, slowly, and raises it again. He does this three times. Then, in one smooth motion, he tosses the dirt behind him and presents his empty hand to me. "See? Gone," he declares.

There's an instant of silence. Then I burst out laughing.

The magician just watches me. Within moments, Doll peers around the edge of the doorway, her dirty face etched with curiosity. "You'd…you'd best show her your trick," I manage. For the first time since falling into Under, I'm grateful I don't need to breathe.

Smoke raises his brows at the child. "Is that true, young miss? Would you like to see my magic?"

Her eye is huge as she nods. But Smoke doesn't move to do the trick; he twists his lips in thought. "Let's make a bargain," he suggests. "If you let me wash your face with the water Spoon has saved up, I'll show you some magic."

Her small nose scrunches as she considers his proposition. Eventually Doll nods again, albeit with obvious reluctance. Smoke gets to his feet. The girl's hand is already stretched out, waiting for him to take it, as if they've done this a thousand times. His fingers curl around hers, a tenderness in the way he does it. Before they round the corner and disappear from sight, Smoke turns to give me a look. "Just remember. You can't kill what's already dead."

My voice is dry. "Thank you for such a lovely reminder."

I'm still smiling when the two of them depart. Once the sound of their voices fades, I refocus on the dirt wall across from me. This time, it takes my mind a while to return to the riddle of Under. Eventually, deep in thought, my hand creeps up to the key. Once again I injure myself holding it so relentlessly, pressing the ridges too deeply into my palm.

There must've been a reason I was buried with it; most of the others seemed to be left with books, clothing, toys, tokens. Keys unlock things, don't they?

A strange and urgent feeling seizes me, and I get on

my hands and knees. With the tip of my finger, I begin to
create shapes in the dirt. Some of them are meaningless,
but some almost seem familiar.

Another sound comes from the alleyway, a heavy
footstep. I jerk upright, forgetting all the words and
shapes. The silence seems to tremble from the force of my
fear. It can't be Ribbon, Smoke, or Doll—they would've
announced themselves in some way. "Who's there?" I
call after a minute or so, trying to hide the quiver in my
voice. Unbidden, an image comes to me of Splinter's
blackened body. I hear Spoon's voice telling me how his
tongue was cut out so he could not scream. Apprehension
burns through my veins with all the force of an electric
current, and it seems bizarre that it doesn't start my heart
up again. I muster the courage to call out a second time.
Just as I begin to, my third visitor shuffles forward and
the light creeps over his face. "Oh, Handkerchief," I say
with relief. The feeling is short-lived when I remember
how disconcerting I find this boy, Journal's apprentice.

The boy's countenance is the same as it was before—
pasty and bland. He doesn't bother with pleasantries. "I
came to deliver this," he mumbles. He holds a book out to
me. "Journal thought you might've finished the other one."

Startled, I take it automatically, stroking the ridges of
the pages with my thumb, and a thrill goes through me.
"Why, thank you."

But Handkerchief is not listening; he's studying the
lines I've drawn at his feet. There are more than I realized,
because he slowly turns around and looks at all of them.
There is a lantern, a book, a dog. Then he takes notice
of the message on the wall. I don't expect Handkerchief

to make any sort of remark—*he hardly speaks*, Journal had said—so I'm taken aback yet again when he tells me, "You're not like the others who've fallen."

I blink. "What do you mean?"

His eyes meet mine, and even now there is no spark of emotion within those depths. He is entirely fact and purpose. "Everyone has accepted this place and what we are. They don't question the rules. They might've asked some things their first day, but after that, they let it go. Yet you sit in this room, drawing in the dirt and still looking thoughtful."

Hesitating, I shake my head. There is little point in hiding my suspicions, as he has already seen everything. "I'm afraid I must disagree with you, Handkerchief. I'm not the only one who is trying to remember."

The writing on the wall is proof of that. Someone out there knows more. Much more.

There is a pause as Handkerchief absorbs this. He raises his brows, and despite that being a universal gesture of interest, it still seems false on him. "Really? Do you think so?"

"Yes." I finally get to my feet, clumsily adjusting my skirt so my shift doesn't show. "I also believe we're wrong in assuming we have no memories."

Handkerchief tilts his head to the side slightly, like a curious bird. "What have you discovered?"

I find it odd that he's chosen not to acknowledge the message behind him. I'm on the verge of mentioning it myself when more of Journal's words echo through my consciousness. *You can read? Very few in Under have the ability*. But wouldn't Journal have taught him how to do so? Frowning, I decide to follow my instincts again and refrain from revealing too much. "Nothing in particular," I say, hoping Handkerchief didn't take note of the silence between his question and my answer.

His face gives nothing away as he turns to go without responding. Just when he reaches the doorway, though, he stops. For the third time during our brief conversation, the boy called Handkerchief surprises me. "Be careful, miss," he advises, glancing back. "Seems to me nothing good can come of the past. We ended up here for a reason."

He's quicker than he looks and vanishes before I can say anything else.

Taking two steps back, I hit the wall and slide down until I'm sitting again. At the same moment my bottom touches the ground, the torch quakes as though taking its last gasp. It goes out and the darkness closes in. Wishing I had left with Handkerchief or listened to Ribbon, I silently command myself to get up and find the alleyway. But before I can obey, a wave of nausea crashes over me. I sit there, helpless against it.

As the awful sensation begins to ebb, a hand grasps mine. I'm about to shriek when I realize it's *warm*. I make a quieter sound of shock. "Handkerchief, how—" I start, thinking he came back.

But it's not Handkerchief.

This person is wearing a pale nightgown and holds a candle. Wax oozes down the slender column of white.

I raise my eyes slowly. The tiny flame is not enough to illuminate anything above the hollow of the girl's throat, but her voice is low and urgent as she says, "Follow me."

She doesn't leave any other option, for she pulls so hard I am forced to either stand or allow my arm to be yanked off my body. I am so flustered that I don't ask questions at first. I stumble into the alley after her, and it takes several seconds to understand what I'm seeing.

This is not Under. Instead of dirt and torches, we are in a carpeted hallway. Painted portraits line the walls, and elegant doors stand erect on either side. The girl releases me and rushes ahead. *It can't be real*, I tell myself, but even as the thought occurs, my chest feels tight with hope. The wall is solid to the touch. There's a distinct scent of lemons in the air, as if the maids have just finished cleaning the floors.

"Who are you? What is this place?" I demand, finding my voice at last. The girl doesn't answer and slips out of sight, the skirt of her nightgown fluttering behind her. "Wait!"

She's gone. Panicked, I break into a run, my shoes making muffled thumps on the floor. I round the corner and spot the candle; the girl has halted. She still holds it so low that I can't see her features.

"Calm down," she chides when I appear. "You're awake now."

"Have I been *dreaming* all this time?" I breathe. My relief is so overwhelming I nearly sag. I'm not dead. I'm not alone in the world. I'm not desperately trying to recover memories of another life. There's no killer burning people below the ground.

But that means there's no Smoke either, the voice reminds me. It causes a strange tightness in my chest.

The girl ignores this, seeking my hand again. She holds it tight and drags me through an open doorway. The lighting is no better in here, and I try to study the room while she closes the door. There's a large bed and a gloomy fireplace. A narrow window stands at the far end, with just enough space between the curtains to allow a faint stream of moonlight through. Walking past me, the girl carefully places the candle in the center of a rug. The scent of lavender follows in her wake. She has dark hair that hangs down her back. "Kneel," she instructs, mindless of my scrutiny. "And be careful. There's broken glass here somewhere."

"Glass? Why?"

"I dropped a vase earlier. Now hush."

I move to obey, my eyes drawn to the girl's bare feet and ankles. Her skin is pale, but she's undeniably alive. She can't possibly be in Under. But which reality is the truth? My thoughts writhe and tangle until they are a hopeless, meaningless mass. And every single one of them dissolves into nothing once the girl begins to whisper. The words are utterly foreign. There's something on the floor I didn't notice before, an odd collection of objects in a bowl that seem to have no significance to one another. A feather, a bone, a golden ring.

Ingredients, a voice in my head whispers.

Alarmed, I open my mouth to ask the girl what she's doing…and all the trinkets around the room lift into the air.

I gape. They bob up and down as though there is a

breeze. Then, slowly, they begin to move. The things circle us, faster and faster, until they're nearly impossible to follow. "What is this?" I breathe, awed.

The girl ceases her string of words for an instant to say, "Magic."

There's obvious pleasure in the response. She starts to chant anew, apparently too late, and all the floating objects crash to the floor. With that, I know how the vase must have shattered. The girl swears vehemently and jumps up, almost tripping on her long nightgown. "Hurry, we must get you back to bed. Father might have heard that." There is a trace of anxiety in her voice now. She shoves the bowl beneath the bed and grabs hold of my arm.

But when she pulls at me this time, I resist. "Show me your face."

She hisses and her nails bite into my skin. I make a startled sound at the pain—more proof that we're not in Under.

"We don't have time for this!" she urges. "You know the danger. Rest assured, he won't be able to hurt me for much longer. Now come." Though I'm tempted to push the issue, her fear is so strong that it begins affecting me, too. I scramble up and follow her back down the hallway. The people in the paintings are more ominous now, their eyes piercing as they track our progress. I tell myself not to look at them, and seconds later the girl twists another doorknob. The hinges moan as the door opens.

Then, from far off, comes a different sound. Footsteps. Heavy and deliberate.

The girl freezes. "He's coming."

"Who's—"

Cursing again, the girl shoves me into the room. Before I can turn, she snuffs the candle out. "I can't see!" I say, holding out my hands. The only answer is the click of a closing door and the faint smell of smoke. Is she in here with me? I strain to listen for anything. Yes, someone is breathing.

I'm about to speak when I realize those ominous footsteps are getting closer. The floorboards creak and groan. I swallow the words in my throat just as the man pauses near the door. I don't move. Five seconds go by. Then, at last, whoever is in the hallway continues on. The noise of his heavy tread fades.

Still, I wait a few more seconds, the silence ringing in my ears. "All right, he's gone. Light another candle and show me your face!" I repeat, strangely desperate. Knowing this girl's identity feels vital. The darkness doesn't move, and for a moment, I worry that I'm wrong and the girl already left. Even the sound of breathing has vanished.

But then, as if I hadn't spoken, her voice emerges from the dim. It's a sorrowful whisper that moves over my skin like a shiver. "Sleep well, little sister."

CHAPTER FIVE

My mind has no sooner registered her words than it's all gone. The moonlight, the bedroom, the house. I'm exactly where I was when it all began, and I stand there in the middle of my earthen house, dazed and bewildered. Am I going insane?

As though it's heard my thought, the torch quivers. The flame struggles to survive, fading and brightening in agonizing bursts. It makes a sound my mind hears as a whimper.

All at once, I no longer want to be alone. The silence is too heavy, the stillness too loud. Earth crunches beneath my shoes as I go in search of Ribbon. Madness and murderers breathe down my neck. I wander through the passages, not only because I don't know the way but also because I'm not able to pay attention to the twists and turns of the maze.

Foolish girl. You shouldn't be alone with a killer on the loose, that inner voice chides. I've begun to envision it as a beetle or a worm lodged in my brain. The reminder sends a tremor down my spine. I blink rapidly in an effort to be more alert. But like the lovely objects the girl sent flying through the air, my mind goes around and around. I come up with multiple explanations for the encounter with that faceless girl: Hallucination. Dream. Memory.

Whatever it was, I know only one thing for certain—I want to learn more. Was she truly my sister? Did she fall into Under, too? Was the magic real?

Luckily, Ribbon spots me, else I would have gone right past her. She pops out of the tavern doorway, smiling. There's the faintest tinge of relief in her expression. For a wild moment, I consider the possibility that Ribbon is the girl from that strange dream, but then she speaks. *The voices aren't the same*, I think with some disappointment. "Key, what a lovely surprise! I see you've decided to emerge from the darkness. Like a phoenix from the ashes, as it were. In the future, though, you should really have someone escort you. Please, join us." Giving me no other choice, she puts her arm around my waist and guides me over the threshold.

The room is even fuller than it was the last time I was here. Every chair is occupied and people line the walls. It's so loud I feel as though I've entered a hive. Shilling and Spoon are sitting together, and I automatically start toward them, but Ribbon shakes her head and pulls me away. She brings me to every other table and makes more introductions, putting names and identities to these rotting creatures. Earring, Gloves, Buttons, Pistol, Collarino. I murmur polite responses and do my best not to stare.

Once I have met everyone, Ribbon and I stand next

to the bar—the only space left. I catch myself listening to the conversations happening all around. Everyone is still feeling the effects of the murder, voices thick with fear and confusion. I lean over to ask Ribbon if anyone else has been harmed, but she straightens, her attention fixed on something across the room. "I think a disagreement is escalating," she says. "I'd best go over there."

I watch Ribbon make her way in the direction of two men. Their fists are clenched and they stand so close their foreheads are nearly touching. Unlike the others, Ribbon does not have to struggle through the crowd; people notice her and step aside. Not from fear, as it was for Smoke, but clearly from respect.

There's a hesitant tap on my arm. I turn and my gaze meets that of a boy. He has so many freckles that at first glance, it could be mistaken for dirt. "Ribbon is our voice of reason," he says. "She's been here longer than almost anyone. Maybe even the first."

He reaches for a cup on the counter behind me, probably his purpose for coming over here. Before I can respond to his comment, something touches my fingers. I glance down. Someone has put a piece of paper on the bar. No one else seems to notice it, not even the freckled boy. They're all observing as Ribbon puts an end to the dispute. I pick it up and unfurl the edges. My eyes scan the single sentence written there.

Swim across the river.

It's the same handwriting as the message on my wall.

Without thinking, I jump to my feet and wildly search the room. No one is looking back or slipping out the door. Freckles has returned to his group of friends in the corner.

As I glare at the unwitting crowd, Fiddle brushes by. "Did you see who left this here?" I demand, grabbing his wrist. There's a tear in his shirt and my palm presses down on his skin. Ignoring the shock that touching him causes, I shove the note in Fiddle's face. "Do you know anything about a river?"

Looking mildly alarmed, Fiddle shakes his head and pulls away. His finger brushes a string on the instrument he carries and it whines. While the man makes his escape, I settle back in the chair, clenching my jaw in frustration and reading the words again and again. What does it mean?

Now someone else is standing at my elbow. I lift my head and say, "Oh, hello, Shilling."

The soft-spoken girl studies my shoes as though they are the most fascinating pair to ever fall into Under. "I 'eard you talking," she mutters. It's the first time I've heard Shilling speak, and her Cockney accent is strong. "Fiddle just arrived 'imself. The boy doesn't know nothin'."

Sighing, I fold the paper in half and tuck it away. "Then perhaps *you* know something about a river?"

"Ain't any water in Under, miss." I nod, resigning myself to another riddle without solution when she adds, "But there's a place. A bunch of old tree roots, all gnarled an' twisted together. It stretches from one end ov da earf ter anuvver. I've 'eard uvvers talking. They're always sayin' 'ow much i' *looks* like a river."

My stomach flutters at her words. This place must be where the writer is referring to. It has to be. "Will you take me there?" I ask eagerly. It flits through my mind that such an excursion could be dangerous—the image of Splinter's charred body is still fresh—but the allure of answers is too strong.

Shilling doesn't seem to possess the same sense of urgency. She pauses, as though debating. She still doesn't raise her gaze above my ankles, but there's a dry humor to her voice as she eventually says, "I don't suppose I 'ave much else ter do."

"I suppose not." My smile is genuine.

In unison, we leave the counter and head for the doorway. Ribbon is still preoccupied with the two men and doesn't see us. Once we're outside, Shilling immediately takes a sharp left, then a right. The noise of the tavern gradually fades. My guide walks like a spirit, silent and swift through the narrow spaces.

After a time, a new sound reaches my ears. At first I wonder if a fly has somehow found its way beneath the earth, but then I hear the note of melancholy in it. Someone is humming. "Who's doing that?" I ask Shilling, nearly tripping from a crevice in our path.

The girl doesn't stop or turn, but her answer floats back. "Her name is Brooch. She never leaves 'er room."

"Why?"

"By da time she fell, she was more skeleton van anything. She 'ad decomposed so much what she 'ad no arms or legs. She barely 'as a face. But there's still a red brooch pinned ter 'er collar."

I fall into a horrified silence. Brooch's sorrow follows us like an eerie dream. The two of us don't speak again, and as the silence wraps around us, it begins to feel like there isn't an end to this city of dirt and shadows. Finally, though, Shilling comes to a halt and points. "There."

With no torches nearby, it takes my eyes a few

moments to adjust in the dark. We're at the edge of our makeshift city. The wall looms up before us, curved, and nestling within its embrace is an enormous tangle of roots. They resemble a mass of snakes or twisting vines in the jungle. It's impossible to tell where one begins and another ends. But then I blink, and the tangle seems to change shape as though it really is water. Just like Journal's tower, there is an otherworldly beauty to it. I study every inch of the wooden water, and as Shilling said, it travels the entire expanse of Under.

Swim across the river, the note said. Why would someone lead me here?

"Has anyone tried to see if there is something beyond the roots?" I ask without looking away.

Shilling's response is hushed, as if she feels the power of it, too. "Yes. There's just da wall. A few even tried ter dig ter da surface. But every time they put their *brass bands* ter da dirt, i' was as if it turned ter stone."

"Magic," I whisper, thinking of the faceless girl. Her voice echoes through my memory. Magic is the only explanation for any of this. Somehow it must all tie together.

Shilling doesn't reply. She stares at the wonder with me for several minutes. I imagine us petrifying, becoming roots ourselves. Relentlessly and silently, I go over every strange occurrence, every detail, every word spoken and written since my arrival. The roots stare back, but if they hold any answers, they're not parting with them.

Finally, Shilling shatters the stillness by saying, "Should we go back, then?"

There is a weight to the question that makes me think

this isn't the first time she's asked it. I shake my head, still unable to tear my gaze from the unmoving river. "Not yet."

"It isn't safe. Ribbon'll worry." When I don't respond, Shilling takes a step back. "Fine. I'll leave you ter it, miss."

You're being rude, the beetle hisses. With effort, I focus on the worried girl before me. "Thank you for showing me the way, Shilling. I truly appreciate it."

Perhaps she expects me to change my mind, because she lingers a bit longer. She fidgets with her tattered sleeve. "Are you certain dis is a parf you wan' ter go down?" Shilling whispers. "The uvver one who tried ter remember ended up killin' 'imself."

I look at her. "I don't think there is another path for me."

Without replying, the tall girl retreats. The sound of her footsteps fades. I suspect I might have been the stubborn sort in life, because killer or no, I stay where I am. *What about Shilling? Is her safety so unimportant?* the beetle questions. Guilt settles in my stomach like a stone.

I'm about to go after her when it happens. That strange, sudden lightheadedness, which is so powerful that I stay where I am, fighting not to collapse.

Then I open my eyes. Everything has melted away—the dirt, the darkness, the graves—and I am standing on an imaginary shore. Just as before, I can *feel* again. My toes wiggle in crisp grass and the sunlight is warm on my skin. A river parts the land in front of me. Brown and rushing, making the journey to somewhere different. Somewhere better.

Somewhere I can't go.

"It *was* a memory, wasn't it?" I murmur. The girl with the candle doesn't materialize to respond, but it doesn't matter. Something in me senses she will return, along with the rest of my story. It will just require time and patience.

For now, the river runs on.

Afterward, I find myself returning to Journal's tower. It's not difficult to find—it stands over the rest of everything. I can't decide whether this is superior or wistful. The openings at the top glow yellow, like fresh-churned butter. According to Ribbon, the strange boy hardly leaves his tower since he and Handkerchief finished constructing it long ago.

Following her example from our last visit, I don't hesitate at the bottom of the stairs. The steps seem even more uneven than the last time, if that's possible, and I focus so intently on them that I'm in the beautiful library before I realize it.

I spot Journal instantly. He kneels on the lopsided floor, several stacks of books in front of him. One is open in his hands. Unaware of my presence, he traces something with his index finger, his carefully combed hair gleaming.

"Hello?" I finally venture. Journal startles, nearly dropping the volume he holds. He turns and his dark eyes find me. Suddenly I feel foolish for this impulsive visit. I take a step back. "I'm sorry, I didn't mean to intrude."

"Key," he says, clearing his throat. He stands in one

movement, closing the book with a *thump*. Dust motes drift through the air. "What brings you here?"

"I finished the books you lent me." Noticing Handkerchief in the shadows, I smile tentatively. His odd kindness during our last conversation has made him less frightening. The pudgy boy doesn't smile back.

"And what did you think?"

Turning back to Journal, I find him staring at me. The intensity of his expression is discomfiting; I try and fail to answer. Eventually Journal clears his throat again and reaches his hand out, intending to take his books. The pose strikes a chord within me. "Were they to your liking?" I hear Journal ask over a vast distance. I'm swaying. The world tilts again. I close my eyes and try not to crumple.

"Give back the book, you little imp."

My eyes snap open. Journal stands before me, but it's not the same boy I've known thus far. His skin, while pale as ever, is not sickly anymore. He wears a different waistcoat, and the green brings out the color in his eyes. Golden buttons shine in the light. His short brown hair is styled to perfection. He's still slight in stature, but there's nothing gaunt about him now.

It's instantly apparent this memory is different. Instead of being a participant, I am a spectator. Words come out of my mouth without thought or urge. It's as though the real me—the dead me—is watching everything from within. "Not until you agree," I hear myself say. My voice sounds strange. After a moment, I realize it's the voice of a girl who's never known death. Never known fear.

"Fat chance of that," Journal replies, still holding his

hand out for the book I've hidden behind me. He twitches
ink-stained fingers. "You already push the boundaries of
propriety far too often. One of these days, someone is
going to see you."

"I'm sure I don't know what you mean," I retort. My
grasp tightens on my prize.

"Oh? So it wasn't you I saw through the window last
night, walking around like a common street urchin?"
Journal dives forward and attempts to snatch the book
away. I evade him and rush behind a chair.

We're in a room that seems more like a study than
a library. Though the walls are lined with shelves, and
the colorful spines of books wait patiently upon them,
the desk is more striking. The size of it seems enough to
accommodate two men, and even the chair holds a sense
of power. Neatly stacked papers rest beside an oil lamp
on its surface. A wide window behind the desk allows
more light in, though heavy curtains hang in the sun's way.
As I inhale the familiar scent of dust, I notice a painting
above the fireplace—the child sitting on a woman's lap
is clearly Journal.

"I have trouble sleeping sometimes," I say defensively,
tearing my gaze away from the portrait. "Where's the
harm in going for a stroll?"

"There's harm when it's midnight and you have no
chaperone."

"Well then, it's a good thing I have one now." I look
around with exaggerated consternation. "Oh dear. Where
did she go?"

Journal doesn't rise to the bait. His expression is sober,
and it's difficult to stay cross with him when his caring is

so evident, it's nearly a perfume on the air. "That's not the same thing and you know it. Promise me you won't go."

Just like that, all the fight seeps out of me like blood from a cut. I sink into the chair with a defeated sigh, and Journal takes the opportunity to pluck the book out of my hand. He seats himself beside me and waits. He keeps his eyes on the book—turning it this way and that, flipping the pages, searching for any damage I might have caused— but I feel the weight of his attention. "Fine. I won't," I mumble.

Journal looks at me sidelong and raises his finely arched brows. "And no asking *her* to go with you, either."

Now I glare. I'm many things, but I'm not a liar. "I already said I wouldn't go, didn't I?"

This seems to satisfy my friend. The chair creaks as Journal stands and brings the book toward the shelves. He carefully slides it into place. Then he asks, without looking at me, "Why is this so important, anyhow?"

I bring my legs up and tuck them beneath me. Some of the excitement returns to my voice. "He's an *American*. I've always been curious about them. Haven't you?"

"Yes, of course, but I've never been tempted to go to the boarding house they're staying at and peer through their window like a Peeping Tom."

I don't grace this with a response, especially since I've given up on the idea. Instead I gaze in the direction of the window, to the street beyond. Twilight sets the cobblestones aglow in hues of pink and orange. I hardly notice; my mind is running down the road and into the village. It creeps up to Mrs. Ivanov's boarding house, along the side, where I know the American's room is because gossip spreads like disease among us. Perhaps he's sleeping in the bed, dreaming of his faraway home. Or, more likely, he's off somewhere finding himself surrounded by every girl of marriageable age in the village.

"I suppose we'll meet him sooner or later," I say absently.

"You can't let any mystery go unsolved, can you?" Journal remarks. There's affection in the way he says it, though. He goes about choosing another book to read, speaking to me over his shoulder. "How is the packing coming along?"

At once, I'm absorbed by my skirt. I fuss at a nonexistent string. "I'm sure the servants are almost finished. I'm not home very often; you know that. Father doesn't like it when I'm underfoot."

Journal plucks a new volume from the shelf and flips it open. "I don't think that's true. He mentioned how strange it will be to go so long without seeing you."

Frowning, I lift my head. "When did you talk to him?"

I watch Journal's spine stiffen. He turns, only slightly, but I'm still able to see the color spreading up his neck and into his cheeks. His tone is too offhand, his grip on the book too tight. "We saw each other recently. Last week, was it? Oh, did you hear that?"

"Hear what?" I stand from the chair. Journal is already at the door, poking his head out. He won't look at me.

"I think Mother is calling," he says. I strain to hear, but the only sound my ears detect is the grandfather clock in the corner, marking the seconds and making the silence between them feel stark. Journal finally faces me, his gaze landing somewhere over my shoulder. I start to ask why he's lying to me, but he's quicker. "I should check on her. May I see you out?"

With that, the memory ends.

Under reappears around me. No sign of the study or the sun. Journal is staring, his hand still outstretched. I'm about to tell him what just transpired when Ribbon's voice, laden with pity and disbelief, whispers through me. *That's impossible, Key.* The idea of Journal looking at me the same way is unbearable. I don't want anyone's pity; I want them to believe.

Still shaken from the memory, I finally return the books. Then I fold my hands and determinedly concentrate on Journal. "Mr. Dickens is a superb writer."

He regards me with a thoughtful expression. Then, slowly, he nods and places the books on a pile beside his desk. "I agree. Though my tastes are more inclined toward the factual." Grasping the twisting armrests of a chair made from roots, Journal drags it around so it's facing me. A strand of hair hangs in his eyes.

I settle into the uncomfortable seat and pluck at my skirts. Silence hovers in the tower, and I'm not sure what to say next. I long for the easy familiarity of the friends we once were. As he waits for a response, Journal moves to sit on yet another precarious stack of books. He links his hands loosely between his knees. "Forgive me," he sighs. "I'm unpracticed in regular conversation."

At this, I meet his gaze. Compassion stirs in my chest. "Then I shall borrow more of your books, so that we may discuss them."

Journal's eyes widen. Clearly taken aback, he says

nothing, and I wonder if—for all his books, his formality, and the constant presence of Handkerchief—this boy is lonely. After another stretch of uncertainty, I make my voice brisk as I ask, "I assume you were buried with a journal, since that's what you're called?"

"Yes."

"How interesting." I pause, hoping he will volunteer more information. He doesn't. When Ribbon was here, he spoke constantly. Is it me who makes him so uneasy, or is there something else preying on his mind?

Journal is intelligent, and he has been here longer than I; perhaps he's made discoveries I haven't. Perhaps he's even remembered something about our shared past. But, like the river, he refuses to reveal anything. *You must earn his trust,* that small beetle advises. It's not wrong. My resolve hardens into something as unyielding as the walls of Under.

Journal speaks before I can. "My companion tells me you paid a visit to the river recently." Noting my quizzical look, he adds, "Handkerchief went to the tavern and overheard someone talking about it."

"Yes. I was curious. It was very beautiful." I hesitate. "While we were there, Shilling mentioned that someone in Under might've started to regain his or her memories."

His gaze narrows. It darts to Handkerchief and back to me. "Shilling shouldn't go spreading tales," he says, his voice becoming a razor with a glinting surface and jagged edges. "It only breeds false hope."

My spine presses against the gnarled back of the chair in an instinctive retreat. Journal notices and his mouth tightens. "Forgive me," he says again.

He looks so upset that I force myself to relax. "Think nothing of it."

By the wall, Handkerchief shifts. We both glance in his direction and back at each other. The sense of shared history is overwhelming, and it's obvious Journal feels it, too. Something holds my tongue, though: a sense that I might regret opening this particular door. Instead I tell him, "I find I am much like Oliver Twist, in that I want more."

Frowning, Journal tilts his head. "More what?" he asks, sounding genuinely interested in the answer. There's the faintest coloring of...frustration there, as well, as if he believes he should already know it.

I raise my eyebrows. "Why, soup, of course!" Journal doesn't laugh, and seconds later my mirth dies. "I want more than death," I whisper. More than the objects we fell with and more than the wounds that were our last. I want the chance to gain more wounds, to stand on a real riverbank, to experience the weight of memories instead of this emptiness. I want more than an existence; I want a life. But how?

As if he hears my thoughts, Journal mutely gets to his feet. He walks toward the makeshift shelves and ignores Handkerchief as he searches through his collection. A few seconds tick past. Eventually Journal plucks one of the books free. "Ah. Here it is." He comes back and offers it to me.

Taking the book from him, I notice the glint of a title on its spine. "*Persuasion* by Jane Austen," I read.

"She was a woman ahead of her time. I believe you'll enjoy her work."

With a pleased smile, I stand and attempt to smooth my skirts. "Thank you. I'll come back once I've finished it." I turn toward the doorway and my footsteps echo through the dusty tower.

"He committed suicide. The man who tried to remember."

Startled by the sound of his voice, I face Journal again. "How do you know it was a suicide?" Both Ribbon and Shilling mentioned it, of course, but I can't help wanting to know more.

"He left a note."

What did it say? I should have asked. But I think of a comment in the square—how someone wondered whether or not it's murder if the person is already dead— and say, "Some would not consider it suicide, since he was simply returning to his grave."

Another frown tugs at the corners of Journal's mouth. I wait eagerly for his answer, to understand what sort of person he is. Instead, he approaches me abruptly. I jump, but it feels as if my feet have become roots themselves, rendering me motionless. "Here," Journal mutters. He takes my hand and places it on his heart. It's the last thing I ever expected him to do. Still, I don't pull away for fear of offending him.

We stare at each other, so close that if he had breath, I would know the warmth of it on my cheek. "I don't feel anything," I say, reluctant to admit it; he seems so earnest.

Journal doesn't look surprised or disappointed. "No," he replies. "But it's a heart just the same. Even if it does not pump blood. This heart experiences longing and hope and despair as much as a beating one. Therefore, wouldn't you consider its permanent end an unjust event?"

I feel my expression clear as I understand. "I didn't think of it that way."

He just looks at me. We've passed the boundaries of propriety, as well as my own comfort, and I know one of us should pull away. Journal must see something in my gaze, because he drops my hand. It doesn't make sense, but it feels colder now. Awkwardly, I hold the book to my chest. "I'll return once I'm fully acquainted with Miss Austen," I promise once again, retreating into the stairwell.

"Until then, Key." Before I can say anything else, Journal focuses on retrieving some of the clutter from the floor and making new stacks. Handkerchief watches from his corner, and I realize that I'd completely forgotten he was there.

When neither of them glances my way again, I take the torch down and leave. Ribbon would most assuredly lecture Journal for not escorting me, or sending Handkerchief as one, but I'm against the idea of being alone with either right now. It probably slipped Journal's mind, for which I'm grateful.

And should the killer strike—however unlikely that is—I'll die fighting. At least I would have chosen my own death.

It doesn't take me long to reach the ground. As I step out into Under, the maze seems darker than it did just a short time ago, as though several of the torches went out. Unease whispers down my spine. Using the dirt wall as a guide, I struggle to remember the way back to my room. There are too many footprints to follow a trail, and soon it becomes obvious that I must have taken a wrong turn. I quell the beginning trickles of panic.

An odd smell suddenly permeates the air. I'm frowning, trying to place it when my shoe collides with a hard object in the path. Losing my balance, I hit the ground with a cry and drop the flame in my hand. It bounces and settles a few feet away, thankfully unaffected. The shadows flicker and tremble.

What did I trip over? Frowning, I pick up the torch and turn. The lump blends with the darkness, so I lean closer. It takes me several seconds to comprehend what my eyes are seeing. Then I scream, recoiling. My back slams into the wall and yet I still keep attempting to scramble away. My heels scar the earth. "Help! Someone help!" I shriek.

But of course it's too late for this poor soul. Regaining my senses, I swallow my horror and stare. Like the other body, it's charred beyond the point of recognition. There is nothing left of a face or clothing. Faintly, I notice that there is something beside the body, untouched by flame or death. Something with strings and a long crack down the center.

A fiddle.

CHAPTER SIX

Shouts reverberate off the walls of Under.

Fiddle's corpse rests at the front of the crowd, fuel for their terror and rage. I stand next to Ribbon and Spoon, quietly observing. The most outspoken individuals are the same as before, the man with the eye patch and the man with white hair. They don't notice Doll kneeling on the ground behind them, stroking the silent instrument that will never be played again.

While their argument continues, I search the sea of faces for Journal or Handkerchief. They're nowhere in sight, and Smoke catches my eye instead, leaning against a building in the shadows. Once again, I feel something inexplicable and powerful pass between us.

"But why bother to kill *him*?" someone snaps, drawing my gaze away from the dark-haired boy. "Fiddle had recently fallen. He had no time to insult or offend anyone."

Pocket Watch—the man with white hair—stands on top of the crate, hands tightly folded. His response is strained and his appearance is more mussed than usual. I imagine beads of sweat on his forehead. "We must assume, then, that these murders are not of a personal nature," he counters. "They serve a purpose."

Spoon scoffs. "What possible—"

"That is the question, isn't it?" he interrupts, his composure visibly slipping. The panic in the square rises, a palpable pressure in the air, and Pocket Watch once again struggles to speak over the cries. His hand is hidden behind the flap of his coat, and somehow I know that he's clutching his watch just as assuredly as I'm holding my key. Ribbon murmurs something to Spoon, but I'm too caught up in the commotion to make out the words.

Once again, violence breaks out, and even without his arm, Eye Patch is in the center of it. This time Smoke does nothing to intervene. Perhaps even he doesn't dare. Emotions are too high, too volatile. I search for Doll to make sure she isn't in harm's way, and it seems that she's taken the fiddle and disappeared. Seconds later a hand wraps around my arm and tugs me away—Ribbon. Willingly, I follow her.

It isn't until we've put some distance between ourselves and the square that Ribbon turns. A nearby torch makes makes her skin orange and her eyes luminescent. "Are you coming, Key?"

"The tavern?" I clarify. She nods, and I shake my head. "Not this time. I'd like to continue reading the book Journal lent me."

Beside Ribbon, the shapely cook clucks her tongue. "You shouldn't be alone, girl. In case you haven't heard, there's a murderer running about."

She's right. The thought of being set on fire, my tongue cut out, is enough to silence any protests. I'm about to acquiesce when both Spoon and Ribbon tense, and I turn to see a dark silhouette making its way toward us. "Luckily, she has a neighbor who doesn't find her company completely intolerable," Smoke's voice says.

We all relax.

"You're making a habit of this, I see," Spoon comments, her tone knowing. "If we were topside, I'd say your intentions were not as innocent as they seem, sir."

"How fortunate that we are not topside, then." Smoke stops beside me, hands shoved in his pockets.

The gray-haired cook winks at me. "I'd wager he's the sort who likes being on top, though, wouldn't you say?"

I frown a little, feeling as though I'm missing something. Before I can construct a response, Ribbon takes me by surprise by wrapping her arms around my shoulders. She smells of rich, wet soil. "I shall come by afterward," she promises. I smile at her and nod. Ribbon releases her hold to go our separate ways.

The instant they're gone, I wait for Smoke to start a conversation, to taunt or mock in the dry manner I'm beginning to expect. Instead he ambles along in that loose way of his, all swinging arms and light steps. Not a single sound passes from his lips or mine. It's not from a lack of words, but because there are too many. They feel like memories, blurry and just out of reach.

As we walk, our shoulders brush once or twice. Each occurrence sends embers scattering through me. I try to concentrate on the turns and markings of the passageways, but my mind is too consumed by images of Fiddle, lying there in the path, utterly burnt.

The passageway narrows and forces us closer together. I'm pretending not to notice when, without warning, my head feels light and hazy. I pause and press my hand against a wall for balance. "Are you all right?" I hear Smoke's voice say from far away.

Another memory is upon me. By now I know what to expect, and once the world stops spinning, I slowly straighten. As usual, Under is nowhere to be seen. This time I'm outside, beneath a wide yellow moon. A short distance away, streetlamps glow. Ice shines on the road. My nostrils flare as I inhale, thrilling in the sensation of fresh, open air.

God, how I've missed this.

"Are you all right, miss?" a voice asks from behind.

A sound of panic tears from my throat. I whirl to face whoever it is, and something strong and strange steals over me. Once again, my words slice the stillness without any bidding or thought. "Don't come any closer!"

So this is another memory in which I have no control. Oblivious to my consternation, the stranger takes a step back and sweeps off a bowler hat, revealing his face. Deep within the body in which I reside, I shiver from the thrill of realization.

It's Smoke, but this is a version of him I've not seen before. His cheeks are flushed with cold, and there's no hard edge of bitterness around him. "I do apologize," he says. There's something different about his voice, too. An absence of mocking or pain. "I didn't mean to frighten you."

Belying his sincere words, there's a mischievous glint

in his blue eyes. The girl I once was studies his face. My heart responds, picking up strength and speed. *So this is the American everyone is talking about*, I think. The very one I'd wanted to spy on through a window, before Journal extinguished that notion like breath to a candle. He's as handsome as the other girls claimed—worthy of every dreamy sigh and wistful remark.

As the gentleman waits for my response, I take stock of my own appearance. I'm leaning against the outside of a house, wearing a coat with fur lining. A matching muff lies forgotten on the ground. Noticing this at the same time I do, he moves to retrieve it. There are cigars scattered all over the ground, as well. "Where's your chaperone?" he asks, presenting the muff to me with a playful flourish. His hair glints in the moonlight, resting against his neck in dark curls. I notice the smell of smoke clinging to him. "A lady such as yourself shouldn't be alone."

"I couldn't sleep," I murmur, accepting the muff. "I thought a walk would clear my head. Were you following me, sir? Or were you just lurking outside my home?"

Never mind that I'd wanted to do the very same thing to him.

Unperturbed by the accusation, the boy puts his hat back on. He's still smiling. "You're lovely enough to inspire such behavior, miss, but I'm afraid I was merely on my way to a boxing match," he replies easily. "I always smoke beforehand, and this seemed as good a spot as any to admire the moon."

"A boxing match?" I raise my brows, curious in spite of myself. "How barbaric."

The boy tilts his head and appraises me. "I'll offer you

a bargain. If you can remember my name, I shall allow you to accompany me."

I scoff at this. But this foreigner has my interest, and he knows it.

It's improper and dangerous and intriguing—I shouldn't even be speaking to him—yet it feels impossible to walk away. Studying his features anew, I pretend to struggle in my recollection. After a few moments I say, "You're Mr. James Alistair. But I'm sorry to say I couldn't possibly go with you to a boxing match."

"And why not?" he demands.

"I'm in my nightgown!"

The gentleman pretends to notice this for the first time. His gaze travels the length of me, and I can't think straight enough to act offended. When he replies, his voice is thicker. "So you are." He offers his arm with a wink that should be gallant. Instead, it's utterly devilish. "Let me see you safely inside, then."

His smile is infectious, and my mouth twitches in response. I resist it and put my hand in the crook of his arm. We walk the few steps down the street—staying in the shadows, avoiding prying eyes—to the front door of a grand house. I bid the charismatic stranger goodbye and begin to go inside, moving much slower than usual. At the doorway, I follow some instinct and turn back around, though I have no idea what to say.

Without warning, Mr. Alistair leans forward. "Meet me here," he whispers, his lips nearly touching my ear. "Tomorrow night. We'll have an adventure."

A denial rises to my lips. Our gazes lock and hold. Before I can think about it, I hear myself agreeing.

"Tomorrow."

Another slow, pleased grin spreads across his face. And suddenly, in that instant, the houses around us disappear. The cobblestones transform to dirt. The streetlamp becomes a torch. Mr. Alistair's clothing becomes ragged, and a horrifying scar appears across his throat.

Reality returns in full force. We're dead. Whatever choices I made that night, they cannot be undone.

However lengthy it felt, the memory must've taken only a few moments; Smoke is frowning at me and still awaiting a response. His hand is on my elbow. When we first met, there was only a slight tingle. Now it has evolved to a sensation that travels through my entire arm, like feathers beneath my skin.

"I apologize," I manage to say. "I was lost in thought."

Smoke doesn't pursue the matter, for which I'm grateful. We walk the rest of the way in silence, and I don't notice how he's looking at me until we reach the doorway. "Do I have something on my face?" Now my hand goes to my cheek self-consciously.

"No. Nothing."

I frown. "Smoke?"

The force of his gaze diminishes. The boy blinks. He looks around like he'd forgotten where we were. "Here you are. Sweet nightmares." He tries to act normally, arrogant and unaffected, but it's too late. I witnessed a flash of vulnerability, recognized the distant way he spoke. I know the cause, for I've experienced it myself. I stay where I am and watch him hasten toward his room.

Smoke remembered something, too.

CHAPTER SEVEN

A pattern begins to emerge during my time in Under.

Throughout the hours I consider to be day, I draw in the dirt of my room and struggle to put a meaning to the shapes. I mull over the memories I've recovered and ponder the messages the mysterious stranger has left. I walk to the river of roots and search for anything that might be reason enough to send me there. I sit in the doorway next to Doll and teach her new words from the book Journal has lent me. After that, I seek out Ribbon and Spoon to enjoy their company.

Once I've had my fill of the girl's kindness and the cook's vulgar humor, I retreat back to my room. For a time, Ribbon always sends someone to accompany me. But as the days pass and there are no more murders, everyone begins to relax and forget their fear. In the quiet solitude of my room, nestled among the rags I've used to make a bed for myself, I read whatever book Journal has given me. There are days when I finish and visit his tower, where we explore the text together.

Sometimes we argue more than we agree, and those are the occasions I like best.

"It's a story about redemption and one man's ability to forgive the transgressions that have been done to him," I say heatedly, brandishing the book through the air.

The boy—and I daresay, my friend—shakes his head, and though he is not quite as impassioned, there is more animation to his countenance than before. For once we are alone, and we sit on the floor beneath one of the torches to better view the pages. His outstretched leg nearly brushes my hip. "Key, *The Count of Monte Cristo* is entirely about revenge. It may appear that Edmond moves on in the end, but it should be noted that it is only after he confronts Fernand and the rest. Ultimately, he could only rest once his need for vengeance had been fulfilled." He takes the title from me, and his tapered fingers skim the words at the end, as if looking for deeper evidence within the ink.

"No!" I persist. There's an abandoned piece of twine on the floor, and I pick it up. "If he were so single-minded he would not have forgiven Mercédès."

"*After* he punished her, of course," Journal counters doggedly.

I let out a needless breath, just to display how infuriating I find him, and settle back on my elbows. I pinch the twine tighter between my fingers and fiddle with it. There will be no winning with Journal—at least not today—so I ask, "Where's your shadow this afternoon?"

"My shadow?" he repeats absently, distracted by a piece of paper resting near his foot. The drawing on it displays details of human anatomy.

"Handkerchief. He never seems to leave your side. What inspires such loyalty?"

There's a note of teasing in my voice, but as Journal meets my gaze, his expression is thoughtful. "I couldn't tell you. One day, he was just there. Watching me, following me, helping me. I found it a bit unsettling, at first, but eventually I found his presence…comforting."

Journal bends to retrieve the drawing. He studies it more closely, the crown of his head all I can see. As usual, there's hair in his eyes, no matter how tidy he tries to keep it.

Without thinking, I straighten the twine and reach around Journal. My cheek touches his as I wind the string about his hair and tie the tightest knot I can manage. "There," I say triumphantly as I finish.

That's when I notice how still Journal has gone. He stares at me.

I pull away quickly. Calling myself every kind of fool, I scramble for something that will distract him. "I think I'm remembering things. About my life before Under," I blurt.

Journal blinks. It takes him a moment to reply. "Oh?"

It's too late to take the words back. But Journal is the most open-minded person in Under. It's silly to be afraid, and now that I've told him, it feels as though a weight has lifted from me. And perhaps my words will help him remember something, too. I bring my legs up and hug them against my chest, conscious of how ragged and stained my skirt is.

"There was a girl," I say. "I don't know her name, but she was always scared of someone. I remembered Smoke, the dashing American who all the village girls wanted. And...I've also seen you. We were friends, I think. Very good friends."

Silence reigns in the tower as he takes this in, and I can practically see the gears in his head turning. Slowly, Journal stands. Leaving our spot under the torch, he strides to a small pile and places the book with the others that I have read and returned. He does not look for another one, as he has all the other times. "And why are you so certain these are memories?" Journal asks finally, avoiding my gaze. Going to his desk, he traces the path of a twisting root with his palm. "Couldn't it be — "

"I just know, Journal." My desperation changes to hurt, causing his name to sound poisonous from my lips. Of all the people here, I convinced myself he would be the last one to question me.

Though he must hear the venom in my response, Journal continues to caress the desk as though it is the first time he's laid eyes on it. There's a sound behind us, and I see that Handkerchief has returned.

"I'm sure it felt very real, Key," Journal says, nodding a greeting to him. He focuses on me again. "But you're not the first to claim having memories, and last time it was a result of madness. Be wary."

I gape at him. How could we go from laughing one moment to this so quickly? It's evident that I imagined the strength of the camaraderie between us.

Handkerchief steps forward and hands Journal a scroll. "What's that?" I ask faintly.

He unfurls the old paper, bends over the desk, and jots something down with what looks like a sharpened bone dipped in ink. "Some notes of mine. Doll keeps coming up here and taking this particular scroll, for some reason. Years ago one of us began to rant nonsensically, and I made sure to record every word. I believe that—"

"Journal," Handkerchief says suddenly. The name is sharp from his lips, a warning.

There's a noticeable pause, and Journal stops writing. He drops the bone and rolls the paper again. Now his expression looks cross. "It's all very complex; I'm sure you have no interest in listening to me ramble on."

I make one final attempt to redeem the afternoon. "No, I do. Please continue."

"Perhaps another time." He tucks the scroll into one of the makeshift bookshelves, behind a stack of thick volumes where small girls won't be able to find it.

Suddenly I can't be in this tower another second. The serene flickers of the torches have become harsh and disparaging. The air tastes of death and dust rather than stories and lively discourse. Standing clumsily, I clear my throat and study the grooves in the floor with as much intensity as Journal with his desk. "I'd best go. Ribbon worries if I'm not there when she walks by my doorway."

He doesn't protest. Our eyes meet briefly before he glances away again. "Handkerchief, you will accompany her. I insist, Key, so don't bother arguing."

Handkerchief is already vanishing down the stairs, and after a brief hesitation, I murmur a polite farewell to Journal and follow.

Our progress is swift and sure. I am beginning to know the way on my own, and we walk alongside each other. Once again, it seems as if our shoes shuffling through the dirt is the only sound in Under. Seeking a distraction, I study the strange boy escorting me back. He walks with his hands at his sides, his expression hidden beneath the brim of his cap.

"I would offer you my handkerchief, except you can't cry and it's covered in filth," he says unexpectedly. He's waited until we are a safe distance away to speak. The lights of Journal's tower are still visible above our heads, but there's no breeze to carry our words to him.

I consider pretending confusion. My world is so rife with half-truths and secrets, though, that I can't bring myself to do it. "I don't know why he affects me," I sigh, relenting. "Is it so obvious?"

"Not to him. Ribbon says that Journal is oblivious to affairs of the heart."

"Of the heart?" I echo, startled. "No, I don't—"

The torch to our right sputters out. It was the only one in this particular passageway, and the dimness is so thick I can barely see my own hand when I hold it out. "Handkerchief?" I call timidly, my fingers brushing the opposite wall. "Where are you?"

Something cold touches me. "I'm here, miss. Take—" His voice cuts off abruptly, and I hear footsteps and grunts, the unmistakable sounds of a struggle.

"Handkerchief?" I cry, searching for him blindly.

"Key, run!" he shouts, and there's more emotion in those two words than in the dozens we've exchanged since I fell out of the grave.

Fear.

Images race through my mind, the crisp skeletons of Splinter and Fiddle lying in the dirt, and instinct takes over.

Screaming, I stumble backward, deeper into the darkness.
I slam into the corner of a structure and a jarring sensation
travels up and down my spine, cutting the scream short.
Part of me wants to run, just as Handkerchief instructed.
But I can't leave him—by the time I found help, it might
be too late—so I scrape together a bit of courage and
start searching for something to use as a weapon. Dimly,
I hope that someone heard me scream.

The unseen battle continues, more scuffling and blows.
I listen with mute dismay, still feeling the ground and
walls. It's impossible to tell who's winning or losing. *What
should I do?* I think frantically. Then Handkerchief shouts
and something *crunch*es, like a fist meeting bone.

Everything stops.

The silence is worse than the fight. Whimpering, I
abandon the search and rush forward to help, weapon
be damned. The attacker hears it; hands clamp around
my shoulders and shove me. There must be a doorway
behind us, because instead of hitting a wall, I stumble into
emptiness. I begin to scream again, but my foe cuts it off
by pushing me. As I hit the back wall, he's there, trapping
me by pressing a forearm to my throat. A rasping sound
is all that emerges, and an instant later two fingers grasp
my tongue.

Now I go wild, bucking and clawing. Flesh clumps
beneath my nails. He grunts but still manages to hold
me in place. Something cold and hard touches my lip—a
knife. *He's going to cut it out*, I realize with horror.

Just as the edge of the blade begins its work, shadows
reach inside the room. There's the unmistakable flicker
of a torch in the distance.

We both freeze.

I'm the first to recover. *"Help!"* I shriek. *"Help me!"*

The stillness shatters into a thousand pieces. The killer grabs a fistful of my hair and drags me into the corner, probably to hide. A futile attempt—someone is calling out and running to intervene. The shadows stretch and brighten. The knife comes down again, and I see it just in time to grab the hand that holds it. My muscles tremble as I strain to make out the face of our attacker, catch any sort of scent, but his back is to the light. I know only that he has broad shoulders.

"Why are you doing this?" I say through my teeth.

He doesn't answer. A moment later, he wrenches himself out of my grasp. The thundering approach of our rescuer is undeniable. In a final, desperate act, the killer reaches out and snatches my key.

"No!" I cry, the sound ringing with anguish. Instead of breaking, though, the chain cuts into my neck and hauls my entire body upright. Fury fills me, and any sense of self-preservation evaporates as I scream and wrestle the key back from him. My foot lashes out and connects with his leg. He doesn't make a sound, but the pressure on the chain disappears. The suddenness of it makes me flop back, and I feel a gust of air as he dives into the alley and away from here.

Seconds after that, someone bursts into the room, a torch in his fist, causing me to scream from the suddenness of it. One side of the boy's face is revealed by the flickering flames. When I realize it's Smoke, I nearly sag with relief. He sees me cowering there and goes still. "Are you hurt?"

But I can't answer, because the familiar nausea is back. "Handkerchief…"

A memory is digging its claws into my mind, dragging me down into the depths. This is neither the time nor place; I struggle against the sensation. It's no use; the struggling seems to make the nausea worse. By the time I'm able to open my eyes, Under has been replaced by the past once again.

I'm standing in the exact spot I met James. This time, I'm fully dressed and concealed by a wool cloak. The design is so simple that it must be meant for a man. I'm also holding a book. Plumes of air leave my mouth with every breath, and for a moment, I'm distracted by the thrill of such a simple thing. To breathe, to need air.

Suddenly, voices slice through the stillness like a knife to butter. Driven by some instinct, I turn aside, hiding my face with the hood. Now my breathing feels loud and ragged as I press against the side of the house. Two men pass without noticing me, not entirely sober, if the slur in their words is any indication. Even so, I wait until their sounds have completely faded before I turn around again. Trepidation and doubt creep through my veins. Why am I out at this hour? What am I waiting for?

I decide to wait a bit longer in hopes of getting answers. The minutes drag on, and I draw the cloak more securely around me to ward off the cold. An owl calls somewhere nearby. There are no stars to admire, as clouds are guarding them jealously, but I can see the moon. It's only a sliver tonight, hardly more than a fingernail in the sky. That doesn't deter its glow, however; if anything, the moon shines brighter. As if to say, *I need not be full to be significant. I need not be whole to be beautiful.*

Once more, the sound of footsteps reaches my ears. My nerves are terribly frayed, and this time I'm tempted to rush back into the house, never mind the intrigue of this memory. But, unable to resist, I dare to glance up. When I see who's walking toward me, I'm unsettled for an entirely different reason. It feels as though the bottoms of my boots grow roots, burrowing deep into the ground, rendering me unable to move.

Despite the hour, James Alistair looks fresh and animated. The glow from a street lamp reveals his well-tailored clothing. The brim of a hat shadows his eyes and his shoes clip against the cobblestones. "I must confess to some surprise," he says by way of greeting, dipping into a bow. "I didn't expect you to come."

"Well, you promised me an adventure." Again, the words emerge without command. I curtsy back, using the precious seconds to gather my composure.

"So I did. Shall we?" With a grin, he offers his arm. A nervous flutter goes through me as I accept. I can't feel his skin through his coat, but just the proximity is affecting; my cheeks feel warm and my stomach is full of birds.

We set out toward the center of the village, and I keep my head low to avoid being recognized. The sensible part of me is going wild, bleating like a sheep, insisting that this is a bad idea. The other part, though... I grip Mr. Alistair's arm tighter without meaning to, overcome with exhilaration, but he doesn't comment.

At first, we meet no one else on the road, as this is not a part of town respectable folk leave their homes for. A few trees appear along the way. Leaves rustle overhead, disturbed by a sudden gust of wind. It feels like the only sound in the world. Just as I'm about to ask Mr. Alistair where this boxing match is supposed to take place, he looks over and notices the object in my hand. "Is that a *book*?"

I glance down as though I've never seen it before; I'd completely forgotten about it. "Oh. Yes. Habit, really. I take one with me wherever I go. My governess used to tell me it's terribly rude, but it's better than falling asleep at Mrs. Graham's ball or Miss Marshall's tea party."

Never breaking his stride, the gentleman tilts his head in an attempt to see the spine. "Is it a romance novel? Poetry?"

Some of my discomfort dissipates at this turn of conversation. "Though there's nothing wrong with such choices, my preferences are a bit different," I say. "This text explores the mechanisms of a locomotive. Did you know that the first railway service was called The Elephant? I find it fitting, as the energy released by the combustion sounds very much like a great beast."

He stares openly now, and my enthusiasm dies as I feel the stirrings of shame. Proper young women are not supposed to know such things, as I'm always being reminded.

I've begun to stammer out an excuse when that grin of his appears. "Well, what do you know?" Mr. Alistair drawls. "A girl with a brain."

"Every girl has a brain, sir. We're simply taught not to use it," I counter. My tone isn't curt or unkind, but I've seemed to put him at a loss. There's another awkward silence—he's probably regretting our bargain.

Desperately I grapple for something to say. "What are *your* interests?"

There's movement up ahead. Erring on the side of caution, Mr. Alistair guides me to the edge of the road, beneath the shadow of a rooftop. His reply is distracted. "Travel, mostly. Games of chance. Meeting new people. A good joke. Coffee and a well-made cigar."

The air now smells of frost and manure. Buildings and bright windows embrace the ice-slickened road. A group of drunken men, arms slung over one another's shoulders, stumble past, singing at the top of their lungs. A carriage clatters by. Prostitutes call from doorways, promising unforgettable nights and unimaginable pleasure. The American ignores them all; the lines of his body seem tense and thrumming. Like a horse at the starting line. But I take it in with wide eyes, thrilled and intrigued.

"And where do you hail from?" I ask next, raising my voice to be heard over the commotion. Logically, I know it's silly to attempt further conversation in this setting, but there's a strange urgency in me to know him.

Shutters close over his eyes before the question has fully left my mouth. As he answers, Mr. Alistair searches the buildings to our right. "I spent my childhood in Boston," he says, his face turned away from me.

"What was it like? Do you have any brothers or sisters?" I press before I can stop myself. I try to imagine America, but having never left home, I'm only able to conjure images of the village we walk through now.

Mr. Alistair comes to an abrupt halt. It seems very deliberate when he says, "Ah, here we are."

It's our local leatherworker's shop—his name escapes

me at the moment. Mr. Alistair bounds up the steps and knocks on the door, then winks at me over his shoulder. We wait. All sorts of questions race through my mind, but I've embarrassed myself enough for one evening, so I remain silent. People continue to walk by, their voices boisterous. Once again I hold the edge of my hood in fear that one of them will catch sight of my face. Eventually the door opens a crack, too dark within to make out whoever stands on the other side.

Mr. Alistair speaks first, and the cheer is back in his voice. "Good evening. Wouldn't you believe it, but I spotted a bear earlier!" he exclaims.

I frown at the bizarre statement. It must be a code of some sort, because the door swings fully open a moment later. Mr. Alistair hurries to my side, offers his arm again, and propels us over the threshold. I go easily enough, eager to escape any prying eyes. Inside, the shop is still and shadowed. The smell of leather is prominent but not unpleasant. As the door closes behind us, I twist around, instinctively seeking a glimpse of the person who let us in. A gasp catches in my throat.

"This way," Freckles mumbles, not quite meeting our eyes. I bite my tongue to keep from saying something; he wouldn't remember me. Technically, we haven't met yet.

We head to the back of the shop, where Freckles leads us to another door, this one much smaller. It opens to reveal a set of narrow stairs. Our guide stands off to the side and doesn't offer any advice or instruction. Clearly, we're meant to go down.

I start forward, but Mr. Alistair bends to murmur in my ear, "Perhaps I should go first."

My thoughts are buzzing like a beehive from the intensity of my curiosity and uncertainty, so I just nod. The American is so tall that he ducks his head as he enters the stairwell. In doing so, he's forced to drop his arm, but he reaches back and laces his fingers through mine. If he notices the way I jump, he makes no comment. His hold is unexpectedly gentle. I silently pray that my palm isn't as clammy as I think it is.

We begin a rickety descent. Within moments, noise rushes up like a wave of hot air. Shouting, clapping, cheering, a din like nothing I've ever heard before. Mr. Alistair must sense my discomfort; his grip tightens. We reach the bottom and immediately find ourselves at the edge of a crowd. The cellar is larger than any other I've seen, devoid of any shelves or supplies a leatherworker might need.

Mr. Alistair doesn't ask permission before he puts a protective arm around me, but I don't protest. His hold is warm and firm. Before I have a chance to reconsider the foolishness of coming here, he pulls me into the chaos.

As we make our way through the throng, an assortment of smells assails me, most powerful of all the unmistakable stench of unwashed bodies. I'm trying to place another—it's almost salty, in a way—when a red spray flies through the air. There are sounds of surprise and encouragement. That's when it hits me, the exact smell filling my nostrils.

Blood.

Two men stand in the center of it all. Their bare shoulders gleam in the light, hair sticking to their scalps. I see one of the fighters get struck in the chest and he vanishes from sight. Somehow Mr. Alistair finds us a spot near the excitement, and we're able to see the fallen man again. He's on his knees, swaying slightly, a dazed look in his eyes. *Or eye*, I think, noting that the other one is pink and beginning to swell shut.

Slowly, he pushes himself up into a standing position. His opponent waits at the edge of the makeshift ring, lips tilted in a satisfied smile. He thinks he's won.

"Yes, that's it, back on your feet!" Mr. Alistair calls. He lets go of me to clap his hands.

I should be afraid. I should be appalled. But when the man looks like he's about to topple over, I'm swept away by the excitement of it all. I lean forward and join in the clamor. "Don't you dare give up!" I snap. The fighter's head swings toward me and his good eye widens. My hood has fallen. I feel a strand of hair against my cheek.

For some reason, the sight of me seems to reinvigorate him, and the man raises his fists. The other boxer—a very unappealing man, I decide, with his thick neck and pasty skin—laughs. The two of them circle each other. It looks like a game of cat and mouse, especially as one of them is so much bigger. My heart pounds and I can feel Mr. Alistair staring, but I can't tear away from the fight long enough to say something.

The man with the injured eye stops suddenly and blinks rapidly. The other takes advantage of the opening. Without any hint of pity, he moves closer and swings. His fist looks like a hunk of beef hung out to dry. A moment later, it connects with the poor man's face. More spittle and blood flies.

This time, when the man crashes to the ground, he

doesn't get up.

Dust floats through the air. I stare at him, so shocked and dismayed that I barely hear another man counting, giving him a chance to recover. But it's done. The fighter lying in the dirt doesn't move.

A roar goes up all around me. The victor raises both arms in the air, grinning from ear to ear. He's missing a front tooth.

I look at Mr. Alistair, but his attention is fixed on a round-faced young man across the way. My companion must make some sort of motion, because the stranger begins to come toward us. The moment he's within earshot, Mr. Alistair turns to me. "This is my friend, Bernard. And this, my dear fellow, is…" He trails off, remembering belatedly that we're trying to keep my presence here a secret. Mr. Alistair just grins and shrugs. "Well, who she is is still quite a mystery. Bernard, will you keep her company for a bit?"

"Of course," his friend says, nodding at me as though we've agreed on something. Mr. Alistair begins to pull away.

"Where are you going?" I ask in alarm.

He raises his brows. The crowd parts, allowing the fallen man to be carried through. "Why, to avenge your new friend, of course."

CHAPTER EIGHT

"T he night isn't over yet, lads!" the announcer—
if that's the proper term for his role in this
dusty cellar—calls. He's a short man with ill-
fitting clothes; his stomach strains against the brown vest
buttoned over it. "We have another contender!"

I watch, openmouthed, as Mr. Alistair enters the circle
and stands beside the sweaty, bloody victor from the
fight we just witnessed. "Is he mad?" I hiss to Bernard,
missing the announcer's next words. The boy appears at
a loss for how to reply; he stares at me like I've let out a
string of Russian.

I look back at Mr. Alistair, who only winks again, as
though we share a naughty secret. Then someone else says
his name, capturing his attention, and he turns away. A
woman at the front of the crowd—the only other female
here, it seems—makes a gesture I don't understand. The
American nods, reaches up, and begins to unbutton his
waistcoat. A minute later, he's naked from the waist up.

My face is on fire. Thankfully, Mr. Alistair still isn't looking at me, making it possible to take in the sight of him without being observed. Every line of his body is like something out of a painting, elegant and thought-out. His skin is golden, evidence that he's the sort of person who spends most of his time beneath the sun. His hair is a bit too long, though, the unchecked blue-black waves giving him a slightly wild look. Removing his shirt only made it worse. The muscles in his back tense and ripple as he stretches, still listening intently to a man next to him.

I had thought I'd known beauty, but this American sets a new standard.

Mr. Alistair glances in our direction, and I instantly drop my gaze. Flustered, I pretend to be preoccupied with fixing a loose strand of hair. The cellar feels like an oven. As the fighters prepare to begin, I remove my cloak and drape it over my arm. I focus on Mr. Alistair again, thinking of all the questions I'm going to ask him when this is over.

If he's actually conscious to answer them.

To our right, a few of the spectators are making wild bets. Money flashes as it exchanges hands. I glance from Mr. Alistair to them, and Bernard notices my interest. Without a word, he shoves some of the men aside to make room and nods at me. I hesitate for an instant. A hundred thoughts race through my mind and my heart pounds.

"Fifty quid on the American," I declare.

My words are met with stares of disbelief. One of the men is older and vaguely familiar. The leatherworker, I realize. With that, his name also comes to me. Mr. Coyle.

He is the first to recover. "Right," the man says. "Very

well, then. Anyone else? No? What about you, Bernard?"

Shouts fill every corner of the cellar, and I whirl to find that the fight has begun. I hold my cloak tight, helpless on the sidelines. Mr. Alistair makes it look like a dance; again and again, he dodges the big man's swings but lands none of his own. From the size of his opponent's fists, I have no doubt that if one of them were to land, Mr. Alistair wouldn't be getting back up.

It feels like my heart is in my throat. I lean close to Bernard and yell, "I'm afraid I don't understand the rules!"

"The round ends when one ov 'em is knocked down," he yells back, not taking his eyes off the brawl. "After that, they get fr'y seconds ter rest. There are no limits ter 'ow many times they go."

The big man strikes out again. I wince, but Mr. Alistair reappears in another spot, like magic. "And they fight with their bare hands?"

It's not a question that requires an answer, of course. We watch in tense silence for a few moments, but the rest of the room isn't silent. They're getting restless. They want blood.

Within moments, Bernard leans over again. His hot breath fans my ear. "They call 'im da Bear, miss. Nuff said, yeah?"

"What do they call Mr. Alistair?" I ask.

Before Bernard can reply, the man we speak of darts forward at last. Almost in a blur, he punches in quick succession, making the Bear's great head snap from side to side. When he finally manages to react, Mr. Alistair is gone. The Bear spins around, his dull features tight with shock and fury. Blood runs from a cut near his eye.

Like the animal he's named after, the large man charges, the crowd at that end of the room scattering in a panic. Once again, Mr. Alistair astounds us all with his agility; he steps out of the way and retreats in the opposite direction. He doesn't smile or taunt, as I half expect him to. He merely waits, emanating a cool control that seems to infuriate the Bear further.

He spits at the American and the glob lands in the dirt between them. "Thee don't fight nawmal," he snarls.

Now Mr. Alistair does grin. "I'm afraid I find normality frightfully boring," he drawls. He finds me in the crowd and winks.

Pay attention! I want to scream. As if he heard my unspoken cry, the Bear sees his opportunity. With a speed that startles everyone, I think, he rushes at Mr. Alistair. This time, the confident American moves too late. I watch in horror as the Bear jumps up and brings his fist down. In my mind, the entire room trembles upon his landing. Mr. Alistair goes sprawling gracelessly along the floor, leaving a trail through the dirt. Bright blood stains the earth.

It's all I can do not to bolt into the ring and put a stop to this. With an expression of triumph, the Bear draws his leg back, intending to kick his fallen opponent.

Just as I'm about to run to his aid and humiliate both of us, Mr. Alistair rolls out of the way and jumps to his feet. His lip is split open and the corner of his mouth is already swelling. The Bear stumbles and Mr. Alistair wastes no time. As though he were only playing a game before, he goes after the big man without a trace of hesitation or pain. He puts strength behind every strike and doesn't give the Bear any chances to retaliate. The cellar is so loud that my ears begin to ache.

There are only so many blows a man can take, even one as big as the Bear. After what feels like hours, he doesn't straighten. He sways back and forth, his eyes fluttering. Time seems to slow.

Yes, that's it. Give up, you nasty man, I think.

Finally, the Bear topples over. The ring fills with more dust as the announcer hastens between them and does his counting. I hold my breath and silently pray that the Bear doesn't get up.

He doesn't.

It seems to be the last fight of the evening—all at once, men flood the ring and it ceases to exist. I crane my neck but lose sight of Mr. Alistair. There is a familiar face working his way toward me, though, and I turn to him.

"Here you are, miss," Mr. Coyle says without preamble. He places some bills in my palm. Truth be told, I'd forgotten all about it.

Mr. Alistair chooses that moment to materialize. He's bloody and filthy, but he managed to locate his shirt. It hangs on his frame haphazardly, sticking here and there because of sweat. His coat and hat balance on one arm.

"Did you bet on me?" he asks with surprise. Wordlessly, the leatherworker moves on to continue dispersing money.

"Of course I did." I hardly notice that we are now alone; all my efforts go into taking stock of Mr. Alistair's injuries. "Are you hurt?"

These are the exact words Smoke spoke in Under just before the memory claimed me. Doubtless they're what triggered it. Without thinking, I reach for Mr. Alistair's shirt and pull the collar down to expose a rapidly forming bruise. In doing so, my fingertips brush against his skin. I catch a glimpse of dark chest hair before I remember myself, and I jerk back as though I've been burned.

Mr. Alistair smiles, slow and secret, his blue eyes brighter than ever. "Never better," he answers. It feels like someone has put a candle against both my cheeks.

A few of the young men have begun clearing out of the cellar, and one of them knocks into us, saving me from a response. The smell of alcohol surrounds him like a fog. Mr. Alistair's hand shoots out to steady me while the boy stumbles on; he doesn't seem to notice either of us.

"We should be getting back. Before someone realizes I'm gone," I say, my voice just as wobbly as the rest of me; Mr. Alistair still hasn't removed his hand.

He nods. "A moment, if you please. I must collect my winnings."

Together, we find a scruffy-looking man in the corner. He stands in the middle of a gathering like some famous opera singer at court. Questions fly at him. When will the next fight be? Who are the participants? Will the American defend his title as champion? Mr. Alistair catches the man's eye and money discreetly changes hands. I watch from a distance, attempting to hide my worry about another fight by fussing with my cloak.

After that, we join the multitude climbing the stairs. Freckles still stands by the door, trying for all the world to be nothing more than another shadow.

"What's your name?" I ask impulsively, stopping next to him. I hold the hood aside so he can see my face.

To say he's startled would be putting it lightly; I could

knock the boy down with a feather, should I have the urge. It takes him several seconds to answer. "My name is Abe, miss. That is, Abraham Green," he mutters. He's so much younger than he looks in Under. Much too young to be put in a grave.

"Well, it was very nice to meet you, Abe." My voice is gentle, and I catch Mr. Alistair giving me a bemused look as we leave the leatherworker's shop and step into the night. Raucous laughter echoes down the street.

The boxing matches may be over, but the night is far from it.

As we did on the journey here, Mr. Alistair and I cling to the darkness, if at all possible. Now I have so much to say, so much to ask him, but the American beats me to it. "Will anyone know you've been gone?" he questions, pulling his coat on.

A stray dog runs across our path. We pause to stay out of its way. "No, I don't think so. At least, no one who will betray me. Do you plan to fight again?"

He shrugs. "Most likely, if I haven't left town by then. How do you spend your days?"

At his mention of leaving, my heart experiences a strange little quiver. But I stop myself from asking about it further, for fear of seeming more invested than he is. "Well, until last summer, I had a tutor who came every day," I reply evenly. "But as I'm to be officially presented to society in the fall, there's not much else to do between now and then. I read, mostly. Write letters. Solve riddles or do puzzles, as silly as that sounds. Or I visit my best friend."

"Is this the young woman I've seen you with?"

"No. I speak of a boy, actually. My family lived next door to his most of my life."

Mr. Alistair quirks a brow. We've left the busy street behind, and quiet creeps around us like morning over the horizon. Darkened houses chaperone us on either side of the narrow street. "Ah, so it's another fellow, then," he replies, swirls of air accompanying each word. "Do I have competition for your affections?"

At this, I cringe and stop walking. My conscience clangs like church bells, though I'm not entirely sure why. "Mr. Alistair—"

"This 'Mr. Alistair' business is so dreary. I prefer James."

"As you are a gentleman, I should call you by your proper name," I reply. "In any case, there's something I need to tell you."

He falls silent and waits. Somehow, despite the cuts and bruises, he's as handsome as ever. Knowing it may be the last time I'm able to admire him like this, I hesitate. His hair shines an ethereal silver in the moonlight. His blue irises are like a blanket of fresh-fallen snow, so lovely and glittering.

When a frown begins to pull down the corners of his generous mouth, I swallow and force the next words out. The time for cowardice is past. "I'm engaged to be married, sir."

At this revelation, the being trapped inside this body—a dead girl named Key—silently gasps.

"And you should know that I'm not a gentleman," Mr. Alistair counters, his manner as affable as ever.

I blink. "I beg your pardon?"

Mr. Alistair tucks my hand in the crook of his elbow. We start walking again, though I don't take my eyes off him even to watch where I'm going. "My supposed childhood was in a Boston orphanage," he informs me. "I have no family to speak of and hardly a penny to my name. The suits you see me wearing aren't even mine; I won some unlucky soul's clothing in a card game. So I suppose we've both been dishonest. Although you kept your secret much longer than I thought you would. What would the minister think?"

"You *knew*?" I ask, trying not to gape.

A ghost of a smile curves those lips. There's a trace of sadness about it, somehow. "You're not the only one who likes puzzles. Before we met, I asked all sorts of questions about you."

I absorb this and find that I'm many things—flattered, pleased, nervous. "And what did you discover?"

"More than I bargained for, I'll tell you that. People in this village love to talk."

"Yes, they do."

"There's a rumor this marriage was arranged against your will."

He says it so casually that it takes me a moment to comprehend the words. When I do, I step on the hem of my skirt in shock. It's on the tip of my tongue to ask for more details, but just as I start to, Mr. Alistair draws to a halt. Startled, I glance up and recognize the house. The walk was far too short and I attempt to hide my disappointment. I decide not to address his bold comment, however true it is. "I suppose this is it. Thank you for a… stimulating evening, Mr. Alistair."

"James," he corrects. "And when will I see you again?"

My stomach flutters. "Again? I'm sorry, but I just don't think — "

Slowly, he reaches beneath the hood to cup my face, and whatever I'd been about to say flaps off into the velvet sky.

His thumbs skim the edges of my jaw, and for such a light touch, I can hardly remember how to breathe. James pauses, probably waiting for a rejection or a protest, but I stare back at him. My heart is a stallion on the moors, wild and racing. He lowers his head and our lips touch. His nose brushes my cheek. It's such a foreign sensation, having someone else's face so close to mine, and then it's gone. He's treating me like some fragile, frightened thing.

When James stoops to kiss me again, I open my mouth to his, utterly ignoring the cut. He makes a sound of surprise and digs his fingers into my hair. He tastes of tobacco leaves, gin, and a hint of blood. Forbidden.

I put my hand on his chest, thinking to end it, but I'm on fire. We move backward, deeper into the shadows. Parts of me that I've been taught to ignore awaken with an eagerness that steals all sense and reason.

James is the one to pull away. We both stand there, our breaths coming short and ragged. Desire radiates from him like heat from a furnace, and it's all too tempting to pull him back. Needing a distraction, or I won't have the strength to go inside, I take hold of his wrists and bring them down. I trace the length of each finger with the tip of mine. "You're going to ruin your hands," I say breathlessly.

It's somewhat gratifying that he sounds shaken as well. "That's the price, I'm afraid."

Almost absently, I stroke a wound on his knuckle that's healing. James shudders, but it doesn't seem to be in pain. My voice is steadier now as I wonder, "Why fight at all?"

"Why bet on it?" he retorts.

He has me there, and oddly enough, I like it. Being made to think, being presented with a challenge beyond decorum, books, or securing an advantageous marriage. I could argue with him all night. Alas, we've pressed our luck too much as it is. Shocking myself, I drop a tender kiss to his knuckles before releasing him. "I'll write when it's safe to meet again. Good night…James."

He smiles. It's different from his usual grin. Softer. "Sleep well."

With those words, his features begin to change. The healthy bronze of his skin fades into a pale hue. A familiar gap appears across his throat, held closed by stitches. Suddenly I'm on the ground, the cloak vanished and replaced by a tattered gown. Seconds tick past as I struggle to orient myself.

I am Key. This is Under. We are dead.

"Smoke?" I rasp. The memory has faded now. "Did you… Did you see all that?"

I'm shocked when he gives a barely perceptible nod. I'd experienced a memory in Journal's tower and he knew nothing of it. What makes this instance different from that one?

At some point, before we became lost in remembering, Smoke must've drawn close and knelt beside me. His expression is twisted, a myriad of feelings from concern to anger to…want. Something within me responds, like there's a knot in my stomach, attached to a string, and he tugs at the end of it. It makes no sense; I've just been attacked by Under's killer. In addition, we hardly know each other—even a handful of memories doesn't change that.

I should move away, say something, resist the pull.

Carefully, Smoke's finger brushes a strand of hair off my forehead. The touch is meant to comfort, but I remember the inexorable attraction between us. I put my palm on his chest in an instinctual attempt to defy it. The air shifts. His hands cup my face. When I don't protest, they trail down my shoulders, whisper the length of my torso, become fists in my skirt.

And he kisses me.

We have no wild pulses, no overwhelming heat. Yet the urges are there, the same as they were in life. To wrap myself around him and push so close that we resemble the river of roots, in that there is no way of discerning where I end and he begins. The memory of our late-night adventure to that leatherworker's cellar is so fresh.

I lean into him and eagerly respond. For the first time since arriving in Under, I feel achingly and wonderfully alive.

Smoke flattens one palm on the small of my back while the other roughly tangles in my hair. He tastes so familiar. We're still against the wall, and I use it as leverage to jump up and fold my legs around his waist. Smoke makes a sound deep in his throat, and I know I'll never think of him as a boy again. There is something at work here, something that banishes logic and reason and any lingering thoughts of Journal or "affairs of the heart."

Journal.

Just like that, I feel sick with guilt. But why? What does it mean?

Smoke senses my confusion and our frenzy ends as quickly as it began. He lifts his head and stares at me. Slowly, I release him and take two steps back. Smoke lets me, his arms falling away. He breathes hard, his chest rapidly rising and falling even though we have no need for air. And in that moment, another image brands my mind. Smoke, covered in blood, hand outstretched toward me. His mouth forms a word, and somehow I know it's my name. My real name. His face is made of pain and betrayal while my chest fills with regret and guilt. This Smoke struggles to breathe, too, and we both know his last breath is coming.

It's undeniably another memory, as demanding and short-lived as all the rest. Feeling as though I may vomit, despite the lack of food inside me, I retreat. I press a hand to my stomach, and Smoke frowns. His kiss still tingles on my lips.

"I think I killed you," I whisper, horrified. He goes still.

Before he can say anything, I run.

CHAPTER NINE

Once again, we convene in the town square.

This time, I know the routine. The dead argue and shout and resolve nothing. The fear in the air is so palpable I can almost taste it on my tongue, like something metallic. Soon, the violence will come. I stand along the far wall and wait, expecting that we'll slip away to the tavern like before.

This time, I won't make excuses in order to visit Journal's tower. My mind is a roiling mass as I avoid thoughts of him, the attack, and a certain dark-haired American. I'm not very successful. Every time the image of Smoke's final moments pops into my head, or I relive that rush of guilt after our heady kiss, self-loathing and dread twist my insides like some ancient torture device.

Attempting to forget about the past few hours is even more difficult to do when Handkerchief stands so near. He tries to seem nonchalant, but I know he's here to protect me. No reassurances or kind words would assuage his guilt about the attack. Soon after I fled from Smoke, the soft-spoken boy found me and begged forgiveness. His nose, which had been struck in the struggle, is bent permanently to the side.

"The bloody bastard moved too fast and he hit me *hard*. It was difficult to walk for a few moments. By the time I recovered, I couldn't find you," he said, his eyes dark. "I could hear you screaming, but it was dark and everything echoed."

His concern made me feel guilty for ever disliking him. "Handkerchief—"

Something sharp jabs at my ribs, jerking me to attention. Turning, I see that it's Ribbon nudging me. Her gaze is directed toward the front of the crowd, and I comprehend that someone is saying my name. "...a terrible ordeal for a young lady! Are you well?" Pocket Watch asks, looking directly at me. I nod, a jerky movement, and he clears his throat. His mustache twitches. "Right. As we were discussing, you are the first to survive, Key. Did the killer say anything?"

His words bring a memory to the surface—the cold sensation of a knife and fingers holding my tongue in place. I clench my fists so tightly that my nails break the skin. Everyone is watching me now. Feeling the weight of all their gazes, I force myself to answer. "No. The most I can tell you is that my attacker had a male build. I'm sorry."

"Don't apologize," Pocket Watch says soothingly. I imagine him as someone's grandfather, the one who always has sweets in his pockets and a joke to tell.

Unrest stirs in the crowd again. It feels as though the

size of the square is shrinking, and I want nothing more than to leave. "How can we know she's tellin' da truth?" someone demands. It's impossible to tell who. "Like you said, no one else 'as lived ter tell da tale. Not even Splin'er. How did one slip ov a girl escape?"

"You forget that I was there," a familiar voice drawls. A hush falls over them at the sight of Smoke. The American strides through the throng like they're water. He stops beside Pocket Watch and his crate. With his hands shoved in his pockets, Smoke faces them unflinchingly. Thinking of our last exchange—the kiss and, afterward, my horrified confession—I concentrate on the tips of my shoes so our eyes don't meet. "I heard her scream," he says. "I didn't see the assailant, but I did find his tracks afterward. His and Key's were the only fresh ones in that room. I would've kept trailing him, but there were too many in the alleyway."

Eye Patch shoves to the front now. His left sleeve dangles, ragged and empty. "If what you say is true, then we can still find him!" There's excitement in his movements. He seems to have dismissed Smoke's violent removal of his arm in light of this new development. "We'll simply compare everyone's footprint to the one."

His eagerness catches on, and as his followers form a plan, I recall an important detail. "I scratched him."

Everyone silences. "What did you say?" Eye Patch asks, his voice even. But his eyes burn.

Sensing his doubt, I raise my chin. "I scratched him. I'm sure of it. There's still something under my nails."

If the crowd was enthusiastic before, they're frantic now. While the noise increases, Pocket Watch looks thoughtful. He raises his voice to be heard. "Everyone will be examined. However, we should also pursue the footprints. It's important that we don't make any false accusations, and we'll know who our killer is for certain if we find both the scratches and his tracks. Do you remember the place, Smoke?"

He nods. Without another word, the boy quits the square. "Wait!" Pocket Watch calls. "We still have to conduct the examinations. Confound it, *wait*!"

Nearly every citizen of Under follows Smoke, too excited to listen. I watch them go, one by one, until only three of us are left. Huffing, Pocket Watch gives up and jumps off the crate to hurry after them.

"Are you coming?" Ribbon asks, touching my arm. Spoon is already rushing after the group. I shake my head, and Ribbon glances from the alley back to me, obviously torn.

"Go." I manage a smile. "I need someone to tell me what happens. I'm not keen on returning to that place."

Understanding flits through her expression. "But you shouldn't be alone, especially since now we know you're a target."

I shrug, as if her words don't strike new apprehension in my heart. "I'll go to the tavern and read. There haven't been any attacks on this side of Under. Not with so many witnesses wandering about."

"Well… I suppose." My friend gives my arm a squeeze before releasing it. She runs to catch up with Spoon.

The moment she's gone, small fingers grip mine. Jumping, I look down. Despite the many times our paths have crossed, Doll's dangling eye is still unnerving. I pray it doesn't show on my face. The child doesn't say anything; she just holds my hand and her toy. "Will you walk with me to the tavern?" I ask.

She nods, and together we leave the brightness of the square.

Halfway there, Doll lets go of me. She walks ahead and squats in the alley, sweeping dirt away to reveal something buried. The doll in her other hand stares at me with its black eyes.

"What do you have there?" I ask, worried that she's discovered another body part. I crouch beside the child and gasp at the sight of Journal's scroll. She must've stolen it from the tower again; it would be impossible to find unless she already knew where it was. Doll probably doesn't understand the writing, but I do. I read it over her shoulder.

It's in the touch. I didn't believe the rumors at first. Witchcraft isn't real. Not real, not real. But it is! They said there were two of them. One, two. The maid heard them in the attic. Black magic. Then the pretty one died. Dead as a doornail. I was the undertaker. I touched her cold skin. Cold like a fish. I saw the other one at the funeral. Dropped my watch, she picked it up. Touched my wrist. One killed me. It's in the touch. But which one?

The beginnings of an idea stir at the back of my mind. I frown, reaching for it, tugging at it, pulling it free. But just as I succeed, that familiar queasiness overtakes me. I try to hold back a moan. Bile rises in my throat. As I struggle to keep it down, I sense something moving and changing. Like before, the dirt all around fades into proper walls and hallways. I blink in wonder, but there's no time to study my surroundings.

"I have something else to show you."

Gasping, I spin toward the sound of her voice, certain my mind is playing tricks on me. But there she is. The girl from the first memory I experienced in Under—my sister, if these visions can be trusted—stands in the mouth of an alley, wearing the same nightgown as before. The candle in her hand quivers. I struggle to forget the scroll and focus on her. "More magic?" I manage.

The girl doesn't answer. She steps back and disappears into the darkness.

"Wait!" I hiss, rushing after her without a thought. She halts at the end of the passage, a faceless silhouette. The girl's bare feet slap the floor, and she leads me to the far end of the house. It's night again, and the sound of snoring echoes. I strain to see her features while she opens a narrow door on the left.

Oblivious, my sister holds the candle higher. "Up here," she says. I peer around the corner, and a steep flight of stairs beckons.

She brushes past and begins the climb. Flattening my palms against the walls on either side, I follow her. Each step moans. I count them silently, and when I reach the eleventh step, my head collides with a hard object. Wincing, I make out the dim shape of a ceiling beam, low and slanted.

"Sorry," the girl says. "I forgot to warn you."

She places the candle down on something. A strange shadow appears on the wall, and it takes me a few moments to realize it's the shape of a harp. Beside it is an old wedding dress, displayed prettily for no one to see.

We are in an attic. The girl kneels before one of the trunks. She uncurls her fingers, revealing a key that nestles in the center of her palm.

The key.

I feel my eyes widen, and I automatically look down at my chest, but of course the necklace is gone. She puts it in the trunk, undoes the latches, and lifts the lid so quickly that dust billows out. We both cough. Once she's recovered, my sister rummages through the contents within.

While she's distracted, I see something move out of the corner of my eye. Turning quickly, I'm startled when I see another girl standing there. One I've never encountered before. I step back, and so does she. Frowning, I raise my hand. The girl raises hers at the same time. The girl's eyes widen in the reflection, and I watch as she studies herself.

She is not tall or stately—her head barely reaches the top of the glass and her shape is more boyish than womanly. But she has elegant hands and a delicately defined collarbone. The green gown is gone, and her nightgown glows in the candlelight, thin and made of lace. It nearly draws attention away from the girl's face, which is pale and solemn. Her eyes are dark, fringed with even darker lashes. Her hair is a tangled mess. She has a small mouth that does not appear accustomed to smiling.

"Here it is."

Dazed, I turn away from the glass in time to see my sister reemerging from the trunk with a large book. The pages are stained and uneven and I can't find a title. "This is how I learned the magic," she whispers, answering my unspoken question. She touches the cover reverently, as though it's made of glass. I lean forward, curious, and she adjusts her hold on the volume so it's propped against her thighs. The spine creaks as she opens it. "I keep it here, where I first found it, so none of the maids stumble upon the book when they're cleaning."

I take it in. My interest is so overpowering that I settle on the floor beside her. The entire page is covered in strange pictures and shapes, like the walls of this attic. Only there's something more eerie and exotic about these.

"What is that language?" I breathe, awed.

"I've no idea. It's not Latin, Greek, or anything else I've studied."

"What made you look in the trunk in the first place?" I know it's not my imagination, the sense of power emanating from the book. I bend closer, and the scent of it reaches for me, old paper and the terrifying lure of the unknown.

The girl turns to a different page, and I examine this one closely while she answers. "I was awake one night, thinking about...Mother," she says, faltering. I sit up straighter, eager to know anything about our parents. "I knew that Father had removed all her things and brought them up here, and I wanted something of hers. To smell or hold. Anything just to remember. This was hidden in a false bottom of the trunk, along with a key. I wouldn't have found it if a shilling hadn't lodged in the casing. I tugged it free, and the bottom shifted."

As if it wanted to be found. Instead of voicing the unsettling thought, I ask, "Do you think she knew about it?"

"I don't know." She strokes the ancient paper. "It

wouldn't surprise me. There was always an...otherworldly quality about her, don't you think?"

The sorrow in her voice compels me to agree, though I don't remember our mother and we may as well be talking about a stranger. "Yes. There was."

Clearing her throat, the girl sits straighter and makes her voice brisk. "There are dozens of spells in here. Levitation is the only one I've been able to manage. I'm probably pronouncing all the words wrong. And many of the ingredients in the sketches are impossible to obtain. For instance, where does one find 'eye of newt'?"

It's a wonder she's been able to accomplish even one spell. I squint at the foreign words, as if that will help make sense of them. Suddenly it occurs to me that, were my sister to succeed at another spell, she would not know the result until it was actually occurring. "What if the other spells are dangerous?" I ask, picturing those glittering trinkets crashing to the ground.

"What if they are? The world holds countless dangers. Most are worse than some old spells in a moldy book." She says this so faintly I almost don't hear it. I don't know how to respond, and the girl saves me by getting to her feet and lowering the book back into the trunk. The latches click shut. She fetches her candle and says, "We'd best return to bed."

Murmuring a reluctant agreement, I quickly follow her toward the stairs so I'm not left in the dark. In my haste, I step on the edge of the nightgown I'm wearing and stumble. The girl quickly reaches back to grab my elbow and steady me. Her fingers are soft and warm. "Careful," she warns, and now she's holding the candle in such a way that I catch a glimpse of dark hair. My heart pounds. I want so badly to ask her name, but by now I know the futility of it. What I've learned in the attic must be enough. For now.

My chance to speak disappears as the girl turns away. Sighing, I tread more carefully down the stairs and into the hallway. For a third time, we make the journey through the moonlit house and arrive at what I am beginning to recognize as my bedroom door. Feeling the girl's eyes on me, I twist the doorknob as if I do it every day, and step inside. I face her, watching the small flame tremble. "Well, good —"

She steps forward, bringing a rush of air and lavender with her. "Meet me in the attic tomorrow night," she whispers, the words eerily similar to James's when he asked me to the boxing match.

A thrill goes through me. The little beetle in my head is saying something, urgent and cautious, but the words are easily drowned out at the prospect of another memory, another night of being alive, another chance to see magic and obtain answers. "Tomorrow," I whisper back. The girl kisses my cheek, startling me, and hurries away. A few moments later I hear a door close.

Smiling, I turn to go into my room.

But I'm back in Under.

Dirt walls stare back, unaffected by my disappointment. What happened to Doll? I touch the key resting against me and absorb the absence of a heartbeat all over again. I allow myself a few moments of self-pity before straightening my shoulders. I should find Doll, make sure she's all right, and get the scroll from her; I want to read the undertaker's strange words again. Anything to stop myself from obsessing over Smoke and my role in his demise.

Since there's no way of knowing where Doll went, I decide to check her room before going to the tavern. I retrace our steps quickly. My room appears first, on the left.Out of habit, I retrieve the torch and walk along its perimeter before continuing on, moving the flame high and low so as not to miss anything. The light reveals nothing but earth and familiar words. I'm about to give up when I see it. I smother a gasp.

Tucked in a corner where no one but me will see it, there is a new message on the wall. These fresh ridges are deeper and sloppier than the others, as if the writer was running out of time.

You are not safe in Under. You must find the door.

CHAPTER TEN

The smell of wood and earth fills my senses.

The river of roots guards my back. I'm kneeling next to the wall, exploring the surface with my hands in hopes of discovering some unseen crevice or outline. I become so intent on my task that I forget about the roots, and when I shift, one of the sharp edges snags my dress. The sound of ripping disrupts the stillness. Growling with frustration, I run my fingers along the tear to assess the damage. Bare skin greets my touch. My already-foul mood darkens further. I can't find the door, I can't find Doll, and now my dress is shabbier than ever.

"What are you doing?"

I let out a shriek and recoil. Since there's nowhere to go, I slam into the wall. My eyes narrow to slits as I search through the wooden tangle and spot Smoke lounging against a particularly large root, arms crossed. My ire fades into something else—a combination of wariness and shame. Beneath that, buried deeper than a grave, is desire.

Smoke watches me with obvious amusement, and I wonder if he knows I've been avoiding him. "I'm trying to get some of these roots loose," I lie, raising my voice. "I want to build a bookshelf."

There's a pause, and he studies me. I wonder if he sees the girl from the mirror in the attic or the girl who killed him. If only I could remember the truth of what happened that night.

"Well, you'd better find Tintype, then," Smoke says, his tone mild. "He probably has a few spare blades."

So he's not going to mention what I said the last time we were alone. *I think I killed you.* Relieved and confused, I look down at the roots. I can still feel his penetrating gaze. To occupy my hands, I yank at one of the wooden tangles. "Where does he reside?"

Smoke shrugs. He begins fiddling with his cigar. "Nowhere and everywhere. He can't be found unless he wants to be."

"Lot of help you are, then." My movements become jerkier and the root refuses to budge. "Why are you here?"

"Because you're not supposed to be alone. Ribbon was worried."

The guilt within me grows stronger. He says it without judgment, but it's easy to picture Ribbon standing in my empty room. She's probably imagining the worst—the killer snatching me a second time and succeeding in his task.

"I'm sorry. I just needed a moment," I tell Smoke, sounding more like myself. Realizing that part of my side is exposed from the tear, I quickly face him again. "She recently informed me that no one has any scratches.

She also mentioned the footprints in the place I was attacked. Or the lack of them, rather." The killer must have returned to remove all traces of his presence, but the others don't see it that way. It's obvious in how they look at me, half contemptuous, half suspicious. In their minds I'm either lying or toying with them, and both are dangerous.

The people of Under are looking for someone to blame, and if the identity of the real killer isn't discovered soon, I will have more to worry about than finding memories or doors.

Smoke, ever perceptive, watches me and the dark parade of thoughts that are no doubt marching across my face. Abruptly he says, "Come. I know a few places we can look for Tintype." He puts the cigar back into his pocket and holds his hand out to me.

I frown. "But you just said—"

"Perhaps we'll get lucky." Smoke's demeanor doesn't waver, and after a moment I lift my skirt to climb over the wooden river. I choose my steps carefully, and once I'm close enough, I take hold of his proffered hand. His fingers wrap around mine firmly and I involuntarily think of our kiss. In that instant, I lose my footing and fall. Smoke catches my waist and slowly lowers me to the ground. The feel of his hands banishes all thoughts. We stare at each other, neither of us moving or speaking.

How can he look at you like that? Especially when you could be responsible for his death? the beetle in my head wonders. Blinking, I finally take a step back. "Thank y-you."

Smoke stays where he is, head tilted, appraising me

again. Why isn't he furious? Why isn't he demanding the truth?

"Should we go, then?" I ask, attempting to sound normal. Smoke swings away without replying. As the darkness swallows him, I consider returning to my room instead of embarking on this search for Tintype. But I've wanted to ask the old man how he finds items like the ones in Journal's tower, and he has not appeared since the first murder. I think of how he stared at me. Why is it that no one suspects him?

I rush to catch up with Smoke and ask about it—he's looking back now, waiting for me—but he isn't Smoke anymore. Not the one I know, at least. Gone is the faint, crooked smile. The gruesome scar. The sad shadow in his eyes. Instead, after the usual bout of nausea, I blink rapidly and find James Alistair grinning at me through a window. His skin glows in the moonlight, and tendons stand out in his arms as he maintains a grip on the frame. He's so beautiful, so alive.

Gasping, I bolt out of bed and rush to lift the latch. "What are you doing?" I hiss, narrowly missing his head as the window swings open. "You'll fall to your death!"

"I received your letter," he tells me, seeming unconcerned. "I must ask, how did you know where I'm staying?"

Any further words of admonishment die in my throat, and I know I'm blushing. The sight of it just makes James's grin even wider. There's a cold wind this evening, and it flattens my thin nightgown against me. I clear my throat and ask primly, "So you received my letter. Good. What shall we do tonight, then?"

Surprising me, James hesitates. He looks down, and I follow his gaze. I've been so absorbed in looking at his face that I didn't notice our hands; we both hold the sill tightly. Our fingers fit in the spaces between each other's, nearly touching.

Ever so slowly, James moves them closer. "...may not sound all that adventurous," he is saying, "but the truth is, I should very much like to speak with you all night long. Until the roosters crow and the sun rises, if you'll allow it."

I meet his eyes again, and a happy warmth spreads through my chest. "Well, I can't stay so long as that, but how about until the moon and stars begin to fade?" I ask shyly.

"You have yourself another bargain, my lady."

The softness in his voice carries a promise. Somehow I manage to say, "I need to fetch my coat. Try not to break your neck as you're climbing down."

He replies, but I don't hear the words as I'm already rushing away. Cautiously, I open my bedroom door and peek in both directions. The hallway is empty, with only shadows and furniture to stare back at me. My heart races. Though I'm tempted to wake the girl who calls me her sister, the allure of James is stronger. I duck back inside to grab a dressing gown, then tiptoe through the house. When I reach the stairs, I fly.

Seconds later, clad in a thick coat, I sneak through the front door. The hinges let out a long groan. I freeze, cringing, but nothing stirs. James is leaning against the house, bold as you please. Once again, he offers his arm. Once again, I take it.

We stroll down the street like any other couple, as

though it's broad daylight and we have nothing to hide. The daring of it makes my heart hammer. For a time we speak of small things, easy things, until we come upon a bench. It's on the edge of a park, which lies serene and empty. James looks at me with raised brows, a question in the gesture, and I smile. He brushes off a fine powdering of snow and bows with a flourish. Heedless of the cold, I sit.

James follows suit and we face each other. In that instant, it's obvious his eyes aren't entirely blue; there's a ring of gold around the pupil, vivid in the light of the streetlamp.

There's so much I still don't know, I think. *I want to know everything.*

"What would you like to know first?" James asks, laughing a little, and I realize I've spoken the thought out loud.

"Tell me how it began. The fighting, I mean." My words are met with silence. I watch James struggle with himself for a moment or two and guess the reason. "If you're embarrassed or ashamed, James, please don't be. None of that matters. Not to me."

He exhales through his nose, sending puffs of air into the darkness. He puts his elbow on the back of the bench, a deliberate effort to appear at ease, I think. "It's a funny story, actually," he says. "I was fourteen at the time. My only friend was a beggar, and I'd slip him some food from the orphanage whenever I could. One day I brought a bit of bread and found him beaten half to death. Turns out he'd been fighting for money. He was supposed to box that very night, in fact, but of course George was in no shape for it. So I went in his place."

"Goodness. And you'd never fought before? Did you win?"

"No." The answer is so surprising that I let out a startled laugh. James's smile is sheepish now. "No one in history has lost more horribly than I did that night. Still, I got a taste for it after that, so I kept going back. Eventually, I did win. I left that warehouse beaten more often than not, but over time that changed. Now it's how I earn enough for passage from place to place."

"Where else have you been?"

"Now that's a story. I first began in Boston, as you know. Then I bought a ticket and made my way to Canada…"

The scene begins to fade. *No, please,* I think. But it's no use; between one blink and the next, everything returns to the way it was. Rocks and dirt and darkness.

"Key, what's wrong?" Smoke asks, frowning at me.

He called me Key, which means I'm truly back in Under. The image of us endures, though. A boy and a girl, sitting on a bench beneath a lone streetlight. Snow falls gently all around them. Stars twinkle above, a full moon shines, and they have eyes only for each other.

The lingering feelings are powerful enough to stir my gray, shriveled heart. Swallowing, I raise my face to his. "I beg your pardon, Smoke. Have you…that is, is there anything you've…"

"What?"

It's tempting to share these brief glimpses of our lives before. But Journal's reaction is still fresh in my mind; he didn't believe my tales. *Smoke is different, though, isn't he? He saw something, too.*

"Where are we going?" I ask quickly, courage failing me. I start walking, forcing Smoke to do the same or be left behind. "It seems like we're walking in circles."

"Tintype has odd hiding places," he answers, fixing his concentration on the path. "Doll showed me a few."

A flicker of fear goes through me as I realize how far we are from everyone else. Maybe it's foolish of me to be so trusting of Smoke, especially if he's remembered anything of how he died. "Doll?" I echo, ready to bolt in the other direction. If he moves toward me...

"She may not speak, but she has more to say than anyone else here."

Before I can respond, Smoke slows again. His expression intensifies. My phantom pulse picks up speed, thundering in my ears, and this time when I look ahead, there's more than dirt and darkness. Tintype is in the alley down the way, sitting directly beneath a torch. His back is to the wall, legs brought up against his gaunt chest. He's staring at something in his hand. It's square and metal. I remember Ribbon telling me that he has a picture of his wife.

"There he is," I murmur, as though he's a wild animal easily spooked.

Smoke raises his brows. "Well? Ask him if we can borrow a knife."

"We?" I echo.

"You think I'm going to let you use it? There's a better chance of you lopping off your own hand than cutting those roots loose."

I huff, but there's mirth in the sound. "What poppycock. I could be quite skilled with a knife. There's no way of knowing until I have one in my hand."

"I heard you coming," Tintype says, startling both of us. My amusement dies. "Worse than a herd of elephants, the lot of you." He tucks the picture back into his uniform and looks at me.

Seconds tick by, thick with tension, and Smoke elbows me. Hesitantly, I step closer. Tintype waits, the buttons on his shirt gleaming. I start to ask him about his talent for finding things, but it doesn't feel right with Smoke here. "If I may, I would like to borrow your knife, sir."

Tintype is silent. He's staring again, and I don't think he's aware of it. His eyes are so pale they seem colorless. I don't know what to say or do, but my earlier sense of foreboding is gone. I don't know him, and yet my instincts say his interest is not a threat.

Some part of him must have heard the question, though, because Tintype stands. He digs in his pocket and presents a small knife. As the soldier continues to watch me, the folded blade slips from his fingers. It hits the ground with a dull *thud*.

At the same moment, both of us bend to retrieve it. Something else falls out of his pocket and flutters to the ground. He must not notice, and while he wraps his fingers around the handle, I pick up the tiny piece of paper. *The curse must be broken.* The handwriting is the same as all the others.

Shocked, my gaze flies up to his. "You," I whisper.

CHAPTER ELEVEN

The man tenses, and I have no doubt that were it not for his leg, he would already be gone. My grip tightens on the piece of paper as I ask, "Who are you?"

He begins to answer, but whatever he says is lost to me. There's a familiar sensation of falling, and though I try to keep my eyes open, it's too fast and too dizzying. Then I open them again and I'm standing in front of a house. It's dusk, the sun barely peering over the horizon. The light is enough to see a man in a uniform walking away. His boots make crunching sounds on the gravel. He takes the proffered reins from a stable boy, runs his hand over the horse's shining mane. I wait. Finally, hesitating, he turns to me.

This face is different from the one in Under. There are still lines, still marks that give away times of sorrow and hardship, but his eyes are different. I wouldn't say they have hope, exactly, but there's more than death and darkness. A sort of…tired determination.

"Please," I say. Tintype's mouth is a thin, hard line. I know there's no purpose in saying it, but I hear myself do it anyway. "Don't go."

He climbs up into the saddle, overly preoccupied with adjusting the straps holding his bags in place. The servants have deliberately drifted away, off to other tasks. Packing the rest of my things and covering the furniture. "I can't," the soldier answers. He swiftly changes the subject. "I've seen to all the arrangements. Mrs. Thompson will accompany you to town later today. Your arrival is expected. Make sure to treat your hosts with respect, dear girl."

After he finishes speaking, I linger on the steps, certain he means to say more. But he doesn't offer any promises or sentiments. With a click of his tongue, the man jolts into motion. I watch him go down the road, toward the brightening sky, and into the sudden darkness that doesn't belong.

I'm back in Under. I stare at Tintype, surrounded by dirt and lies, and another memory returns. A truth that maybe part of me knew all along, from the moment I laid eyes on him. It's fortunate that I have no need for air, because it feels as if my lungs have contracted.

Though I don't say the words out loud, Tintype must see it in my expression. "I wondered when you would remember," he says simply. He isn't surprised.

My father.

"Why not just tell me?" I demand. I clench my fists, glaring now, torn between a dozen emotions. Anger, joy, sorrow. Even now, grown and battered by far more than a distant father, I feel the sting of his leaving.

Tintype shifts from foot to foot. "To avoid this very conversation. There's not much beyond that to tell. I knew you would want to know everything. And I have nothing."

I might have believed him, were it not for the way he's looking at everything but me. Evading a discussion between us is not the true reason he withheld this for so long. When I respond, my voice is colder than dead flesh. "You were ashamed."

He doesn't deny it. Tintype may not have his memories, but he knows as certainly as I do that he was my father in name only. I can still feel the ache as I watched him ride away, echoes of feeling so desperately unwanted.

In the silence that follows, I realize that I'd completely forgotten Smoke. But now the spot beside me is empty. He must have retreated to give us privacy, a surprising gesture. Dimly I realize that Tintype is speaking.

"...my fall, I began to remember. The memories were faint, but I knew that I had a daughter. I saw myself at your funeral. As time went on and you didn't arrive with the others, I decided it was necessary to take matters into my own hands."

The revelation triggers something, and just like that I'm back in the grave. Silence, cold, oblivion. Then something happened to make me stir.

"Your voice," I whisper in a burst of comprehension. Somehow, I'd forgotten those words that drifted down to my resting place. *Wake up. Please wake up.* "I remember it now. You called to me while I was in the grave. It was the sound of your voice that made me fall."

He nods. "Long before that, I found the key in one

of the alleyways here. Doll eventually led me to the door. Every day I would open it, lock it behind me, and go up to the graveyard."

"The door," I cut in faintly, remembering now. "Am I to understand that it's possible to leave Under?"

"Anyone can if they have the key."

Tintype says this as though it's so simple, so obvious. But my mind staggers. All this time, we could have been above. Away from a murderer. Out of the darkness. Feeling ill, I press a shaking hand to my forehead. "I don't understand. Why haven't you shared this knowledge? Why haven't you—"

"Think, girl," the soldier snaps. "What if they all wanted to go topside?"

It seems that even in death, I long for the approval of my father. Without hesitation, I obey him and imagine it. Every one of the dead—Eye Patch, Smoke, Pocket Watch—walking about in the daylight. Anyone who saw us would be terrified. And even if some of us have family left who'd be able to accept such a bewildering turn of events, what kind of life could we lead? Never aging, never belonging.

Loath as I am to admit it, Tintype's decision to remain silent had probably been the correct one.

"I apologize for interrupting," I say stiffly. "Please continue."

His tone is matter-of-fact as he does so. "Sometimes I walked to town. I couldn't ask questions or risk being seen, so I just took things from houses to make our lives in Under more comfortable. I also hoped to overhear something about the circumstances of our deaths. I always returned to you before the sun came up. For hours I sat by your headstone and spoke to you. Finally, the night came that I unearthed your casket and put the key inside. I had an inkling that you would need it once you awoke. Of course, I had no way to return because I had given you the only means into Under. So when the way was clear, I followed you through the hole."

Almost involuntarily, his gaze flicks down. His limp. So there was a cost in waking me.

Sadness fills my throat and makes it impossible to speak. It occurs to me that I should thank him for what he did; without his efforts I could very well still be in that cold grave. Never knowing Smoke, or Doll, or Ribbon, or Journal, or all the rest. But the words won't come.

Tintype waits for another moment. Slowly, he takes a step back. I know he means to disappear again, and desperation loosens my tongue. I'd been meaning to ask him the first question that should've occurred to me—my name—but a more important one arises.

Lunging forward, I seize his arm. "My sister! Do you know who she is; is she here in Under?"

Confusion clouds his eyes. He shakes his head. "You never had a sister. Not that I remember, at least."

"No, that can't—"

Tintype pulls free. "My role in this is finished. The townspeople spoke of a curse—it must be true, else why would we be here?—and I had a sense that you might be the one to break it. That's all I can say. If I remember anything else, trust that I'll seek you out."

Part of me knows I should stop him, that I may not have another chance to speak with this man. But I watch him limp away and do nothing. His eagerness to escape makes the wound in my back seem harmless compared to the pain in my heart.

The darkness swallows him and, after that, the alleyway is silent. I linger for a time, hoping Smoke will return. When there's no sign of him, I begin to make my way back. A new thought pops into my head, though, and I jerk to a halt. *The wretched door.* I spin back around. "Tintype! I still don't know where—"

He's gone, of course.

I swallow a curse and continue on my way. Soon I reach the house that still doesn't quite feel like home. I stand in the doorway and stare at Tintype's first message. *I remember you.* With a cry, I run at the wall and claw it with all the strength in me. Chunks of earth fall at my feet. When it's done, I drop to the ground and weep. Great, heaving, dry sobs. No tears fall, of course, and it's never seemed so cruel, the inability to fully grieve. No one comes to comfort me, and I wouldn't let them if they tried.

Some grieving must be done alone.

After a time, I curl on my side, shuddering. My eyelids flutter. Though it's not truly possible, I succumb to something that feels like sleep. Wonderful, soothing sleep.

I send a prayer above that I'll never wake.

"Wake up."

A puff of warm air envelops my face. I open one eye. Moonlight streams through the filmy curtains, and someone is kneeling next to the bed, her elbows leaving indents in the mattress. The girl must see that I'm awake and adds, "Hurry. It'll be morning soon." She stands and picks something up from the floor—the book. Then she moves to the door.

Once again, I have no control over the words that leave my mouth. "What are we doing tonight?" I ask, sitting up reluctantly, though I should be eager. I want to ask why she made me believe we're sisters, who we are, what the end of this story is. But my mouth won't obey any commands.

Without a candle to illuminate her presence, the girl's voice drifts from the darkness. There's a note of excitement in it that belies the solemnity of our surroundings. "I've a confession; I started without you. And I'm fairly certain I learned how to do a love spell! Do you remember our neighbor's dog? The crusty old poodle?" She doesn't give me a chance to answer. "Well, it was sniffing about the house again, so I brought it up to the attic with me. And once I spoke the words, it's been enamored with me, I swear! I had to put it back outside to get away from that horrid breath. There, can you hear it whining at the door? The thing won't go home now!"

The last dregs of sleep are still fading, and I fail to hear most of her confession. Only certain words stand out. "A love spell?" I repeat warily, rubbing at my eyes. I peel the covers away and touch my feet to the cold floor. "I'm not sure about this, Kathleen…"

Shock travels through me. Kathleen. Her name is Kathleen. Dimly I comprehend that she's speaking again and force myself to pay attention. These memories hold the answers to everything, and they're too vague and brief as it is. "…worrying!" she insists, so enthusiastic that she forgets there are others in the house. "It's nothing drastic, just a bit of magic that will make him turn my way. Now come!"

"Make who turn your way?" I ask, finally obeying. I drift after her into the hallway, and she surprises me by taking a right instead of a left.

"James Alistair, of course. The dashing American. He's not like the other boys, wouldn't you agree?" There's a dreaminess to her voice I haven't heard before.

"Have you two spoken?" I manage. Now that we're talking of him, my mind goes back to our first kiss beneath the streetlamp. To our long conversation on that bench. I'd known Kathleen was intrigued by James, but so was every girl in town. She'd concealed the depth of her fascination. Realizing that I'm once again missing her words, I shake myself.

"…visited the house once, most unexpectedly," she tells me. "Muriel was appalled. I think that's why he didn't stay long. But it was proof that he once felt the same way I do, or was interested, at the very least!"

The house is unusually bright. Outside, the moon is full. Kathleen is walking away, making it impossible to see her face, but part of her nightgown droops and something on the back of her shoulder catches my eye. The whiteness of her skin is marred by a large bruise.

"What happened?" I ask without thinking, studying the colorful mark of pain.

Her response is sharp. "Don't ask questions you already know the answer to."

Cowed, I don't speak again, and she leads me down a wide staircase. We've entered what is clearly the foyer, and it's the grandest room I've ever seen. A chandelier hangs from the ceiling, dripping with pearls and glittering jewels. The walls are adorned in paintings, these more beautiful than ominous, and the marble floor gleams in the silvery light. Gripping the railing, I slow to look at everything.

Kathleen just hurries down the rest of the stairs and opens the door without hesitation. A dark shape launches itself at her. She drops the book as the beast crashes into her. Kathleen grunts and barely manages to maintain her balance. The shadows are so thick it's difficult to see what is happening. I open my mouth to scream, but then she turns toward me. A slant of moonlight falls over the creature, and I realize that her arms are wrapped around a...poodle. All her efforts go into forcing its frantic tongue away from her face.

"Do you see?" she crows at me. "Imagine the potential!"

I'm gawking. All I can think is, *You want to reduce a man to this?*

When I say nothing, Kathleen sets the dog down and pushes it back outside. Just as it starts to leap at her again, she slams the door. The dog whines through the wood. My heart hurts for the poor creature.

Ignoring the sounds, Kathleen rushes at me and takes my hands. Of course her face is hidden in darkness. "I want to test it one more time, just to be certain," she says urgently. "Can you think of another subject we should use?"

"A subject?" I echo. It seems that's all I'm capable of tonight. Suddenly I notice that our palms are slippery, and I gasp at the sight of blood. "Did you cut yourself for this spell?"

Making a sound of impatience, Kathleen turns away again. She surveys the foyer with her hands on her hips, as though something will appear or announce itself. "Oh, I know!" she gasps. "Wait here. No, meet me in the attic. Bring the book. I have an idea."

With that, she leaves. The dog continues to cry, and I know I can't leave it like that. My gaze falls to the book on the floor—Kathleen never lets it out of her sight—and I pick it up to examine the pages. The dog begins to scratch desperately, as though it's going to dig through the door itself. I glance toward the top of the stairs, worried that someone will hear and investigate. When no one stirs or appears, I focus on the book again. A small voice in my head insists that I bring it to the attic, as Kathleen instructed, but I have no control over my hand as it turns the pages one by one. It stops when I reach an incantation toward the middle. All thoughts of danger dissipate.

Kathleen's writing appears on the page. *Love spell*, her scrawl reads. It feels wrong, like a rule has been broken. My mouth goes dry.

There's a strange lump beneath the page. Frowning, I flip it over and find an envelope tucked in the book's spine. The wax seal has been broken. Though my conscience twinges at the knowledge that I'm reading someone's private correspondence, I can't help myself; I pull the letter out. It's written in an elegant feminine script. My eyes consume the words:

My darling daughter,

I've made it so that you will only find this book when there is a true need. I hope that time never comes. If it has, your father must have succumbed to his violent urges again, and for that I'm sorry. Over the years, I have caught glimpses of it, but he always manages to rein it in. Please don't hate him. His own father was a brutal man. We learn how to respond to anger at the knees of our parents. However else it may seem, he does love you.

We have ways to help him that the vicar or the physician do not. You are too young to be taught the old ways, but you have power, Kathleen. It is only possible for women to wield it, and this book has been handed down from every generation in our family. Even so, keep it hidden. The world is full of people who fear the unknown.

There is more to be wary of, darling. The words and ingredients within these pages are simply a guide for that power. The true power rests in our blood. Any words of intent that spill from your lips will be rich with it. Use your veins only if there is true need.

I've also found that whatever emotion we're feeling affects the outcome of the spell. Many of our ancestors misused their power and went mad. It can be dark and addicting, if we let it. Keep a clear mind and an open heart, daughter.

I wish there had been more time to properly show you how beautiful this gift is. But there are some things even magic shouldn't reverse. As such, think of me whenever you feel that prickling in your fingertips and a shift in the air. I'm here, even if my body isn't. I love you, Kathleen.

Your mother

Slowly, I put the letter back in its hiding place. My mind resembles a ballroom, chaotic with movement and sound and color. Kathleen must've found this recently; when she first showed me the book, she hadn't known anything of its origins.

Before I can truly absorb what I've just read, something draws my gaze toward the bottom of the love spell, where there is a smaller block of text. It stands apart from the original words, yet somehow I know it still relates to them. One looks similar to the English version of *undo*, despite its strangeness. Following a hopeful whim, I read this bit over and over, memorizing it. My blood sings, as if this is what I was born for.

Finished, I set the book down on the table where I know we normally receive calling cards. I have no idea what I intend to do or what I've just learned. Still, I don't fight it. Like the kiss with James, there is an unseen force compelling me.

Walking to the door, I step aside and twist the knob. The dog instantly tries to bolt past in search of Kathleen, but I haul it back by its scruff. As I have no ingredients, I sink a savage bite into the fleshy part of my palm. Red drops swell through the new, ragged openings.

Under my breath, I say the words burning in my memory. A tingling sensation travels my entire body. It feels like I'm falling from a great height. The creature fights me for a few moments, but the second I utter the final syllable, the tension eases out of its body. To be certain, though, I hold on a bit longer. The dog doesn't whine or struggle. Gradually, I release my hold and ease back on my haunches. It pants happily now and scratches its stomach with its hind leg. Its claws hit the floor. *Click-click-click*. Then, moving so swiftly I have no chance to avoid it, the dog gives me a sloppy kiss.

I gag and push it away. The poodle sneezes and looks at me with innocent eyes. "She was right," I whisper, wiping my face with the back of my sleeve. "You *do* have horrible breath."

Unperturbed, it gives me one more lick and prances off into the night, those claws clicking against the cobblestones. I stand and watch it go, thinking about the words I can still taste on my tongue. I may not have seen Kathleen's face or learned anything of the curse my father mentioned, but I know something more. Something vastly important, even more so than the contents of the letter.

I knew how to do magic, too.

CHAPTER TWELVE

Doll finds the third body.

This one takes a bit longer to identify. Using a sad sort of roll call, we eventually discern that the victim is Freckles. Tintype is missing, as well, but this body is too slender to be his. I stare at the remains, ignoring the chaos all around. To everyone else, he is the quiet boy with a speckled face. To me, he is the boy who once sat beside me in the tavern. Grief is becoming a constant companion, and it holds my hand, there in the square. "Farewell, Abe," I say to his corpse, hoping that he's no longer able to hear it.

The memories are returning too slowly, I think, hiding clenched fists in the folds of my skirt. *I need to find the murderer before he strikes again.*

The truth waits in my past, I know it. And if I can't find it in my head, then perhaps I can among the living. I need to go topside.

It's my fourth visit to this particular place since my

arrival in Under. As everyone else succumbs to hysterics, I remember what Freckles told me. *Ribbon is our voice of reason. She's been here longer than almost anyone.* He stared at me with those blue eyes and I recoiled at the brush of cold skin. I didn't even try to hide my revulsion.

Ribbon doesn't attempt to assert that reason now. Pocket Watch is losing control more than ever before, and Eye Patch is shouting so loudly the living must be able to hear him. There's no sign of Smoke or Journal. I consider leaving, but that would place even more suspicion on me than there already is. Someone mentions Tintype—who's been absent since the day I remembered who he was, and whom no one has much knowledge of whenever I ask— and shouts begin for a search. A few men disappear with torches. The dead who remain continue to argue.

"What about the girl?" a woman demands, pointing at me.

"None of this started until she got 'ere," someone else mutters.

I freeze, knowing I should say something but uncertain what will assure them of my innocence.

Ribbon darts to the front. Spoon moves closer to me, winking, and I try to smile back. Then we both focus on Ribbon, who gives Pocket Watch a coy bump with her hip. He's so startled that he steps off the crate.

My friend nimbly hops up and looks out at the crowd without a trace of fear. Her ribbon is the only splash of color in the square. "We must take our minds off these dreadful murders!" she announces. "It is clear that nothing is being resolved today. I propose a dance!"

"A dance?" I echo incredulously. Heads swivel in my

direction, and some scowls return. Spoon steps on my foot, and her girth is enough to cause discomfort. *Shut up*, her look says. I give her a baffled look in return. "But how—"

Ribbon lifts her chin. The rumbling quiets once again. "We still have the fiddle, don't we?" she counters. "There must be someone who can play. And we have our hands for clapping, as well as our feet for stomping. It shall be a grand event, I promise you."

Her fervor is contagious, spreading as quickly as rage or fear, and people are nodding. One man volunteers his harmonica while another promises to light as many torches as possible. I have no interest in planning a party. While everyone is distracted, I escape into the alley that will take me to my room. The passageway is brightly lit and busy enough that the killer wouldn't dare attack here.

Reaching the doorway, I notice that a tiny figure sits in the one opposite mine. She makes no sound as she plays with her toy. I sit beside Doll, letting out a breath, and she merely edges over to give me room.

For a minute or so, I observe. Her movements are graceful, the dirt coating her skin making them all the more entrancing. I am reminded that beauty can be found even amidst so much grime and death.

"Would that I had fallen with a pint," I say, leaning back on my elbows. "I don't know if I drank in life, but in death I surely would enjoy one."

The little girl doesn't respond. I'm about to ask her for the scroll when laughter echoes through the alleyways. Somehow Ribbon has brought them from the brink of violence to excitement about a dance. I listen in disbelief. It occurs to me that with everyone occupied, it might be a good time to slip away to the river again. But there is no telling how long they will be in the square, and I don't dare venture to the roots by myself. Not when so many suspect me and the murderer is becoming bolder.

"At this rate, I'll never have time to find the blasted door," I confide in Doll. She surprises me by going still. Our eyes meet, and all at once, I remember something Tintype said. *Doll eventually led me to the door.* "You… you know where it is, don't you?"

Whatever she sees in my face convinces her of something, because Doll takes my hand. Despite my qualms about traversing the empty places of Under, I allow her to pull me away. This is too important.

Silently, she guides me through the maze. The group searching for Tintype still roams the outskirts; I can hear their frustrated shouts. "Will they find him?" I whisper. Doll shakes her head. We continue on, passing Journal's tower, and I allow myself one look toward the lights at the top. It is too far up to see him, of course. Every time I am tempted to visit, I recall his doubt. *Why are you so certain this is a memory?*

Our friendship must have meant far more to me than it did to him, anyway; he has not sought me out or questioned my absence.

Do you really care? the beetle asks snidely. *You seem quite occupied with Smoke.*

Resisting the urge to sling a childish insult at it, I silence my thoughts and try to pinpoint which passage we're in. The faint sound of humming is a giveaway — I still have not met the unfortunate Brooch — and by the time we reach our destination, I already know where

we're going. The river of roots awaits, usually cold and
elegant in its strange splendor. But no one has thought
to replace the dying torches, and the veins of the ancient
tree suddenly seem menacing. "I've looked everywhere,"
I tell Doll, sighing.

She tugs insistently and releases my hand to climb
over. "Careful!" I call, hushed. Doll maneuvers to the
other side with ease, and gestures for me to follow. The
intensity of her expression makes me swallow further
protests.

My progress is slower as I try to keep my dress from
tearing again. Doll is patient. The eyes of her dangling
toy watch, too, as I finally jump down next to her. Doll
takes hold of my hand once more. Somehow she's able
to see well enough to navigate through the narrow space
between the wall and the roots. I count the steps quietly.
Fourteen…fifteen…sixteen…

Doll halts. She looks directly at me and points down.

Lowering myself to my knees, I strain to see. There's
nothing. More dirt and rocks and darkness. Was this all
a game to her? Straightening, I clench my jaw to keep
barbed words from escaping. I remind myself she's only
a child. "Very funny," I grind out. "You fooled me. We
should—"

But Doll stomps her foot and points again, more
emphatically this time. Her blue mouth forms a word.
Look.

Humoring her, I kneel again and shift so my shadow
isn't falling over the wall. As I did the time Smoke
interrupted me, I lean close and run my fingers over it.
And there, just where Doll said it would be, is a hole in

the earth. It's so small that it would be impossible to find, unless you knew where it was. Exploring it, examining it, I notice the odd shape of the hole and feel my eyes widen. Because I know there's only one thing that would fit into it. One thing that would turn the inner latch and open this door without a knob. One thing that would let me out of Under.

Tintype told me it would be so, but it's still thrilling. Smiling, I touch the chain around my neck.

A key.

I wait for my chance.

Ribbon flits this way and that, trying to make the tavern festive. I obey whatever instructions she throws my way, but the door is all I can think about.

It's been hours since Doll led me to it. I had been just about to leave, the key poised over the hole, when my name echoed through all of Under, panic laced in the familiar voice. *"Key!"*

Of course it was Ribbon, thinking I had been taken and killed. It would've been cruel to worry her that way, so I reluctantly followed Doll back to reassure our friend. Though everything within me wants to bolt, I know I need more than a few minutes to explore the outside world. Ribbon, who is far too protective for her own good, has occupied nearly every moment of my time preparing for the dance. Endeavoring to make the tavern as clean as possible, seeking anyone who was not in the square when the invitation was issued, amending our own appearances so that we look more like the living. The tear in my dress is finally seen to.

Ribbon also insists on finding decorations of some sort. "Was Tintype brought back?" she asks, surveying the space critically. "I don't know how he does it, but the man can find anything. Perhaps there's some...old flag buried around here. Wouldn't that add a splash of color?"

I'm saved from having to answer when a group of people shuffles through the door. Ribbon beams and moves to greet them. In preparation for the occasion, she's been teaching the citizens of Under *how* to dance. Thankfully, there's no need for me to participate in the lessons, as it seems I know the steps quite well. I go to a spot out of the way and Ribbon begins. Briefly, I allow myself to wonder where Smoke is during all this.

"Now, today I would like to focus on the waltz. It's a fairly easy one. Simply count in your head. One-two-three, one-two-three." Her voice is high and clear, like a bell. She puts them into pairs and positions their arms. It's an unnerving sight, all these corpses swaying in their rags, the torchlight revealing the wounds or illnesses that took their lives.

The lesson goes on, and even I have difficulty looking away from Ribbon. She glides past her clumsy pupils, makes an adjustment here and offers encouragement there. Her hair begins to come loose from its pins and brushes her lower back in dark waves. One boy openly gawks while a man forgets to concentrate and steps on his partner's foot.

The sound of the woman's annoyed exclamation jars

me. I cast a furtive glance around the room; everyone is consumed by the waltz. Seeing that this might be my only opportunity, I ease around the edge of the room, creeping toward the door. No one turns or notices. When I reach the threshold, I don't look back.

The moment I duck outside, a memory accosts me in a burst of dizziness and confusion. My eyes are open the entire time and I watch the worlds collide, like paint for two different landscapes blending on a single canvas. When it's over, I'm on the verge of vomiting. It takes momentous concentration to force it back down. After a few moments, I'm able to dart a glance to my surroundings. I'm in a bedroom. It's night once more. I stand in front of the window, staring down at the street. Am I meeting James again?

I press my palm to the glass and strain to see beyond the veil of mist hovering over the village. Anticipation flutters within me.

"It didn't work."

Somehow I manage not to scream. Whirling toward the familiar voice, I press a hand to my chest, as though my heart is pounding. Kathleen stands behind me, and as always, her face is still obscured by shadows. Those boney toes peek out from beneath the hem of her nightgown. "What didn't work?" I ask.

Kathleen doesn't move. "The love spell," she answers. There's something in her voice, a bleakness that wasn't there before. Not even when I mentioned the bruises on her back.

Kathleen's hand fists in the material against her thigh. Before I can say anything, she continues, "I did it incorrectly, I suppose. Or perhaps not even magic can get Mr. Alistair to love me."

I take a step toward her, and she responds by retreating deeper into the dim, toward the door. Uncertain as to what I should say, how to comfort her, I make a helpless gesture. "Perhaps you just need to—"

She cuts me off. "No."

"Let's distract ourselves!" I say abruptly. There's an edge of desperation in my voice. "Let's try to learn a new spell."

"I'm not in the mood tonight," Kathleen manages.

Despite this, she allows me to pull her toward the window, where a shaft of moonlight falls upon the floorboards. Gently, I tug the book out from beneath Kathleen's arm. I settle on my knees and put it between us. The sight of its worn cover is familiar now; we've been attempting a different spell every night. More often than not, nothing happens. This time the pages fall open to a spot near the middle, sending a waft of scent up at me. Unable to resist, I inhale the lovely perfume of aged paper.

"All right, what shall we try tonight?" I ask briskly, rubbing my hands to warm them. Kathleen gives no reply. Very well, then. I set about choosing it on my own. I flip past the spell for levitation, the spell to make oneself undetectable, the spell to light a fire. Soon I come across a page with a drawing of a delicate flower. The text beside it looks simple enough. My heart thrums with anticipation as I jump to my feet and fetch a letter opener from a drawer. I return to Kathleen and press its tip into the fleshy part of my thumb. A bead of blood swells. I drop to my knees again.

Hoping to pique Kathleen's interest, I focus on the spell and begin to recite the beautiful words aloud. Their meaning is still lost to us, but it doesn't matter — power fills my veins, heating them as though I've just had several glasses of wine. At first, the room remains hushed and still. Then something moves in front of me. I look down and nearly gasp, which would cut the spell short. I manage to keep chanting, though, as I watch a green sprout grow before me.

Kathleen's voice joins mine. My eyes fly to hers. At some point she must've taken up the letter opener, because a thin line of blood makes its way down her wrist. We hold hands, share a secret smile, and continue the spell. The bit of green stretches and thickens at a speed that's astounding. Within moments a burst of color appears as the thing blooms and unfurls. I'm too distracted to note if the same thing is happening near Kathleen.

When the spell is finished, I've created a rose. I stroke one of its petals in wonderment. It quivers from the touch. "Kathleen," I breathe. "Look at this."

I turn toward her, but she's gone, withdrawn across the room. In the place where she was kneeling, a tiny plant pokes out from between the floorboards. Frowning, I lean over to study it. It's the beginnings of something, more of a weed than a flower. The stem is brown and brittle. One touch and I suspect it would crumble. What does this mean?

Concern burrows deep in my stomach. Maybe she's ill. Maybe performing these spells is draining her. Thinking to comfort her, I turn again and search for Kathleen's face in the dark.

"Don't you see?" she whispers before I can speak. "The power responds to you more than it does to me. I felt it."

I'm already shaking my head. "No, Kathleen, that's not—"

She releases a ragged breath. "It doesn't matter, I suppose. None of it does. You would do well to learn from my folly. Don't ever give your heart away."

She melts even farther into the shadows, and I know she's crying. I want to cry, too. I move to follow the other girl, but the room is beginning to vanish and Under is taking its place. Emptiness radiates from the alleyway where Kathleen must have been standing. My outstretched hand collides with a wall. I curse.

"Key! What are you doing out here?"

Ribbon, of course. I turn and watch her squint into the darkness. She stands beneath a spitting torch, looking like an angel or a demon with her rotting gown and blazing hair. I falter, mentally scrambling to find an explanation for my presence here. "Forgive me," I say after another moment. "I thought I spotted Tintype."

I walk toward her, smiling weakly. She doesn't seem to sense anything amiss. "'Tis a pity about the decorations." My friend sighs, linking our arms and propelling us back to the tavern. Just as we reach the doorway, a man with one leg hops up to Ribbon and shyly thanks her for the lesson. She returns the sentiment warmly. We go inside, where a few still remain, sitting at the tables and drinking their water as though it is life.

When we're settled at the counter, Ribbon's countenance unexpectedly brightens. "Oh! Perhaps you could ask Journal if we might borrow some of his belongings. He's quite taken with you. I daresay he couldn't refuse."

My mind is still spinning from the encounter with Kathleen, but this revelation makes it jerk to a standstill. "Taken with me? Journal?"

She plucks at her skirt with a sly glint in her eye. "He asks about you often when I visit his tower."

"What do you tell him?" I glance around as if Journal is nearby, listening.

"That you're a puzzle. You're constantly disappearing, even though there's a murderer on the loose with his eye on you." Ribbon smiles to soften the admonishment. "And sometimes you get this look on your face, almost like you're traveling to another place. Journal informed me that it's a result of your intelligence and a trait to be admired."

"He did?" I ask with raised brows.

Ribbon kisses my cheek. "It's the truth. Now, why don't I find someone to escort you to the tower?"

She leaves my side and weaves through the tables, making a beeline for a portly gentleman in the back. My eyes follow her but don't really see anything; I feel a thoughtful line deepen between my brows as Kathleen's warning echoes through my head. Absently, I touch my chest again—the heart within lies still and cold. Sometimes I remember how it felt to have a beating one, though. Throughout memories of Kathleen. In Journal's tower, sitting on the floor bent over the withered pages of a book. And during the kiss with Smoke.

As though the thought is a summoning spell, Smoke

himself appears in the doorway. He searches the room, and within seconds, our eyes meet. A slow smile spreads across his face. I respond with one of my own.

Don't ever give your heart away, the anguished girl had said.

But I suspect it may be too late.

CHAPTER THIRTEEN

It begins.

The music draws them to the tavern. As a result of Ribbon's lessons or the need to forget the murders — just for a few hours — their excitement is even more obvious than it was before. There's no hesitation to start the dancing. I stand behind the bar where I can avoid being trampled and Ribbon comes to stand beside me. "Did anyone fetch Brooch?" I ask.

Across the way, a boy bows and asks a girl to dance. She covers her mouth with skinless fingers and giggles.

"She had no wish to come," my friend answers. She doesn't look away from the crowd. Yellowed teeth flash in the light and skirts fly from the fervor of their movements. I watch the terrible loveliness of it all, smiling when Ribbon is coerced into a haphazard waltz with the reverend.

Toward the front, the strange band plays. The harmonica crows over the stomping feet and clapping hands. A young man attempts to play the fiddle, but without much luck. It sounds much worse than it did in its predecessor's hands, the bow shrieking and whining over the ancient strings.

Still, it is better than nothing.

Politely declining a request to dance, I devote myself to being an observer. Courtesy of Handkerchief, since Journal was not present upon my arrival yesterday, the walls are decorated with odd items from their tower. A painting, the pages of a book with words that faded long ago, tree roots. I try not to fidget as I wait for Smoke to reappear. Earlier, upon his arrival, Ribbon had sent him on an errand for more decorations. Now I'm so intent on spotting him, in fact, that I nearly miss the newcomer slipping inside. No one else seems to see him as he drifts through the crowd. They are so unaffected by his presence, in fact, that I begin to doubt my own instincts. But then something catches the light. Though he stands across the room, shrouded in shadow, the gleam of those buttons is unmistakable.

Tintype.

If I don't speak to him now, I never will. Either his ability to disappear or the suspicion on his head will see to that. I make my way in his direction and ignore the irritated glares people give me. Somehow Tintype senses my approach, and our gazes meet for an instant before he turns in an attempt to run.

Moving quickly, I seize his sleeve. "I need to know more!" I demand without preamble, not bothering to lower my voice. Everyone is watching the dancing, and the music is far too loud. "You're my *father*. From what I remember, you denied me that. There's a debt between us. I need more information about the curse."

"Not here," he mutters, trying to pull away again. His eyes shift. "I just came to see what all the fuss was about."

Something hard and desperate comes over me. "You're hiding from Eye Patch and the rest of the men, aren't you? Do you suppose if I scream and announce your presence, you'll live through a trial? Not to mention seeing the curse put to rest?"

The mention of this ceases his efforts to leave. Tintype—I can't think of him as my father—steps forward so his lips are next to my ear. Our faces are so close I can see the flecks of color in his irises and smell the rot on his breath. "Dear girl, I can't tell you anything," he insists. "My own memories are few. You must remember on your own. I've done what I can to help you along."

Just as I am about to argue, the music changes. The harmonica becomes a mournful sound, almost lonely. As if it has seen brighter rooms and sung to warmer gatherings. Laughter dies and conversations cease. Slowly, people leave the floor and others step into it, clasping each other close. Much closer than Ribbon's teachings allowed.

I look back up at Tintype, more determined than ever to coax the answers from him. "But how—"

He stiffens, his gaze focused on something behind me, and I twist to discover what has his attention. Immediately I see that Journal is here and he's fighting through the crowd. His gaze meets mine for an instant. When I turn back, Tintype is gone.

I suppress my frustration by patting my hair and smoothing a wrinkle on my skirt. Spinning again, I find myself face-to-face with Journal. "Hello." There's a note of uncertainty in my voice that is impossible to mask. "I hope you don't mind that Handkerchief lent us some of your things. I would have waited for your permission, but he informed me that you might not be back for some time—"

He shakes his head. "I didn't mind. That's not why I came tonight."

"Oh." I hesitate. For the thousandth time I hear Ribbon's voice in my mind, putting life into something I never allowed to take so much as a breath. *He's quite taken with you.* "Is something wrong?"

Someone shoulders by, causing Journal to stumble forward. He finds his balance just in time, but our bodies brush. He stammers, uttering words like *perhaps* and *dance*, and suddenly I realize what he is attempting to ask. I watch him struggle, and a smile tugs at the corners of my mouth now. All my frustration with Tintype is forgotten.

"Would you do me the honor…" Journal begins. He clears his throat and rakes his hair back. "That is, I would very much like it if…"

In response, I take his hand. It is larger than I thought it would be, engulfing mine like I've thrust my fingers into a bucket of water. I lead Journal through the wall of people observing the dance. They glance our way, and I see several do a double take when they realize who I'm leading to the middle of the floor. Facing Journal, I put one hand on his shoulder and the other in his. He positions his free hand on my waist. The space is confined, and we're only able to dance in short sways and slight turns.

We've been on the floor for a few moments when

Journal takes an unnecessary breath, as though to prepare himself. He speaks quietly. "You've been honest with me, and my conscience demands that I do the same. It wasn't fair, what I said the last time we were in the tower together, because I knew you were telling the truth. But there's a pattern in the killings and I'd finally begun to see it. Key, the pattern is this — anyone who starts to remember their past is killed shortly after. Your confession terrified me. I hoped that if you questioned yourself, the memories would either cease or you would never speak of them again."

Whatever I'd expected him to say, it wasn't that.

I automatically move through the steps of our dance as I think about Journal's revelations. His theory makes sense; why else would someone attempt to kill me? Perhaps they overheard my conversations with Kathleen — it's never clear whether I'm speaking out loud when I experience the memories — or saw me drifting through the alleys. The thought has not even finished when a new kind of terror grips my heart. If what Journal says is true, then more people are in danger. Just that afternoon, Spoon had mentioned she remembered her daughter's face. "Thank you for telling me," I manage.

Now it's your turn, the beetle says snidely. *You haven't been as honest as Journal thinks.*

To my relief, Journal isn't finished yet. "I've been making discreet inquiries," he goes on. "My suspicions were confirmed. Each victim exhibited the same behavior, though perhaps not to the same degree. I've felt the urges myself. Splinter spoke of docks and ships. Fiddle wouldn't stop mumbling about a girl named Beatrice.

Freckles went mad searching for a job so he could send money back to his family. There's no way of knowing what else they would have remembered, given time. It seems that anyone who regains a bit of memory dies shortly thereafter."

More pieces fall into place. Slowly I say, "The first death. The undertaker. You said he was ranting and raving. So he'd started remembering, too."

Journal nods.

That's why he kept the contents of the scroll secret, I realize. He didn't believe the man had killed himself, and he was worried if I read the account of the ramblings, it would awaken something in me. Handkerchief had been protecting me as well, when he stopped Journal from revealing too much.

"There's something else," Journal says. Something in his voice catches my attention—a potent mixture of dread and reluctance—and I refocus on him. His hand tightens around mine and I don't think he's even aware of it. The music changes, but we keep dancing. Journal visibly struggles to find the words. Just when I'm about to lose patience, he speaks. "It's you, Key. You're the link among them."

I frown. "I beg your pardon?"

"I was going mad trying to find the event or trigger that caused the victims to start regaining memories— especially now, after so many quiet years—and it took embarrassingly long for me to realize what had changed in Under. It was you. My own memories began the very day we met. But how? Was it something airborne? Was it a specific phrase or word?"

"Could you get to the point, please?" I ask impatiently.

He acts as though my words fall on deaf ears. Knowing Journal, they may have. "There was a moment with you that I couldn't get out of my head," he says, meeting my gaze. "The first book I lent you. Our hands brushed, do you remember?"

"Of course I…" In a burst of comprehension, I almost jerk to a halt on the middle of the dance floor. My mind goes back, and back, and back. All the way to Splinter and his rough hands on the day of my arrival. Fiddle and the way I grabbed his arm in the tavern. Freckles and his timid tap to gain my attention. Pocket Watch and his comforting pat on my hand.

The truth had been in the scroll—in a supposedly insane man's words—all along. *It's in the touch.*

I'm the reason these innocent people are burning.

But one piece doesn't fit. That first man to die, the one whose ravings Journal recorded. He'd never met me; I'd fallen long after his demise. When would I have had a chance to touch him?

Perhaps you didn't. Perhaps he *touched* you, the beetle suggests.

Oh, God. That's right. The man was the village undertaker; it stood to reason that he'd been the one to prepare my body. Somehow, a single brush with my skin really does bring remembrance. Dead or alive, apparently. I want to vomit at the revelation. How many times have I touched Doll? Ribbon?

Journal has remained silent during all this. Now I look up at him again, and despite the hypocrisy of it, anger shadows my next words. "Why didn't you tell me *sooner*? I could've been more careful. For that matter, why haven't you warned anyone else? It's obvious that more and more are starting to remember. Staying silent won't protect them now."

Just as Journal opens his mouth to reply, something touches my back. Turning, I see that another couple is dancing needlessly close to us. It's Eye Patch—despite his missing arm—and a woman named Bonnet. He's watching me intently, as if his partner isn't attempting a dialogue with him. Eavesdropping in hopes of catching an admission of guilt, most likely.

Noticing at the same time I do, Journal bends his head and lowers his voice even further. "I made efforts to keep you from remembering, Key, because I wanted you to be safe. But warning everyone else might squelch their desire to regain those memories. And that is essential," he murmurs.

"More essential than survival?" I counter, stepping on his toe. I don't apologize. There is a war brewing inside me now. The instinct to protect the friends I've made here and the desperate need to find answers. It's clear that Journal has already made his choice; he would sacrifice lives for the sake of those answers. I search his eyes for proof that I'm wrong and find nothing.

Perhaps he sees the revulsion in my face, because he doesn't answer. A moment later, a familiar voice drawls, "May I cut in?"

We both jump. Smoke stands beside us, a strange look in his eye. For the first time, I'm not eager to speak with him. My fingers dig into Journal's shoulder again, a silent plea to refuse the request. There's so much more to say.

But he steps back and places my hand in Smoke's.

The ice has returned to his demeanor. "Thank you for the dance," Journal intones, avoiding my gaze. "Enjoy the rest of your evening, Key."

When the dance began, I'd thought to tell him that Doll has the scroll again, but now I have no wish to help him. I watch Journal leave the tavern. Without warning, Smoke puts his hand on the small of my back and pulls me close. The place where his palm makes contact feels like it's on fire.

I lose sight of Journal and automatically flatten a hand on my new partner's chest to put some distance between us. Unperturbed, Smoke lifts my arm and spins me. "I hope I wasn't interrupting something," he says when I'm facing him again. "You looked very serious for an occasion that's supposed to lift our spirits."

This time I succeed in pushing him away; we're being observed and I don't enjoy making a spectacle. "Not at all. And I'll endeavor to wear the appropriate expression for this event."

Smoke cocks his head and gives me an exaggerated frown. "So formal. Which puzzles me, since I probably know you better than anyone else in this hellhole."

There's a charged pause. His meaning is all too clear, and I know we're both thinking of that kiss in the dark. Finally, the discussion I've been dreading. I lift my chin and don't pretend to misunderstand. "What happened between us was a mistake," I say quietly, however much I don't want to. "It won't happen again."

"Don't make promises you can't keep." He grins roguishly. It's as if seeing Journal and me together has affected him, uncovered something dark and bitter. There's no glimpse of the kindness I saw the day he brought me to Tintype, or the blind adoration I experienced in the shadows.

"I'm engaged, Smoke," I remind him.

"I should think that *dying* would release you from any prior commitments. Besides, that didn't stop you before."

"It does now," I snap. He has no idea what sort of danger he's in just being near me. In touching me. And perhaps there's also a part of me that is trying to atone for the selfish choices I made back then.

Once again the music changes. I almost sag with relief; one more minute and Smoke would've seen through my mask. The clapping and stomping returns and the tempo quickens. As excited shouts sound all around us, I step away from him. "Thank you for the dance."

A muscle works in Smoke's jaw. "I can think of better ways to pass the time," he quips. There's something suggestive in the way he says it, and I glare at him, forgetting my anguish. Then, as luck would have it, a memory chooses that moment to resurface. I know it's futile to struggle. Expecting it now, I close my eyes against the nausea. It rushes through me like water filling a glass. Distantly, I'm aware of Smoke gripping my waist, offering support as the memory claims me.

Once the dizziness passes, I am not the least surprised to open my eyes and see James. The sight of him unsettles me, though. For once, that wild hair is slicked back and I can see his face fully. He's wearing tails and his shoes must've been recently shined. Mischievous—but alluring— dimples deepen in his cheeks. His cobalt eyes gleam.

With effort, I turn my attention to our surroundings. We're in a local tavern, made of wooden walls and high ceilings. Beams crisscross the open space above us. The air is heady with the smells of hot food, perfume, and sweat. Unlike the last time, James and I are being watched. Men and women alike stare in our direction. Their whispers fill my ears.

"What are you doing?" I hiss. The lights above us are too bright; it feels like our secrets are revealed to the entire room.

James's hand doesn't waver. He stands before me, blatantly out of place among these people. My friends have all backed away, putting distance between them and scandal. "Will you honor me with your hand for a quadrille?" he says, posing the question in such a way that it's obvious he's voiced it more than once.

My heart pounds against the walls containing it. "You know we shouldn't, Mr. Alistair," I remind him, wishing I sounded firmer about it.

"That doesn't answer my question. I'll ask again. Will you honor me with your hand for a quadrille?"

I cast a worried glance around us. *Would there be so much harm in one dance?* I wonder. Just one. The temptation to touch him again is too great.

Resenting my own weakness, I give in and put my hand atop his. James grasps my fingers, and even through the white kid glove, I feel the heat of it. He flashes that familiar, impish grin of his. With a dramatic gesture, he sweeps me onto the dance floor, right in the thick of it. A yellow-haired girl next to us stares, aghast at our daring. My resolve wavers.

"Mr. Alistair—"

"I thought we agreed you wouldn't call me that anymore."

For a few moments, I'm caught up in the quadrille. I've always enjoyed dancing and James is an excellent partner. As he spins me, I notice some girls tittering in the corner, coyly hiding smiles behind their fingers. "Why are you here?" I blurt, tilting my face up, seeking James's gaze.

"In the village?" he asks, every movement like liquid. It reminds me of the night I watched him fight.

"Well, I'm curious about that, as well, but I meant with me," I clarify. "If you look there, nearly ten girls are waiting for you to ask *them* to dance."

Truth be told, there's a part of me that's wondered— from our very first meeting—whether this is all a game to him. I may be innocent, but I'm not naive. There are men in the world who treat women like rags. Use it a few times, then toss it into the rubbish pit. And a man as handsome as James Alistair must have women throwing themselves at him daily.

Perhaps he guesses at my true motives; James frowns and doesn't reply, at first. We continue through the steps and motions. I have an inkling that the last time I tried this dance with my fiancé, it wasn't nearly so natural.

"I have no pretty speeches to offer," James says once we're facing each other. His expression is uncharacteristically agitated. "No bits about how I was enchanted by the sound of your laugh or the secrets in your eyes. All I know is that I saw you and I had to know you."

I almost stumble at his words, for I've had the same

thought about him. "I confess, I'm disappointed you weren't overwhelmed by my beauty," I say lightly, trying to bring James's smile back.

He remains solemn. "The world is full of pretty girls. In all my travels, though, I've only found one like you."

The world around us has faded. There's no tavern, no other dancers, not even music. Not because the memory is retreating, but because he makes me forget everything else. I search James's gaze, painfully aware of every place our bodies touch. "And what's so interesting about me?"

Of course he answers the question with one of his own. "I could ask you the same," James replies, raising his raven brows. "Why are you dancing with me when I'm sure there are a dozen others begging for the chance?"

I almost remind him yet again that I'm engaged, but the words stick in my throat. Instead, I settle for another truth. "I suppose some things don't have a proper explanation. They just are."

"You might be right," James murmurs.

There's no chance to reply; just as quickly as it began, the memory blows away like ashes on the wind. We are surrounded by death and decay once more. Smoke and I still stand in the middle of the other dancers, but our circumstances couldn't be more changed. While I stare, Smoke's hand tightens on me. I barely notice. "We've done this before," I tell him in a whisper.

"Yes." His voice is low so others won't hear. I don't have to ask whether Smoke accompanied me into the memory again; the answer is in his eyes. I open my mouth to ask him what else he's remembered.

Just then, tinkling laughter reaches my ears. I turn to

see that Ribbon is surrounded by her admirers, distracted by all the noise and attention. Recognizing an opportunity, I turn back to Smoke. "I'm sorry," I say. Possible lies or excuses fail me—or maybe I just don't want to give him one—so I leave it at that. He lets me go, but I feel his gaze all the way to the door.

As I slip out of the tavern, there are no ghostly girls or concerned friends to intervene. Equal parts relieved and triumphant, I hasten in the direction of the wooden river. My ears are alert for any sounds of pursuit. Both Journal's discovery and the latest memory with Smoke are fresh in my mind, and I mull over every word exchanged while I walk. For a few minutes I'm worried this isn't the right way, but then I hear the humming of the woman with no limbs. Reassured, I grab hold of my skirts and run.

Soon enough the roots come into view. I glance behind me to be sure there's no one watching, no one lurking. Only the shadows stare back. Having enough sense to claim one of the torches that's still lit, I hurry forward and climb over the tangle. I hold my arm carefully aloft to avoid disaster, and my feet hit the ground on the other side with a dull *thud*. I'm shaking so badly that I have trouble finding the door.

Eventually the flame, bright and crackling, reveals that familiar hole in the wall. Tiny, oddly shaped, and full of possibility. I fumble for the key about my neck and it fits perfectly. Taking a step back, I feel light-headed from a rush of doubt and panic and exhilaration.

And the door creaks open.

CHAPTER FOURTEEN

The first thing I see is light.

Up ahead, at the end of the passage, a line of brightness beckons. The path continues to slant upwards. I finally reach the light, stepping as close as I can, and its soft glow makes my shoes seem less ragged. As if I've ascended into the heavens rather than fallen into the earth. It looks like the space beneath the bottom of a door. Equal parts impatient and fearful, I hold the torch up and search the wall at the end of the path. This one isn't made of dirt, and I touch it apprehensively. Cool stone whispers against my skin.

There doesn't seem to be a doorknob, but eventually I find a familiar-shaped hole. Trembling, I fit the key inside once again. Everything within me leaps at the sound of the latch clicking. I hesitate for just an instant before flattening my hand on the stones. The muscles in my arm tense as I push.

Nothing happens.

"What?" I whisper, frowning. I push it again, but the door doesn't budge.

My resolve hardens; I didn't come all this way to return empty-handed. Clenching my jaw, I brace against the door and dig my feet in. A grunt escapes me. This time the door quivers and dirt rains down. I draw back and return with more force. A scraping sound ruptures the stillness, like two rocks grinding together. Encouraged, I slam into it a third time, and the door finally opens.

It's only a crack, just enough for a draft of air to seep through. I wedge my face into it, straining to see something. Anything. But the space is too narrow. Desperately I stand back and thrust the torch out. The light flickers on another wall, smooth and dusty. Nothing else within sight.

Once again I steel myself, withdrawing in order to put all my weight against the door. It takes several more attempts. Finally there's enough space for me to fit through, and I triumphantly stumble into the world of the living.

The torch crackles as I whirl in a circle, soaking it in. I seem to be in a…mausoleum.

Names are engraved in the four walls around me, and two stone coffins rest in the center. Pale moonlight slips in and illuminates everything. Though I long to stay and read the names, I know there isn't much time until Ribbon discovers my absence. It wouldn't do for her to organize a search party and have everyone realize that I'm nowhere to be found in Under. I go to the exit, the rustling of my skirt the only sound in this sleeping place. The handle lifts without difficulty, and when the door swings open, I freeze on the threshold.

I'm back.

The moon shines from behind wisps of clouds, softly illuminating a cemetery. A layer of snow covers everything, though our headstones burst through like rocks in the ocean. Stepping down, I exhale experimentally. A grin of delight spreads across my face when a plume of air swirls out, visible in the cold. The action brings my attention back toward the sky, and now that I'm beyond the ridge of the mausoleum's roof, stars greet me. I stare up at them, reveling in the sensation of knowing that there are places beyond Under.

A sudden and overwhelming urge comes over me to laugh, scream, and weep all at once. It's not fair. It's just not fair that this is no longer my world.

Unfortunately, there's not enough time to mourn the life I didn't get to have.

Despite the lingering sense of a ticking clock, curiosity drives me to the closest grave. I kneel beside it, and a fine sheen of frost makes the engraved words stand out: THOMAS YOUNG, BELOVED MAYOR. There's a faded portrait beneath this. Though the man in the image is younger, I instantly recognize Pocket Watch. His fine suit, the very essence of leadership that emanates from him. It seems that our traits have not left us, despite our memories doing so.

Thoughtfully, I stand and glance toward the road. A wrought-iron fence surrounds the graveyard. I hurry to the gate, snow crunching underfoot, and push it open. The hinges squeak.

There are no houses or towns nearby, only trees and stars. I glance in both directions down the dirt road, searching for a sign or any indication of where civilization can be found. When it becomes clear there is neither, I choose left and begin my journey. A worry flits through my mind that when I come upon another soul, they will see the truth in my features. The realization that I am not right, not even alive.

But what was it Journal said? *You are remarkably well preserved.*

Praying that it will be enough, I trudge on. For what feels like hours, I walk on ice and snow. With each step, my unease grows. Air whistles in my ears and my limbs begin to stiffen from the cold. I crest a small hill and peer at the stretching road despairingly. Did I pick the wrong way?

Telling myself that I will walk just a little farther, I reach level ground again and tuck my hands beneath my arms. The winter doesn't bother me, but it wouldn't do for something to fall off. I am starting to worry about my legs when the wind carries a new sound to my ears. After a moment I determine that it can only be the creak of wheels and the clattering of hooves. Then, confirming this, a horse emerges from the darkness. It pulls something along behind—a buggy—and I see two silhouettes. Once it draws closer, I see the outlines are two men. One clutches a physician's bag in his lap while the other holds the reins. Frantically I raise my arm and yell, "Please, sir! Where can I find the closest town?"

"Just up the road, miss!" one of them calls back. "I would take you, but my wife is in labor!"

Before I can form a reply, the buggy thunders past. The man I assume is the doctor twists around and stares at me until they roll over the hill and disappear from sight. Does he suspect I don't belong here? Urgency takes hold, stronger now, and I haul my dress up once again to run.

Another copse of trees embraces the road, and it isn't until I reach the other side that I see what can only be the distant lights of homes. A laugh of relief bursts from me.

Don't waste precious time, the beetle urges. Heeding it, I rush headlong toward the living. The dirt becomes cobblestones and the trees transform into buildings that line the street. Nothing looks familiar. A man slumps in a doorway and sings his woes to the night. I foolishly halt, terrified that he'll lift his head and scream at the sight of me. But he's too lost in his pain to see anyone else's. Like Kathleen does in all my memories, I leave the glow of moonlight and step into the shadows.

The deeper I venture into the village, the busier it gets. Windows glimmer from the revelry happening inside. Laughter drifts through walls and music — real music, from instruments without scars or age or unskilled handlers — pours out of an opening door. It slams shut again, but I'm already hurrying across the street toward it. In order to learn about the past, I'll need to speak to someone who was there. Or at least heard about it. I pause to read the golden letters over the doorway: THE CROWN. Beyond the glass, the crowd is so thick that it reminds me of Ribbon's dance for the dead.

There's the thud of footsteps, and I turn to see a man walking past. The flaps of his coat are raised on either side of his face to protect it from the biting wind. Impulsively I reach out and touch his arm. "Excuse me, sir. Sorry to bother, but where am I?"

He shakes my touch off with obvious disgust. "Keep your distance, woman!"

I feel myself blanch and I reel away so hastily that my back slams into the bricks behind me. Something tugs at my sleeve. A boy with a dirty face peers up at me. "You're in Caulfield, miss," he tells me, swiping at his dripping nose.

"Caulfield?" I repeat faintly. The child nods. He struggles with the bundle of papers tucked beneath his arm. I take note of the date, which also means nothing to me. February 6th, 1910. One of the papers slips free and tumbles to the ground. I kneel to pick it up for him, forcing a smile. "Thank you."

He takes it and dashes off. I watch him go, reminded sadly of Doll. It's easy to picture her running through this town with innocent abandon, that strange toy flopping in her grip. When I face the door again, I notice a girl beneath the streetlight giving me a strange look. Her gaze isn't directed at my face, though. I glance at my clothing as if seeing it for the first time. It is undeniably outdated compared to what these strangers are wearing. Self-conscious, I hunch my shoulders and hurry inside.

Warmth immediately envelops me, thawing my stiffened parts. I feel the stares, but for once I'm too preoccupied to care. This is what a real tavern looks like. The floor is filthy and stained, the counter gleams with strokes from a rag, the walls are covered in posters and pictures. Stools and chairs and tables fill the room, and in the corner an old piano stands with an air of affability. A man is bent over the keys, slamming out a lively tune that makes my toes tap. Alcohol—not collected rainwater—flows freely. Smoke curls through the air, and I inadvertently think of the black-haired American I left behind, the feel of his hands on me and the sharp-edged lilt of his voice. *Don't make promises you can't keep.*

Agitated, I approach the man behind the bar. He doesn't notice me. "Mary, fetch that cap from the floor," he calls. The top of his bald head gleams but his face is covered in gray scruff. "I'd wager it belongs to William. He left in a hurry when he heard the baby was coming."

The woman called Mary leans over to pick it up. When she straightens, she unabashedly adjusts her low neckline. She catches me watching. I brace myself for harsh words, like the man outside, but instead, she comes closer and frowns. "Are you feeling well, dear? You're so pale. Where's your coat?" Her voice is kind.

It takes me a moment to reply. "Thank you, I'm all right. I'm looking for information, actually—perhaps you can help me."

"What kind of information?" She puts the hat on the counter, then sits on the stool next to mine and addresses the man behind the bar. "Get me a pint, will you, Jacob? It's been a long night."

I'm so eager that the words trip and stumble over themselves trying to leave my mouth. "I'm looking for a family. They're probably gone by now, but I need to know what happened to them. A man and two girls; one of them was called—"

"You'd best call on Victoria Room," Jacob cuts in, twisting a rag within a glass. "She knows the history of this town like no other. Knows everything else, too. I'd bet she could tell you whether Mayor Young's daughter is having a boy or a girl tonight."

Mary nods in agreement as she gulps down the

sloshing amber liquid he's given her. I focus on Jacob. "Mayor Young's daughter?"

"He was our mayor once," the man clarifies. "Friend of mine, as well. He died years ago, and old habits die hard. I keep thinking he would've been excited to meet his grandchild."

So Pocket Watch is a grandfather. ... and now I'll never be able to tell him. A pinch of sorrow grips my heart. "Where can I find Victoria Room?"

"She lives on the north end of town, just by the park. You can't miss the place; it's the biggest one. Won't be awake at this hour, though."

Blurting out my gratitude, I jump off the stool. Mary sets down her cup and says, "Wait."

I pause. She walks around the bar, and Jacob sighs as he takes a step back. She disappears beneath the counter and reemerges with a coat. She hands it to me with a stern expression, unaware that her neckline is drooping again. "Put this on. Bloody foolish to be walking around without one, you know."

It wouldn't do to tell her I'm not affected by the cold. I swallow my instinctive refusal and simply say, "Thank you."

The woman waves this away. "Come back sometime and tell me what old Mrs. Room had to say. I do love a good story."

Promising her that I will, I pull the coat on—it's so big the material bunches around my elbows—and prepare to face the cold once more. I put my hand on the door. "I didn't catch your name, love," Mary calls suddenly.

Hesitating, I turn back. My gaze drops to the floor as she waits. Trouble is, I don't have a name to give. The coat is wrapped around me like an embrace, a physical reminder of her kindness, and it feels wrong to give her a lie. After a moment I make myself face the generous woman with the tired eyes. "Ask me again the next time we meet."

Mary smiles with bemusement, and this time she doesn't stop me from leaving. "You always did have a soft spot for strays," I hear Jacob say just before the door closes.

Outside, a beggar gives me further directions. His ragged finger points to the left. The park is easy enough to find after that; Caulfield is not a large place. I keep to the side of the road, and soon the buildings fall away again and I find myself facing a large circle of snow. Benches are buried beneath the whiteness, and elegant houses surround it all.

The biggest one, Jacob told me. He was right. It stands with its face toward the town, old and looming. A light glows in one of the windows. The knocker watches my approach—a golden lion—and it almost feels as though it's silently daring me. It doesn't know where I've come from or the depth of my desperation.

Lifting my chin, I slam the ring firmly against the wood.

The door swings open moments later. I am so startled that I take a step back. The woman on the threshold is clearly the owner of this house; there's an air about her that speaks of authority and assurance. Despite this, Victoria Room is a short woman—her head does not even reach my chin. Her gray hair is swept into an untidy bun at the top of her head, and she wears an old dressing gown of yellowed lace. Her face is wrinkled by age and smiles.

"A visitor? At this hour?" she warbles, appraising me.

It takes me several attempts to speak. My instincts shy away from the brightness, where my pallor will be more obvious. Thankfully, the coat Mary gave me hides my old dress. "I apologize for calling late and unannounced," I say eventually. "I know there have been no introductions made between us. But the gentleman at The Crown informed me that you were the one to go to if I wanted to know more about a family that once lived here."

"Well, he spoke correctly, girl. It's fortunate for you that I don't sleep much. Do come in. Goodness, you're not wearing a hat or boots. What's your name, then? Where are you from? What brings you to Caulfield?"

Though I am still reluctant to lie, I see no help for it this time. My mind flashes back to the tavern and the woman who gave me the coat. "I'm Miss Mary…White," I say, eyeing the color of the walls. I step past Mrs. Room, leaving her other questions unanswered. "Thank you."

She closes the door, and the cold retreats. Her watery eyes continue to examine me. "Now, tell me more about this family. What year were they here?"

We appear to be alone. As I speak, I take in the high ceilings and flowered wallpaper. "I don't know, I'm afraid. It was two girls and a man. They lived in a large house just like this, and at least one of them died. Other people in the town died, too, though I'm not sure if it was the same year. There was a young lady with a wound in her back, an American whose throat was slit, many who succumbed to illness—"

She nods with recognition. "Ah, yes. I remember.

Strange business, that. People in this town were dying left and right. No one knew what to think, or how to stop it, and it was a terrifying time. There were rumblings of a curse. Things only got worse when the cholera came. This way." Mrs. Room gestures for me to follow her. Gripping the rail with white knuckles, she lumbers up the stairs. She huffs and wheezes like an old chimney but still manages to talk the entire way. "Superstitious folk thought it was the end of days. Others clung to the belief that the occurrences were nothing but coincidence. There was no one to immediately investigate, as the constable died from a fall off his horse."

"How strange," I murmur. Did Kathleen attempt to put a curse on James and lose control? Or did she go mad and destroy the entire village?

"Quite," she agrees. We reach a hallway that reminds me even more of the house from my memories, only this one is wider and glaring from the glow of electric bulbs. Mrs. Room stops halfway down, still breathing heavily. "It's getting harder and harder for my old bones to make it up those stairs. I'm not sure which family you're looking for, but we'll most likely find the answers to your questions here. This is my collection. Inherited, for the most part. My father had a passion for history, which I share. After those terrible deaths, possessions of the families were discarded. He gathered as much as he could. 'Twas only fifteen years ago—not part of history yet—but Father knew something remarkable had happened. It was his aspiration to write about it, though he died before he could complete his inquiry."

I frown. "Why were the possessions discarded?"

"Mostly because no one wanted them. There was something unholy about it all. But many of the dead also passed on without a will or heir, leaving their things for taking or auction." She opens another door and flips something on the wall. Light floods the room.

Stepping forward, I look at it all with wonder. There's so much. Even if Tintype lived in Under for a hundred years, he would not be able to "find" as many items as this. Paintings and trunks and clothes and instruments and books. In the corner there is a small round table. Four chairs are tucked beneath it.

As I stare at it, a noise begins and becomes louder. Clinking and laughing. The dizziness starts and I know another memory is coming, unstoppable as a train. I blink and suddenly the chairs aren't empty. Men sit on the worn cushions, smoking and squinting at cards in their hands. Haze surrounds the game. The breath catches in my throat when I realize James is one of them. He's grinning, sliding a pile of money toward himself. His companions are groaning.

Once again, my mouth moves of its own volition. "I would like to play," I hear myself announce. I'm sitting behind James, once again wearing a cloak and solid boots. The sight of him—even the back of his head—makes it difficult to breathe normally. "I've watched long enough to understand, I believe."

In response, the gentleman with red hair kicks a vacant chair toward me. I switch seats and gingerly arrange my skirts before picking up the cards he deals. Silence hovers over the table. A line deepens between my brows as I study the hand I've been dealt. James watches me closely, and it's as though I can feel his touch. He's so alive that I want to stare at him instead of the full house I hold.

Suddenly James leans close. His breath tickles. "Have I told you that I find you incredible?" he asks quietly.

My stomach flutters and I forget the others in the game. "As a matter of fact, you haven't, sir."

A new voice disrupts the stillness. "Miss White? Are you well?"

I jump, and the poker game vanishes. James and the two men are gone. Mrs. Room walks past, approaching a different table on the other side of the room, and motions for me to join her. I follow automatically, though it takes several attempts to force my mind back into the present. "…are the other families that lived in this neighborhood," the old woman is telling me. "The Wiselys, the Sandersons, the Nathanials. Such beautiful children."

My footsteps echo as I cross the floor. Families and individuals look at the camera with gray eyes, and it feels as though they're peering through the glass at me. Still reeling from the memory of Smoke, I examine each of them in turn.

One of the images captures my attention. Mrs. Room watches as I pick it up and study the boy more closely. My grip tightens on the frame so severely that it creaks. With trembling fingers, I flip it over and tug at the wood keeping the picture in place. Just as I hoped, there's writing on the back. When I see the name scrawled in the corner, I nearly drop the entire thing. My veins burn with remembrance, a sense of rightness. *Henry Wisely, 1895.*

Journal.

CHAPTER FIFTEEN

I burst into the tower.

They must have heard me coming up the stairs, because both boys are looking toward the doorway. The serene flicker of the torches only agitates me more. I am coated in shame and snow. Chunks of it fall to the floor as I halt before Journal.

"I've been keeping things from you," I blurt. I'm not sure which is the driving force making me confide in him over everyone else—the guilt or the memory of our friendship.

Journal is slow to react. Straightening, he sets a book down on the desk and takes in the sight of me. The snow around my feet starts to melt.

"Handkerchief, would you give us a moment?" he asks the boy politely. Handkerchief doesn't hesitate, but I feel the weight of his stare as he walks past.

The moment he's gone, I move forward, clenching my hands into fists. The picture in Victoria Room's house is branded on my mind, inescapable and permanent. I look at Journal and wonder how I didn't remember him as Henry Wisely. Now that the knowledge is there, it's all I see. The hands that once held more elegant books than the one on that desk. Clothes that were flawless in their tailoring. Features that were once vibrant with affection, not death.

"I can't remain silent anymore," I manage. "I feel like I'm going mad."

Calmly, Journal pulls the chair out, a silent instruction to sit. Only then do I comprehend how my legs are shaking. "Tell me," he says simply.

I do. I tell him everything.

About Tintype, the memories, the door. Everything that transpired fifteen years ago, except what I've remembered about Smoke. "There was more to go through, but I worried the daylight would expose me," I finish, settling back with a weary sigh.

All this time, Journal has listened without a word of interruption. Now he shakes his head. He tucks his hands behind his back and begins to pace. "Incredible. Just incredible. I wonder why it took you fifteen years to wake?"

"I don't know. But now I wonder if the magic has something to do with my lack of decomposition."

Journal purses his lips. His expression is nearly identical to the one in the picture. My sense of guilt is overwhelming. I fiddle with my skirt and swallow. "Journal, there's something else you should…" But I trail off, blinking rapidly. The tower wavers and fades. I fight the memory. At first, Journal doesn't notice. He's talking to himself, absorbing the new information I've given him. His bent head gleams. I try to focus on that, on those shimmering strands, but the memory is stronger. I squeeze my eyes shut and wait for the tower to retreat.

Journal must finally realize something is wrong. He calls my name. His voice grows fainter and fainter. I wonder why he's never able to share in the memories with me, as Smoke sometimes is. Perhaps it has something to do with my own will.

I feel the change happening again, the past closing in. Just before nausea grips me, it's almost as if there's been a gust of wind or there are sparks on the air. Under and Journal melt away like the snow still clinging to my stockings. Then my head swims and it's all I can do not to heave. Eventually, as it always does, the feeling passes.

I am in a bright drawing room. A gentle fire warms the air, and the walls are decorated in patterned wallpaper. The furniture is stylish and refined. I glance down at the clattering cup of tea in my hand. Steam rises from the black surface. I am wearing a lavender dress, and beneath it the whalebone stays of a corset restrict my already shallow breathing.

"My father…" I begin. I stop. Begin again. "My first thought was that it can't be true. That is, you wouldn't have asked him without speaking to me. Did you?"

Henry's jaw clenches. He stands before the fireplace. In a nervous gesture, he tugs at the bottom of his waistcoat. "It's true."

The fire pops and hisses as a log falls. Outside, a carriage goes by. The neat *clip-clop* of hooves on the cobblestones is the only sound between us. I pluck at my skirt, pinching skin in the process. Pain radiates through my leg and I try to hide my wince. Part of me is aware that the quiet has gone too long, and I fumble for something to say. The rattling increases, and I lean forward to put the tea down. My gloved hands clasp painfully in my lap. "I don't understand," I say at last.

"We're a good match, you and I." There's a note of pleading in the way he says it. "Our parents approve. They've been expecting this for years."

"Henry, it's not that I… This is not how I wanted…" Once more, I fail to find the right words. Now frustration clogs my throat. Of course the match occurred to me, but it hadn't lasted longer than the space of a few breaths. This boy is my friend. He doesn't make my heart beat faster or my dreams difficult to leave.

Henry comes close and seizes my hands. His palms are clammy. "I can make you happy. I accept you for who you are and I'll do everything in my power to make sure—"

"I don't want *acceptance*," I cry, yanking free without thinking. I surge to my feet. "I want someone who knows me and *celebrates* it."

Hurt flashes across his face. Henry purses his lips and withdraws into himself. "I can see you've had a shock. Perhaps you just need some time."

I don't know what happened next; suddenly everything is cracking and ripping. I reach out to grab Henry, my mouth forming his name, but he's already gone. In the space of a moment, I find myself grappling at the air.

Someone takes hold of my hand. My senses return and my surroundings solidify into the gnarly walls of the tower. I look down at Journal, who's kneeling in front of me with an expression of concern. "What did you remember?" he asks, somehow knowing. The twine at the back of his neck is coming undone.

An overwhelming sensation of loss clogs my throat. I move his hair aside with gentle fingers. It doesn't surprise me, somehow, that Journal is the one I was promised to. And even though I don't have the memories of how we died, or whether the marriage actually happened, that particular bond between us feels intact. Journal's lack of knowledge about the engagement doesn't make it any less valid. I'm ashamed of the girl I'd once been, who was able to display such a lack of faith or loyalty.

Journal waits for an answer, but I can't bear to lose his friendship all over again. The truth would most assuredly do just that.

"Nothing. It was nothing."

L aughter pours from the doorway of the tavern. Hidden in the shadows, I peek inside. Almost everyone in Under is there. Now that they know how to dance, it's been impossible to get them to stop. The sound of Ribbon's laugh rises above the crowd, exactly the reassurance I need. She won't be searching for me. Retreating, I whirl and run in the direction of the river.

My eagerness and desperation for the truth has increased, despite the risk in slipping away. At the door I turn the key in the lock and slip into the passageway, reaching the mausoleum without difficulty. Leaving footprints in the frost, I poke my head outside to make sure no mourners are here to witness my exit. Only the solemn trees and woeful headstones gaze back. I step into the night and begin the journey to the largest house in Caulfield.

Like before, the old woman answers just moments after my knock. She swings the door open and raises her gray brows. "Back again so soon, Miss White?" She doesn't remark upon the hour this time.

"I was hoping you had more information for me," I say, shivering on her front step. The coat Mary gave me is hidden in Under. In my haste I forgot to fetch it, and I pray Mrs. Room doesn't notice my clothing.

"Well, come inside, then. You're letting the cold in."

Once again Mrs. Room leads me up the stairs and to the room full of history. "Make yourself at home," she invites, though it sounds more like an order. "I'm going to fetch my knitting from downstairs. Be back in a moment or two." Her footsteps retreat, and I move to the table where the picture of Journal stands. I allow myself to look at it for just a few moments before putting it down and going to the next. This image is so faded and grainy that I can't make out the faces. It's a family portrait of a young girl and a clean-shaven man.

I hold it close, squinting. There's something familiar about her face. The shape of it, perhaps, or how it's partly turned away. As if she didn't want anyone to notice her.

Startling me, Mrs. Room's voice comes from behind. "Those are the Talbots. Lovely family. Very charitable. They took in a girl when she had no one. I can't seem to recall her name…"

Before she's finished speaking, I feel my gaze widen
in recognition. Of course, it's Kathleen. And the man
standing behind her, with the square jaw and the hard
eyes, is the father she's so afraid of in my memories. So I
was a ward of her family. When she called me her sister,
she meant a sibling of the heart, not in blood. One more
piece to the puzzle falls into place. But there's still so
much left.

"There was quite a scandal surrounding the family,
if I recall. It was so long ago. If you want to know more
about them, I think I have a few other belongings in that
pile." Mrs. Room settles in a rocking chair and begins
to knit. The *click-click-click* of her needles fills my ears
as I turn, and something inside me sinks at the sight of
all the crates and trunks. *Well, there's no time to waste.*
Squaring my shoulders, I lift one off the stack and begin
sifting through it.

Minutes later, a new sound disturbs us from our tasks.
The knocker.

Mrs. Room sets her project aside and frowns. "Who
could that be?" she mutters to herself. Pressing her
hands to her thighs, she heaves herself up. Bones and
floorboards creak when she leaves. I continue sifting
through artifacts of the past and attempt to listen at the
same time. There's the telltale moan of hinges as Mrs.
Room opens the front door and voices echo through the
house. One of them is distinctly male.

Unease creeps through me, but I tell myself there's
nothing to be afraid of—no one knows I'm here. I kneel
to keep digging for the truth. But then there comes a
scuffing noise, like a heel scraping over the floor, and I

lift my head again.

Journal stands in the doorway.

I drop a photo album in shock. It falls with a clatter. "What are you *doing* here?"

His chair and clothing are stiff with frost. He looks more ill than he did in Under, as though he's just climbed out of bed against the doctor's orders. At least, I hope that's what anyone who might see him will believe.

"I found you using the details from your accounts," Journal says unrepentantly, inspecting the room with obvious curiosity. A pang of realization hits me that I must've left the door ajar. *You imbecile, Key*, I silently fume. Before I can reply, he adds, "There's been another murder, and Ribbon is going frantic looking for you. She thinks you're the one who was killed."

"Blast!" I rush to the door, knowing there will be time for questions and arguments later. Journal moves to follow, but I see the way he looks back at the room, longing in his eyes. Urgency overpowers any uncertainty or guilt, and I seize his elbow to drag him out. We burst into the hallway and keep going.

Mrs. Room, halfway up the stairs, halts at the sight of us. "Finished so soon? I thought—"

"I'm so sorry, but we must go," I cut in, still clutching Journal. He opens his mouth, and I tighten my grip to silence him. "Mr. White and I just received some dreadful news."

The old woman hurries to accompany us outside. "Oh, this is your husband? I didn't realize. And how unfortunate, I hope it's nothing serious!"

Shouting empty reassurances back at her, Journal and

I break into a run the moment we cross the threshold. A square of yellow light stretches over the ice as Mrs. Room watches us go. Soon we leave the cluster of houses behind, moving out of her sight. "Did you go through the village?" I demand, imagining all the lights and people that could have exposed him.

"No one noticed me. And while I was outside debating what to do, I hid behind a hedge."

Praying that he's right, I lead him along the outskirts, taking the longer route in order to avoid prying eyes. Journal is strangely silent. Just as we pass a pond, the surface glinting in the moonlight, something hard hits me in the back of my head. Alarmed, I whip around. Journal stands in the middle of the empty road. The corners of his mouth twitch. His hand drips with swiftly melting snow, and comprehension makes my eyes narrow.

Just like that, the tension between us evaporates. "We don't have time for this!" I insist, even as I bend to scoop together a ball of my own.

"I know." He grins now, and it's the first time I've seen him smile. In that moment, he looks like the child I grew up with. "But it's been so long since I've been around snow!"

I start to reply, and Journal shocks me once again by darting off the road and onto the pond. "What about Ribbon?" I call frantically. He acts as if I haven't spoken, whooping as he slides on the frozen water. Glancing in the direction of the cemetery, I hesitate for an instant, then relent. I fight through the shin-deep mounds to reach his side. The moment I step out, Journal gives chase. He's like a completely different person, and part of me would rather linger and speak with him. But I run, as I'm supposed to, attempting not to fall while evading his grasp. Soon enough, his hands wrap around my waist and he hauls me back. I scream.

Turning, we latch onto each other as though our lives depend on it and spin in wild circles. I shriek with laughter, struggling to keep my balance. Both of us are panting as though we're out of breath, and the air swirls with white clouds. When I lift my head, still smiling, I expect to see Journal laughing, too. Instead, he's staring at me with one of his odd expressions, and for the first time, I know what it is.

Awe.

The moment I have the thought, everything begins to quiver. "Oh no," I moan, bending over. The nausea is particularly vicious. Unable to stop it, I retch.

Journal's hands tighten around mine. "Key, what is it?"

He says something else, but the words come from a vast distance. As always, the feeling gradually passes. When I stand upright, I expect to see a memory that takes place in the ice and snow. Instead, I'm back in the Wisely household, seated in the same infernal chair as before. Henry and I both stare at our cups of tea in another agonizing silence. The grandfather clock mocks us. *Tick. Tick. Tick.*

"Perhaps we could browse the library," Henry finally suggests.

Relieved, I almost jump from the chair. "I would like that."

Without another word, he rises. I follow suit, thinking he's going to offer his arm, but he turns and walks out of the room. After a moment, I trail after him. He leads me past the stairs and down a hallway, toward a door tucked in the back. The busy sounds of a kitchen drift in our direction. Henry twists the knob and stands aside, his gaze firmly on my shoes. This is a room I've entered dozens of times before, but now, I hesitate at the threshold. It doesn't feel as welcoming as it used to.

Silently, I tell myself not to be so foolish. I step inside.

Any other day, I would go to the bookshelves and voice some of the titles, intending to read aloud from whatever we chose. Henry would scoff and come up with reasons why it was the wrong one. After a time, though, we'd find a volume we both liked the sound of.

In an effort to return to those happier days, I move to the shelf. The sound of purposeful footsteps startles me. I turn to watch Henry sit at the desk, open a leatherbound book, and begin to write in it. As if he's completely forgotten me, his mouth puckers in concentration. Disheartened, I trail my fingers along the edge of a shelf and walk the perimeter of the room. When I glance at Henry again, I catch him staring. He quickly looks down at the book in front of him.

"Will you read to me?" I ask impulsively.

Two spots of color appear on his cheeks. "This w-wouldn't interest you," he stammers, slamming it shut.

"And why not?" I tease. Wanting to see the text, I circle the desk and stand beside him. As Henry frantically shoves the mysterious volume into a drawer, my skirt brushes against his thigh. A flush crawls up his neck, joining the blush, and Henry's entire face is red now. I step back, but something in him seems to have cracked open.

"I wasn't entirely forthcoming with you," he blurts.

I back away. My instincts come alive and tell me that I won't like what he's about to say. "What do you mean?"

He forges ahead as though he's riding into battle. "When you learned of our engagement and we spoke, I told you it was a good match." He stands but remains where he is, fingers splayed on the desk as if to balance himself. "But the truth is, I wanted this more than I've ever wanted anything. I have for a long time. Frankly, I've memorized every tiny detail about you. The curve of your neck, the way your brow lowers when you're reading a passage you find interesting, the shape of your fingers where they grip the page. Yes, I know you see only friendship between us. I reassured myself that once we were married, you would come to feel love."

Words elude me; they may as well have become birds and flapped off. I stare at him openmouthed. "I—"

"It began when we were just children. The first time I saw you, I only caught a glimpse. But it was enough. I was sitting on a bench in the park when your carriage went by. You had your head out the window, and your face was lifted toward the sun. Your eyes were closed and you were smiling. A governess was shrieking about decorum, but you ignored her. I wanted more than anything for you to open those eyes and see me. When you didn't, I made inquiries to discover your identity. I didn't rest. And eventually I succeeded. Imagine my surprise when I learned your family lived in the house next to mine."

At last, he falls silent, and I swear I can hear that damn grandfather clock again. *Tick. Tick. Tick.* Henry stares at me, his dear face so hopeful and earnest. Afternoon sunlight pours through the window behind him, setting half the room aglow. The tranquility of it belies the chaos warring inside me. My lips quiver. What can I possibly say to such a confession?

When it's clear the silence has gone on too long, I make a vague gesture. "Henry... I didn't know."

With that, the study crumbles like ashes. There's a moment of disorientation, then I'm on the ice again, midspin with Journal. Slowly, we slide into a standstill. Neither of us moves. This time I find the courage to ask him. "Did you remember?" I whisper.

His heart is in his eyes. "Yes."

But he still doesn't know. He doesn't know that I fell in love with someone else.

"We should g-go." Pulling away, I focus on our feet and straighten my skirt. I don't wait for him to answer before hurrying off in the direction of the road. Henry's eyes bore into my back all the way to the graveyard.

He opens the gate and steps aside. We trudge past the headstones, then silently enter the mausoleum, the distance between us charged. I don't look at him again, even when we reach the door to the passageway and plunge into darkness.

We use the wall for guidance, but the journey back into the earth is slow going. Without a torch, the path is more treacherous, abruptly dipping and dropping. I put all my concentration into the next step. After a while, a distant part of me begins to suspect something isn't right. Frowning, I pause and listen. There's a fluttering sound in the stillness, but the tunnel is so resonant that I can't tell if it's coming from ahead or behind us.

"Journal, did you hear that?" I whisper.

He's closer than I realized, because his breath fans tendrils of hair around my face. I jump. "No. What is it?"

We both go silent, waiting for something to stir in the oblivion, but there's nothing. Did I imagine the sound? "Never mind," I murmur, starting forward again. Journal's hand touches mine on the rocky wall. Jerking away, my toe collides with something jutting in the path and I stumble. He grabs me in an attempt to help, but I wrench myself out of his hands. "I'm fine!"

Journal doesn't snap back, and I childishly wish he would. The guilt has become a bitter taste in my mouth. He deserves to know the entire truth, what kind of girl he loved. Yet the idea of saying the words out loud brings a terror to my soul that wasn't there even when a knife was poised over my tongue.

We keep walking in stilted silence and finally reach the second door. Cautious as ever, I make sure no one is near the roots before emerging.

The instant we land on the other side of the river, I expect Journal to depart in the direction of his tower. He doesn't. We both head for the clamor that is undoubtedly coming from the square.

Standing at the front, Ribbon spots me straightaway. She leaps down from the crate, but the dead are so consumed by their anger and fear that they don't clear the way for her. As she fights to get through, I see the body by the wall. Like all the others, it has been burned. Someone else who had begun to remember and paid the price. Who did I touch? Who did I condemn in one unthinking moment?

Ribbon pushes past the last of the corpses in her way. "Thank heavens," she cries, throwing her arms around me.

"I found her in one of the unoccupied rooms. She was so focused on her book that she didn't even hear me say her name," Journal lies smoothly.

My friend instantly begins admonishing me, and her arms are so tight that I feel my bones grind. "Ribbon." I pause. She doesn't release me. "Really, I'm all right. You can…" I trail off when I catch sight of Shilling's face, who has moved to cower by us. Everyone else within my line of sight wears similar expressions of terror and astonishment. One of them makes a cross on their chest. They all seem to be looking up.

"What is it?" I ask, finally detangling myself from Ribbon's embrace. "What is everyone staring at?"

Wordlessly, Shilling points.

A familiar sound echoes around us. With the chalky taste of dread in my mouth, I glance toward the earthen sky. At first, it looks like nothing but a swift shadow. But then the shadow squeaks.

"A bat, it's a bat," the others are whispering. For a moment I'm confused—has this happened before?—but no, of course they'd still know what a bat is. Our stolen memories don't affect basic knowledge.

The little creature flaps its wings wildly, panicked by this starless and strange world it has found itself trapped within. I remember that moment in the dark when a small sound pierced the stillness. It must have followed us through the tunnel.

This is my fault.

Lowering my chin, I meet Journal's gaze. He's looking

at me instead of the bat, and his mouth is tight. We're both thinking the same thing. Whoever my attacker is, whoever has been trying to keep me from discovering the truth of Under and so desperately tried to snatch the key from around my neck during our last encounter, will draw an inevitable conclusion at the sight of that bat.

They will know I have opened the door.

CHAPTER SIXTEEN

The latest victim is Pocket Watch.

Once one of us finds the courage to search it, his body is easy enough to identify. I stand off to the side, clutching my throat. Though charred and cracked, the trinket he was always carrying managed to survive the flames. It's dropped to the ground, forgotten, where Doll gently picks it up and tries to wipe the glass clean. She tucks it into her pocket. Little thief.

While the typical shouts and chaos ensue—this time without the kind white-haired man to attempt order—I stand there numbly and stare at the remains of the old mayor. Sorrow burrows its way into my heart. "Rest in peace, Thomas Young," I whisper, uncaring if someone hears me. No one appears to.

Ribbon is talking now, using the gentle tones that usually charm them like a snake in a basket, but it's not working this time. Spoon steps up beside her in defense, her stained apron and rumbling voice somehow making her seem formidable. Distantly, I wonder why her loved ones didn't bury her in a nicer dress. Sentimentality, perhaps?

While they keep everyone from descending into anarchy, Journal bends his head close to mine and says, "I want to show you something. Will you come with me?"

It's more dangerous than ever to be associated with me. Glancing back at the crowd, I say loudly, "I haven't finished the book—"

"Please, Key."

He's never pleaded with me before. Giving in, I nod and automatically take the alleyway that will bring us to his tower. Though I don't turn to look, I know Smoke watches us leave. *It's for the best,* I tell myself.

If only my heart would believe it.

Journal and I weave through the maze and he stays right on my heels. I feel the tension rolling off his skin. The joyful, confident boy I glimpsed at the pond is gone. It feels as though his tower is farther away than usual, and by the time we arrive at the door, my own nerves are thrumming. We go inside.

Upon climbing the stairs and entering the wide room, I see that Handkerchief is absent. Journal wastes no time; he strides to the stacks against the far wall while I sit in the chair by the desk and tap on one of the roots with my finger. It sounds like a drum. Eons later, Journal returns with a leather-bound volume. Without explanation, he places it in my lap. Then, folding his hands behind his back, he swings away.

My gaze lingers on him before I look down and gently lift the cover. I already recognize it from the memory

we share, when he led me into the library and read
aloud. He'd tucked this little book into a drawer before
I could see what it was. Now, it takes me a moment to
comprehend the lines of the makeshift ink. Disbelieving,
I turn the page. And the next. And the next.

It's...me.

Drawing after drawing of me in another life. Drinking
tea, riding in a carriage with my head out the window,
reading a novel. The girl Journal remembers is beautiful.
She seems strong and certain. It's clear that some of these
were done while he was alive because of the ink, but
most were undeniably completed after Journal died. The
strokes are rougher from the bone he's forced to use in
place of a quill pen. I recall the way he looked at me when
we first met, as though he were seeing a ghost.

I tear away from the drawings to look up at him. "Why
didn't you tell me when we met?"

Journal turns. He comes to stand in front of me,
obviously stalling. I clutch the sketchbook—which the
others must have mistaken for a journal—and wait.

"I don't know," he admits. "Perhaps because I'm so
used to keeping things to myself. Or perhaps I didn't
want to frighten you."

It seems we've both been keeping things from each
other, then.

Here is my chance to tell my own truths. I stand there,
trying to summon the nerve, but apparently I'm not ready
to make a confession. It's my turn to stall. "Why tell me
now?"

The boy who was once my best friend doesn't answer,
at first. He fiddles with a button on his vest. "I suppose..."

Journal falters. "There's a murderer on the loose. If something should happen to either of us, I didn't want to go back to my grave—or wherever we go—without having told you the truth."

Yet another silence falls. Journal waits for my response, unable to hide his apprehension, and the guilt threatens to break me. I need to leave. I need to get away from the past and the pain. "I—I should go," I say. Standing, I give the book back to Journal and walk to the stairs. He moves to follow. "No, it's fine," I say hurriedly, holding a hand out as if to stop him. "I still have Tintype's knife."

"Key, the killer—"

"Please, don't feel badly. What right do I have to be angry? I'll come back soon; I just need to think."

Grabbing my skirts, I hurry out before Journal can ask any questions. If he calls after me, my noisy escape drowns out the sound. I run down the remaining stairs and stop at the base of the tower to dig Tintype's knife out of my stocking. Pressing on, I focus on putting some distance between the tower and me.

It's immediately obvious that some torches have burned out, casting the passageway in even more shadows than usual. This happened once before, the night I was attacked. Fear takes hold and urges me to *run*. The only safe place is too far from here, on the other side of the wooden river. Even so, it doesn't stop me from trying.

As I fly toward safety, though, I realize this is a chance to learn who the killer is and put a stop to the deaths. Halfway to the river—my progress is hindered by my skirts, despite having hauled them as high as they'll go—I slow down to listen. Yes, there's the distinct sound of footsteps. I start to shake at the prospect of what I'm about to do. But I ignore the terror screaming through me and jerk around to get a glimpse of the killer.

The gaping doorways and dying embers look back. I hide the knife in the folds of my skirt and take a few more steps before halting again. Every time I stop, so does the other person. I feel like a rabbit within the fox's sight. It's all too clear that I could very well die in the next few minutes, and despite my noble thoughts and intentions leading up to this, the possibility is horrifying.

Please, God, save me, I pray desperately, so afraid I can hardly think.

Outrunning him isn't an option now. The tavern is too far and I'd probably trip on my skirt again in the process. So, in a show of false bravado, I glare at the looming alleyway. "Who's there?" I call, hoping Doll will poke her head out of one of the doorways. Nothing moves.

Hands wrap around my arms and yank me into the darkness.

CHAPTER SEVENTEEN

The sound of my scream is muffled. My attacker hauls me into one of the dirt houses and presses the edge of his jaw to my temple. I fight him, wrenching this way and that, kicking my heels fruitlessly into the air. "Quiet! Someone is following you," Smoke's voice hisses into my ear. After an instant of shock, I relax against him, so relieved I could weep.

We wait like that for what feels like hours. Silence reigns. There's still no sign of the killer, and just as I'm about to speak, a shadow flies past the doorway. A gasp catches in my throat and I press harder against Smoke. His hands tighten. We wait a bit longer to be certain he's gone. Eventually I pull away to face Smoke, shuddering. The only source of light is a torch that must be farther down the passageway, and all I can see of him is a dim outline. "Thank y-you." I adjust my clothing as a distraction and an excuse not to meet his gaze.

"You were going to leave him for me."

My head snaps up. I frown in confusion. "What?"

Smoke shoves his hands into his pockets, seeming completely unaffected by our near brush with death. "The hermit. You were going to leave him, and run away with me."

There's a pause, in which I scramble for a response and he watches me. Our gazes catch and hold. My insides quake at the expression on his face; there is more emotion there than he's ever allowed me to see before. It's as if the boy from my memories and the one I know now have finally molded together to become this fiery being. One touch, and I know I'll burn.

"You remembered everything?" I ask, breathless. Inadequate and inane, but it's all I'm able to manage.

He doesn't answer straightaway. Slowly, giving me the chance to turn away, Smoke lifts his finger to brush a stray hair out of my face. "I remember…you," he murmurs. "More and more every day. I know that we were together on the night I died. I know that I loved you until I took my last breath."

It feels as though his words bounce off the walls and come back to me in violent bursts. *Loved you… loved you…* It's utterly unexpected after our last angry encounter. I shake my head, jostling his hand. "You're wrong. I wouldn't have done that to Henry."

Yet even as I deny it, there's a rose of realization growing in my chest, a thorny knowledge that he speaks the truth. Everything begins to make sense. Why I feel so guilty around Journal, why I've been reluctant to tell him about our past. Because then he'll remember what Smoke has, and he'll know that I utterly betrayed him.

I didn't just fall in love with someone else. I shattered

Henry's heart, as well.

I think part of me has suspected this truth for a long time. It was one I didn't want to unbury.

Smoke only seems to hear one word. His expression darkens. "Henry, is it?"

But now I'm remembering the horrific image of James's death, the haunting flash of blood and betrayal on his face. I recall the taste of Smoke on my swollen lips as I stared at him and whispered, *I think I killed you.* Forcing myself to glance up at him, I make a vague gesture, belatedly realizing that the knife is still in my hand. "And I thought…didn't I…"

Somehow Smoke understands what I'm trying to say. "You didn't kill me. That honor was bestowed upon someone else." He turns away and takes a few steps, the line of his shoulders tight and furious. I absorb the revelation. Relief joins the shame. *I'm not a murderer.*

Before the thought is finished, Smoke swings around again. "So you don't remember at all?" he demands. Despite the anger in his eyes, he sounds vulnerable. The question hovers in the space between us.

I yearn to tell him that yes, of course I remember him, if not our ending. That the memories of Smoke are exciting and dark and…shameful. And it's the shame keeping me from giving him what he wants. "We should go to the tavern," I say instead of answering, bending to tuck the knife back into hiding. Smoke's eyes flick toward the pale leg exposed beneath my skirt, and I hurriedly cover it again. "It isn't safe here."

His jaw works. The air thickens, not with lust but with pain. *Too many people,* I think. *I'm hurting too many people.* But I don't know how to put a stop to it. I stand there, trying to think of a way to avoid causing more heartbreak. After a moment, Smoke gives up. He stalks to the doorway and doesn't wait to see if I follow.

He sets a pace that forces me into a run to keep up. We reach the tavern and he ducks inside without hesitation. I pause at the threshold, looking in the direction of Journal's tower. The lights at the top quiver.

Sighing, I hurry in after Smoke. Noise washes over me. The murder of Pocket Watch has made the inhabitants of Under more terrified than ever. The night of the dance is a distant memory; they crowd into this room like pigs waiting for the slaughter.

Smoke has already found a place at one of the tables. He laughs at something the reverend says. If I hadn't just felt the heat of his glare, it would be easy to believe that he's been here all along. That he hadn't just saved me from the killer again or proclaimed his love.

"Sing!"

Distracted from Smoke, I search for the speaker. But then someone else takes up the cry. "Yes, sing!"

Sounds of agreement travel through the room. I have no idea who they mean until Shilling stands. Smiling, she goes to the spot where Fiddle once played. A hush descends on the crowd. Once everyone has quieted, Shilling opens her mouth, and the most beautiful sound I've ever heard comes out.

Another movement catches my attention. Spoon is waving me over, the loose skin on her arm jiggling. Ribbon's seat is empty, and I see her in a darkened corner, talking to Handkerchief. I weave through the tangle of legs and chairs to slide into the rickety seat next to the old cook. It creaks precariously. Shilling keeps singing, transformed from the girl I've known since my fall. The hunch to her shoulders is gone and her gaze is direct. Looking at the rapt expressions all around, it seems as if she's put a spell on them. The sadness is gone from their eyes, the fear forgotten. No one but Journal or I know that as long as they don't possess memories of a life before this, there is no danger.

At the thought, my hands become fists under the table. With one touch, I could make them all remember. But at what cost? Am I willing to sacrifice these people for the sake of knowing who we are?

Journal is, the beetle hisses.

Suddenly the familiar scent of lavender teases my senses. Kathleen? Alert, I straighten in my seat and look around. Shilling finishes her song. Everyone begins to clap, and while they call for more, I mutter an excuse to Spoon. She just nods. Ribbon is still talking to Handkerchief, and not even Smoke glances in my direction. I leave the tavern unnoticed.

Just in time.

A memory begins to swoop in. I rush to an out-of-the-way spot and sit in a particularly dark shadow, gripping my knees like a raft in the sea. Under tilts and falls away. While I'm in the throes of retching, something soft and warm envelops me. Eventually I open my eyes and find myself in a bed. Unlike the last memory, this room is familiar; I'm back in the Talbot house. Kathleen is just closing the door, her back to me. The light from the hallway narrows and disappears completely. Her nightgown glows as she rushes toward the bed.

"How was your afternoon with Mr. Wisely?" the girl whispers, lifting the bedcovers and crawling in beside me. There's no trace of her earlier despair, for which I'm grateful. Her skin is freezing.

I heave a sigh and roll over. The edge of Kathleen's face gleams like hills in the moonlight. "He barely said a word to me," I tell her, cringing in remembrance of all the rebuffed attempts at conversation. "We used to converse so easily. Now everything is ruined."

"You may feel differently about him someday. I've heard affection often blooms after the wedding," she offers.

I tuck the sheets beneath my chin. "I do care about Henry, Kathleen. He's still my friend, despite how things are between us. I just…wanted something different. I even wrote to Father, begging him to reconsider the match, but he dismissed it immediately."

My friend flops onto her back, making the bed frame shake. "Well, at least Mr. Wisely noticed you long enough to ask for your hand. When I saw Mr. Alistair in town, he couldn't be bothered to tip his hat."

I pause. It feels risky to talk of him after Kathleen's failed attempt at a love spell and my secret dalliances with him. "Well, he's an American. Rumor has it they're a very thoughtless bunch."

"I suppose." She falls silent for a moment. "Maybe I should try again."

Alarm slams through me. "No," I say, too quickly, and force myself to calm. "Kathleen, this magic is addictive. I feel it, as well. We should be careful with how often we use it."

"Yes. You're right. Of course you're right."

Her voice is faint. Suddenly I'm desperate to hear her laugh. "You could always marry the butcher's son. I've never seen someone with such devotion."

It works. Kathleen muffles her squeal into the pillow. "Have you seen his teeth?" she demands. "They have more stains than Irene's dusting rag!"

Her voice is too loud. Stiffening, we both stop breathing and listen. There's no telltale whine of hinges or the familiar thunder of approaching footsteps. Relaxing, we giggle until the darkness no longer feels menacing.

Seconds tick by. Slowly, our smiles fade and we become solemn once again. I hear Kathleen swallow. "I've felt a darkness in me of late," she confesses quietly. "I remember Muriel once telling me about the women in our family. So many of them had tragic ends. Perhaps the book is not as wondrous as we believed."

"We should stop." I try to sound firm, but a trace of reluctance seeps through the words. The possibility of never feeling that power again seems unimaginable. Still, if what she says is true, we can't risk her sanity or our lives.

Kathleen gathers breath to respond, but distant footsteps silence whatever she had been about to say. *Thud. Thud. Thud.* She goes rigid and my nails unconsciously dig into the tender flesh of her arm. "He won't find us," she promises, grabbing me. There are no ingredients for a spell, and I have no idea what the girl intends to do until the rusty smell of blood fills the air—she's cut herself.

"Kathleen, no!" I hiss.

She ignores this. It's too late, anyway.

Taking a breath, Kathleen starts to chant. This is a spell strengthened by pure, naked fear, and I think of the warning in her mother's letter. Seconds later, the door opens; a man fills the entrance. The light is to his back, hiding his features, but then he turns. He has a large moustache and bushy sideburns, undoubtedly the man from Mrs. Room's photograph. Kathleen's father.

He searches the room and glowers at us. While Kathleen continues to mutter next to me, I steel myself for confrontation and violence.

Oddly enough, Mr. Talbot strides to the window and whips the curtains aside, causing a shaft of moonlight to fall over our legs. He doesn't move. The silence stretches. Any moment now, he'll yell or yank the covers off our bodies. Instead, though, he growls low in his throat and withdraws. The door shuts.

Once it's certain he's gone, I sit up, frowning. "Why did he leave?"

"Because he thought the bed was empty," Kathleen answers, satisfaction dripping from the words. She doesn't seem concerned about the cut. *What's a little more pain?* I think sadly.

The pale light isn't enough to show her face, but the shoulder of her nightgown is sagging again. My fingers skim her bruised collarbone. The mark has darkened to hues of yellow and violet. "I remember when I first met your father," I murmur. "He seemed so kind. I didn't think him capable of something like this."

"People are capable of anything; it's just a matter of circumstance. Or the right spell. But you would have liked the man he was before Mother died." When I don't respond, Kathleen exhales. "He'll tear the house apart looking for me. I'll go back to my room."

I begin to protest, but her arms wind around me. She presses a kiss to my temple, her lips soft and damp. On bare feet she pads to the door, and I watch her head poke out. Once she's certain the way is safe, Kathleen slips through. *Click*.

A wave of guilt and sorrow crashes over me. I close my eyes and listen to her retreating footsteps, wishing I were strong enough to fight back against Mr. Talbot. Minutes tick past, and though I try to stay awake to listen for any cries from Kathleen's room, the edges of sleep creep in.

Suddenly a new sound disturbs the stillness, yanking me away from the dreams that have begun to pull me under. I fly upright and instinctively scramble backward, away from the door. I hardly feel it when my spine hits the headboard. But no one comes in. A shadow moves against the floor and, panicked, I look toward the window. I see the top of James's head vanish.

I hurry to undo the latch, but he's already left. There are marks in the frost left by his fingers; the American must've climbed the drainpipe again. Quite a feat in this weather. As a gust of wind rakes at my bare skin, a splash of color against the windowsill draws my eye. A single rose lays in the frost, its vibrancy and beauty a defiant stand against the unforgiving winter. Doubtless James purchased it from the hothouse, but it's fun to think he has magic of his own.

I hold the soft petals against my nose and inhale. Its sweet scent makes me smile. I look to the street, toward where the mysterious boy would have run in order to return to the boardinghouse. He's gone. But not for long.

Clutching the rose, I close the window and return to bed.

CHAPTER EIGHTEEN

J ournal waits for me near the door.

His note, delivered by Handkerchief, burns in my pocket. Upon opening it, the sight of his loopy, elegant handwriting made my heart feel like a living organ again. *Meet me at the river.* I was so excited that my grip tore the paper. With Journal helping me, it was almost certain we'd find answers.

The portly messenger couldn't possibly know what the note said, but that didn't stop him from giving me a look as he left. It was a look that spoke volumes, and Handkerchief's warning echoed in my head. *Be careful, miss.*

Halting at the edge of the maze, I see Journal's silhouette. The torchlight casts his outline against the wall like the finger-shapes children make when they're supposed to be in bed. Something in his stance changes, and I know he must have spotted me, as well. Journal doesn't say a word. He just waits.

After another moment of hesitation, I begin the climb over. Halfway across, though, one of the roots snaps. Gasping in panic, I grapple for another one to hold on to. Journal rushes forward, shadows dancing over his skin as he holds his hand out. Trembling and trying to maintain my balance on a much thinner branch, I look down at it. There's no time, yet I foolishly study the lines of his palm. If only there were some way to read the events of the past in them. I've no interest in the future, for it only holds death.

But no matter how long I look, I just see lines. Relenting, I swallow a sigh and take his hand. As soon as my feet hit the ground, I let go. Journal seems unsettled; his hand clenches into a fist. "Thank you," I mutter.

"You're welcome."

There's a pause. Then, grateful for an excuse to put my back to him, I find the hole and fit the key inside. We both duck through, making certain to shut the door tightly behind us, lock it, and begin the trek to the surface. It's far easier this time with the flame to guide the way. But I keep thinking about the bat and peeking toward the low ceiling. On the tenth or eleventh glance I don't see the path slanting up and nearly trip again. Journal offers his hand, but I'm already straightening. I yank at my skirt and we continue on.

Silence hovers in the air. There was once a time when we would not stop between sentences, arguing and enthusing and supposing about whatever book he had lent me. It's unbearable, how awkward I feel around Journal now. Thinking of the reason for it, a hot ball of shame swells in my throat. However inevitable the courtship with Smoke felt, however powerless I was against my passion for him, it still left someone I loved in pain. I couldn't speak even if I wanted to, and we go the rest of the way with the crackling torch as the only sound between us.

Journal steps past me to shove the heavy door open. The mausoleum is undisturbed, glittering with frost and frozen dust. I hasten to the outer door and step into the cemetery. Wind whispers through the trees and headstones. The instant Journal appears beside me, we head for the road, ice cracking and shattering beneath our shoes.

We're nearly to town when he attempts conversation again. His voice startles me. "Have you remembered anything else since our last conversation?"

The question swirls in the air like a snowflake. Thinking about it, I feel Kathleen's breath on my cheek as she asks, *How was your afternoon with Mr. Wisely?*

My mournful answer seems to come from every direction, agonizing and unavoidable.

He barely said a word to me, the stars murmur.

I just wanted something different, the tree branches whisper.

We are ghosts, but we are the ones being haunted.

With a jolt, I realize Journal is looking at me, still hoping for a response. We've reached the outskirts of town. To avoid drawing attention, I take us along a quieter road that goes around everything. "No, nothing else," I say, feeling as though he can see the truth in my face.

There's a pause, and Journal continues appraising my expression. When I refuse to speak further, he purses his lips. Nodding, he then quickens into a pace that is impossible to keep up with. The lights of town beckon ahead. I keep my gaze on them and half walk, half run, pretending not to see the tense line of Journal's shoulders. But the beetle whispers to me, so deeply nestled that I can't ignore its reason. *The memories belong to him, too. If circumstances were reversed, wouldn't you want to know?*

Blast. Gritting my teeth, I halt in the middle of the road. "Wait."

He doesn't seem to hear me, or perhaps he's just ignoring me. I run after him, cursing beneath my breath some more. The moment Journal is within reach I impulsively grasp his sleeve. He faces me with a questioning look, and I lick my lips. My instincts war with each other, a bloody battle between keeping the knowledge secret and doing what's right. "Your name," I blurt, shifting from foot to foot. The voice in my head goes quiet. "It's Henry Wisely. As you know, you asked for my hand. And I... I wasn't pleased about our union."

A whistling wind is the only response. I wait for bitterness or anger. Instead, Journal walks toward me. *Crunch. Crunch. Crunch.* The tips of his boots come into view, stopping only a breath away from mine. I tense.

"What else?"

Something makes my gaze flick toward the horizon. A sense that something isn't right.

"Oh God," I whisper. We're closer to Victoria's than I realized. Otherwise, I would have noticed it earlier. Journal twists to see what has my attention, and his mouth thins in a grim line.

The house has been burned to the ground.

Neither of us speaks the entire way back to Under. The image of those blackened ruins torments me more than the dark. Was it coincidence, just an accident? Somehow, I don't think so. There were answers in that house, and we'd been so close to unburying them. The killer must have followed Journal and me that night, all the way through town and to the old woman's home. The sounds I heard were more than a confused bat.

We make our way through the tunnel, and once again I lock the door behind us. Journal accompanies me to the alley where I live. Smoke and Doll are nowhere to be seen. As we reach my doorway, I pray that Mrs. Room survived. It's encouraging that there were no new graves in the cemetery. "Thank you for walking me to my room," I say to Journal, frowning at the ground. Thoughts buzz in my skull like a hornets' nest, still consumed by Victoria's destroyed home and how someone else in Under has now been topside.

He doesn't give the polite, expected response. "Key, I've been thinking," he begins. Still distracted, I try to focus on him. Journal rushes on. "Perhaps you should go back through the door…and lock it behind you once and for all. Just stay topside, where it's safe."

I'm already shaking my head. The thought of everyone else trapped and burning causes a bitter taste in my mouth. "I won't abandon all of you," I say, digging my fingers into the dirt wall.

"Don't think of it as abandonment. Think of it as survival," he growls.

Survival. The word makes me remember running through the dark, the smell of burnt flesh, listening to the rise of frightened shouts. Then, instead, I think of Smoke. The magic trick he showed me in a shadow-filled room, our banter in the passageways, that heated dance in the tavern. And I know that I don't want to survive; I want to *live*.

But there's no point in telling Journal any of this. When I finally respond, my voice is soft. "I'm already dead, you know. You don't have to protect me."

The truth of it makes his eyes darken. Looking away, Journal clenches his jaw. In the few seconds of silence between us, there comes the distant sound of singing. "Something tells me I've always done a shoddy job of it," he mutters, ignoring Shilling's sweet voice. "Why else would you be here?"

I listen to the sad words of the girl's song. "We both made mistakes," I whisper, more to myself than him. Something in my tone makes Journal frown, but he doesn't ask any questions. Instead, he takes my arm and tugs. I allow it to come away from its hiding place behind me, and Journal stoops to brush a feathery kiss over my cheek. Then he lets me go. I watch him turn and walk in the direction of the tower. A wild desire comes over me to call him back, to ask him if we can ever repair the friendship that once meant everything to me. But fear of his answer keeps me from making a sound.

As soon as Journal is gone, the familiar feeling of a memory descends. I stand strong against the wave of nausea. The alleyway quivers. Then, in the space of a blink, it's gone. To distract myself from the urge to vomit, I gaze around.

Four walls stare back at me, rough and wooden. There's a narrow bed in the corner. The covers are rumpled and tossed aside, as though the sleeper had been eager to face the day. Clothes are scattered over the floor, among them, many that I recognize. There's also a smell in the air that causes a tightness in my chest, like the heart within is torn between overwhelming anxiety and incandescent anticipation.

Something creaks to my left. Already knowing who I'll find, I turn. It feels like a pillow has burst inside me and all its feathers are drifting down, down, down. I forget all the fear and frustration of Under and exist only here. Only now.

James stands in front of a desk, making adjustments to an oil lamp. There were no fights for him today—the cuts on his knuckles are scabbed over. His hair is too long; it spills over his white collar. I admire his long fingers, hardly able to believe I'm really here. Standing in an American's room, unchaperoned, in the middle of the night.

No, he's not just an American, I think. He's strong, adventurous, funny. A bit mysterious, perhaps, but we've only known each other a few weeks. He challenges me. His conversation is thought provoking. He makes it seem possible to achieve more than what's expected of us in this life.

And he occupies my every waking thought, along with every midnight dream, in a way no one ever has before.

James lifts his head and catches me staring. His lips quirk in the beginnings of that smile I so love. "Would you like to—"

In three strides, I'm across the small room. I take hold of his shirt and pull him to me, then I claim his mouth like I've wanted to do almost since the moment we met. If I feel any nervousness, it's pushed out by the thrill of tasting him again. James recovers quickly and responds with a fervor that makes all thought leave my head. Instinct takes over. We move backward, never pausing in our frenzy. My spine hits the wall. His hands are in my hair, making it come hopelessly undone, and mine are buried in his as well. It's as soft as it looks. He smells like soap and sweat, but somehow it's a pleasant combination.

I've never felt like this before. As though time were never invented, as though I've lost myself in another person. There's also an ache deep within me. A desire for *more*.

Without warning, James draws back. I make a sound of protest, but he holds me firmly, his palms two hot spots on my skin. Slowly, he tilts his head to the side and presses his lips to my neck. My breathing intensifies. I grab the bottom of his shirt and pull it free, catching a glimpse of the firm stomach beneath, and can't resist skimming my fingers down it. Muscles clench in reaction to my touch, and James inhales sharply. He grabs my wrists.

"Are you certain?" he asks. We both know there are so many reasons why this shouldn't happen. Scandal. A child. Henry.

No, I don't want to think about Henry. Not right now.

"Don't stop," I whisper. James gives me that melting smile of his. Slowly, much too slowly, he bends down. This kiss starts out leisurely, as though we have all the time in the world. We taste each other again and again. Heat and need build inside me, until I'm almost rough with my explorations. He responds in turn, but he seems to be having trouble with my clothes. Should I be helping him? How on earth will he manage without looking? At the exact moment I have the thought, James steps back, most likely to see the laces better. In doing so, his shoe catches on the edge of my gown. Something tears with a jarring sound, and I can't stop a surprised gasp. James pulls away completely, this time with merriment in his eyes.

I cover my face and wish I would vanish into thin air. "Blast these wretched layers. Now you know why so many families employ a lady's maid."

His laughter makes my heart do strange things. James tugs at my wrists and I peek at him. "You're looking at this the wrong way, darling," he says soothingly. That stubborn strand of hair has fallen in front of his right eye. "We've been given a delicious opportunity."

"Opportunity?" I echo, nonplussed.

James nods. I still haven't the faintest idea what he means. But, as he proceeds to make a torturous game of undressing me, I do understand. One by one, he removes an article of clothing. As he does so, he touches an exposed bit here or leaves a kiss there. My blouse, skirt, and bloomers land on the floor in a careless heap. After these come my garters and stockings.

The sensations coursing through me are so overwhelming that I forget to be embarrassed. By the end of it, I'm biting my lip to hold back a moan. James turns me around so I face the wall. I brace myself against it, no longer trusting my legs to keep me upright. He nips me playfully on the back of the neck before he kneels. A moment later, I feel his fingers on my waist, and I nearly buckle from the anticipation. But more seconds tick past and nothing happens—James has stopped.

Confused, I glance over my shoulder. James is glowering now, locked in a fierce-looking battle with my corset. "Damn it, woman," he growls. I utter a brief, giddy laugh. It's comforting, somehow, knowing he's not quite as experienced with laces as I would've thought. Eventually, though, he triumphs over the knot and pulls them free. The corset falls away.

The air seems to still. Breathing should be easier, but instead, it's suddenly impossible. I stand there in nothing but my chemise as James straightens. He turns me again, and I know everything I'm feeling shows. His emotions are a bit more difficult to discern; he doesn't move, doesn't speak, doesn't smile. My heart pounds harder as I realize he's giving me the chance to undress him, just as he's done with me.

My shyness returns, but I don't let it spoil the moment. Instead, reminding myself to breathe, I put my hand under his shirt and learn the ridges and planes of his body. At my touch, James's eyes go hazy; his lips part with want. His clothing is simpler than mine, and removing it should take only a few moments. Like he did, though, I linger with every piece of it. Savoring the sight of moonlight on his bare skin. Admiring the taut muscles that react to my touch. He is beautiful, much more beautiful than I, and I keep waiting to wake up from what must be a dream.

At last, we have bared ourselves completely. James stares with frank appreciation—his gaze makes me feel like a spring flower beneath a ray of sunlight—but only allows us to look for a smattering of seconds before he takes hold of me. I close my eyes, expecting another shattering kiss, but he stops a hairbreadth away. I look at him questioningly.

"You are so beautiful," he breathes.

No one has ever looked at me that way before.

Just as I'm about to demand another kiss, his mouth is on mine. I'm not frightened by the intensity of it or the knowledge of what comes next. No, it only fans the flames crackling all around us. I wrap my arms around James's neck and, following some instinct, jump up to wrap my legs around his waist. He groans. We move swiftly to the bed, and he sets me gently on my back. The mattress springs creak.

"Leah," he whispers. I freeze, certain that I haven't heard him right. I pull back slightly, looking into his bright, earnest eyes. He hesitates at my expression. "Leah, is everything all right?"

My mind roars. I want to cry and scream and dance. My name, my name, my *name*. The piece of me that I've been missing, like a lost limb or a precious heirloom. It feels so right, fits so perfectly. I am Leah. It echoes through me again and again, more powerful and permanent than any song, memory, or feeling.

Tears prick at the corners of my eyes. Smiling, I pull James back to me. As our kiss goes on, his knee parts my legs. The core of me is aching, yearning for more, and I open wider. James lifts his head, a question in his eyes. I don't let him ask me if I'm sure a second time; I let my body tell him. It moves against his in a way that proper girls would never do.

James hesitates only a bit longer. Then, reaching down, he makes sure to enter slowly. I'm surprised by the pain— my old governess told me it was that way for many girls, but somehow I'd forgotten—and I must grimace, because James freezes. I cup his face in my hands and quirk a brow. "What did I tell you earlier, Mr. Alistair? *Don't stop.*"

After that, neither of us speaks again.

W e must sleep, but it's the sort of sleep where one doesn't remember doing it. Before I know it, morning pours through the window. I awaken gradually, disoriented by the unfamiliar room. Then, all at once, last night comes roaring back like an ocean tide in a storm. I jerk to look. Yes, James is there. Or, rather, I'm here. In his room.

I hold the scratchy blanket against my chest, instinctively hiding my nakedness in the brightness of day. James doesn't stir. My alarm fades as I study him. The sunrise turns one side of his face luminescent, his hair tousled from sleep. Those long lashes cast lovely shadows upon his cheeks. I drink in every detail, knowing I should be taking my leave but unable to make myself move.

Though I've always heard that what we did would change me forever, I don't feel very different. I'm also not ashamed, not yet. I wanted this. But…what if one night of passion was all James wanted? What if he moves on to the next girl and acts as though last night never happened? What if I'm just a gullible fool?

My smile dies. Panic flutters in my chest.

Then there's a knock at the door. I jump and, recovering, glance wildly at the window. I immediately dismiss the possibility—someone would see me. Thankfully, James hears the sound and begins to wake. Before he's fully conscious, I close my own eyes. *Coward*, that small voice whispers. I ignore it and roll toward the wall. This way, whoever is waiting in the hall will only see that the American has some floozy in his bed.

James leaves our warm cocoon, dons the trousers he'd been wearing the night before, and crosses the room. He opens the door strategically, keeping me hidden. He speaks so quietly I'm unable to catch anything. The door closes again and, seconds later, something clatters. I dare to twist my head and look. James stands in front of the desk—there's a tray on it now, laden with breakfast and tea. He turns around to lean against the edge of the desk and takes a large gulp of the tea. Before I can move, he notices me.

"Good morning," he says with a smile. "Are you hungry?"

I realize I'm staring at his mouth and pretend to be fascinated by the pink flowers painted along the rim of the cup instead. "Good morning," I murmur. "No, thank you. In fact, I should probably go home."

He comes back to bed. Is this the part where he dismisses me? Breaks my heart forever? I sit up, avoiding his gaze. James leans forward and presses his forehead to mine. The smell of him wraps around me, thrilling and painful at the same time. I brace for words dripping with pity or condescension.

"Marry me," he whispers.

My eyes fly to his. For an instant, I'm convinced I couldn't have heard him correctly. But James sits there and grins. I make an odd, strangled sound that could be interpreted as a shocked laugh. All my fears melt like frost beneath the sun. "You're mad!" I manage.

He nods. My head moves up and down with his. "Maybe so. But you can't tell me you want to stay here for the rest of your life. Not you."

I lean back and raise a brow. The blanket slips and James's gaze darts down to take note of this. His eyes darken. "Has it ever occurred to you that I needn't marry in order to leave?" I ask, a bit breathless. "That I can do so whenever I please?"

"And it would be my honor to be part of your journey," he says. My regard of him rises even more when he doesn't mock me or talk about the impossibility of a girl venturing out on her own.

"I thought you had no honor," I point out.

"Right. Mustn't let anyone think so. Might ruin my reputation."

I cover my mouth to smother a laugh. Sounds come from the hall and through the wall, clear indications that the rest of the house is awake. James watches me, his expression unexpectedly tender. I know he still awaits an answer, and my mirth soon fades. "May I... May I think about it?" I ask. Inevitably, Henry invades the space between us.

"Of course. But don't take too long."

I frown. "Why?"

James clutches his chest and flops back on the mattress.

The entire bed shudders. "Because the suspense might kill me," he cries.

This time, the laugh won't be contained. It bursts out of me and bounces off the wooden walls. James jerks upright and claps his hand over my mouth, but then he starts laughing, too. We sit there and try to shush each other. Despite our mirth, I can't stop my attention from lingering on his glorious chest. James goes quiet as he, too, admires me.

"I really should go," I whisper. The spell between us breaks when someone walks by the door, singing loudly about an Irish girl named Eileen. I clear my throat and cast a wary glance at the pile of clothing on the floor—it will be nigh impossible to put back on. "The house will already be waking. I'll be lucky if I can sneak in without anyone noticing."

James's eyes twinkle. "I can help you dress, at the very least."

"You would make an excellent lady's maid, sir," I say primly.

He pretends to consider this; his expression becomes speculative and he rubs his chin. "That's good to know. Perhaps my days in dusty cellars are at an end."

I grin and finally leave the bed. James doesn't look away for a second. Suddenly bashful, I hurry into my chemise, a furious blush crawling up my neck and into my face. The breakfast tray beckons from its place on the desk, offering a distraction. I move to inspect its contents. The fare is simple: just bread and butter. As I pick a piece up and bite into it, I notice a match on the desk.

"Oh!" I exclaim.

"Are you all right?"

"Yes, something just completely slipped my mind. I got you a present when my friend and I went shopping the other day." I abandon the bread, return to my discarded clothing, and search for a hidden pocket in the skirt. My hand reemerges with a small package. I thrust it toward James, who sits up fully. The blanket pools around his narrow waist. He looks at me questioningly and, feeling silly, I shrug. "You can open it whenever you'd like."

He makes quick work of the wrapping, and within seconds it falls away to reveal a cigar tucked into a new holder. Part of the holder looks like marble. The pearly portion is carved into an intricate design, something akin to vines or snakes. I fumble over an explanation. "The cigar itself is insignificant, really, but the holder is made from meerschaum. Or so I was told. I saw it and thought of you. Anyway, will you assist me with the corset?"

"Wait." James catches my hand with the one that isn't holding the gift. His voice is different. Strange. I face him, and by now, I recognize the look in his eyes—it's probably reflected in mine. I feel that stirring again. That warmth rising within me. "Come here," he growls throatily.

Smiling, I allow James to pull me back down.

CHAPTER NINETEEN

It's as though my name was a stone in a wall, and now it's been pulled free, sending all the rest tumbling down. The memories continue to bombard me, swift and relentless, and with each one I become more certain that I don't want to know the rest.

I curl up in the corner of my bleak room, struggling to manage the onslaught. There are images of spurting blood, a full moon, bared teeth. Voices come out of the darkness, and it becomes impossible to discern what is real and what isn't. Light flares and fades. Unseen hands brush my skin. I feel myself dancing and curtsying and smiling one moment while weeping and screaming and falling the next.

If anyone in Under tries to reach me, they don't succeed. I'm lost in the past and can't find my way back.

Eventually I learn how to grab hold. Tighten my mind around a single event or conversation. At first they're slippery, like a fish just out of the water, and it takes many failed attempts before I manage to catch one.

I grit my teeth and open my eyes. There. I've done it.

My frustration fades as I take in where I am. I'm standing in a street, the lights casting soft shadows over the cobblestones. The moon gleams from its lofty perch.

Suddenly something separates from the darkness. A silhouette. It moves in my direction, going through the patches of light too quickly to see a face. I'm about to scream when I realize that it's James.

Something in my chest loosens. I run into the street, meeting him halfway, and then we're in each other's arms. *People will see,* reason hisses. But it doesn't matter. Nothing matters but this.

"I've missed you," James whispers between kisses. Eventually, though, he lifts his head to meet my gaze. I make a sound of protest, which coaxes a tender smile from him. It doesn't stop him from asking, a note of worry in his voice, "Have you made a decision, my dear Miss Campbell?"

Like nearly every other occasion that I venture into the past, I experience the sensation of having no control. Like two souls fighting for one body. There's no chance to react at the revelation of my last name. "Soon," I hear myself promise, and my hands clutch his lapels tight. The word *yes* hovers on my lips as I pull him back to me. James Alistair bends his head to kiss me yet again, a heated claiming that makes it impossible to think. Everything in me reacts like chemicals in a vial. His tongue tastes of something sweet and bitter at the same time, like cloves. Though I respond eagerly, pressing closer, something hovers at the edge of my thoughts. A reason that we shouldn't be doing this, why it feels wrong...

"Leah?"

The voice comes from behind, drowsy and confused. I recognize it at once. "Kathleen," I gasp, pushing James away. I spin toward her, making a belated attempt to cover myself with the shawl I brought from my bedroom.

Kathleen shuffles closer. Her bare toes step into the pool of light and the hem of her nightgown flutters. Her face remains hidden. "What are you doing out here in the middle of the night? Is there someone with you? I heard…" At that moment James shifts, and my friend trails off at the sight of him. I know she's staring. Finally noticing my swollen lips and rumpled nightgown and drawing inevitable conclusions.

Then her whisper emerges from the darkness, as powerful as her father's fist. "How could you?"

"Kathleen, I…" There's nothing I could say that would remove the pain and fury from her voice. I swallow.

She runs, her feet slapping against the ground. The front door to the house opens and slams, echoing into the night. With that sound, I feel her closing herself against me. Putting an end to everything I hold dear. Friendship, family, home.

What have I done?

James touches my elbow. He doesn't attempt to comfort me, for which I'm grateful. When minutes go by and still I say nothing, he murmurs, "Leah?"

"Purchase the tickets," I say, feeling as though the stars are crashing down around me. But my pain isn't fair to him, not in this moment. Trying to muster some joy, I stand on tiptoe and brush a gentle kiss across his lips. "I'll meet you tomorrow night, as soon as the sun goes down. Can you arrange a coach?"

"Does this mean…the answer is yes?"

I smile at his expression. "Yes, James Alistair. We're going to be married."

Then, giving him no opportunity to speak or see the sadness in my eyes, I adjust my shawl and walk away. Every step I take makes the details of the street dissolve. The houses become dirt. The light transforms to flame. The stars fade into nothing. The nightgown changes to a frayed gown. By the time I completely return to myself, to Under, two truths are devastatingly clear. Things I have fought to learn and know.

Are you certain dis is a parf you wan' ter go down? Shilling once asked me. As if she knew.

My name was Leah Campbell. And I betrayed everyone I ever loved.

I can feel yet another memory coming; for a moment or two I'm aware of being on the ground in Under, holding my head, and moaning from the onslaught of nausea. Soon—but not soon enough—I open my eyes and find that I'm in a familiar hallway. The attic door is to my right, and I'm about to reach for the knob when a song drifts to my ears. I halt in disbelief. Turning, I spot a girl at the far end. She doesn't look at me, but I still recognize her dark hair and solid build. My mouth goes dry.

Shilling.

"Miss Kathleen went upstairs, miss," she says, rubbing vigorously at a table.

So Shilling was our housemaid. Feeling numb, I open

the door and climb into the attic. This time I remember to
avoid the low ceiling. There's a candle burning on top of a
trunk. It's nearly gone, and melted wax drops to the floor.
A strangled sound disturbs the quiet and all thoughts of
Shilling evaporate. Searching the room, dread roils like acid
in my stomach as I creep through the length of the attic.

The sound reaches my ears again. A sob. The same
instant I realize this, I find her.

Kathleen sits in the farthest corner of the room,
hidden by a crate. All I can see of her is a knee. "What
are you doing?" I ask, rounding the corner.

Twitching in surprise, the girl hunches her shoulders
and twists away from my gaze, making me wish I'd
brought the candle. There's a thump as she hurriedly
closes the book. "Nothing," she mutters.

"We promised we would only come up here with each
other." I say it cautiously, as though she is one of the
caged beasts we saw at the circus once.

Kathleen twists back around, her body curled over
the book as though I'm trying to take it from her. "I'm
the one who found it!" she snarls, teeth glinting in the
dimness. "You wouldn't even know about magic if it
weren't for me."

I shrink back. Kathleen is silent now, her breathing
swift and labored. Then her hand stretches toward me.
The book falls to the floor. "I'm sorry," she says. "Please,
don't be afraid of me. I couldn't bear it."

Despite the severity of the situation, all I can think
is that I haven't betrayed her yet. The evidence is in her
fingers, which are still reaching for mine. In this moment,
we are still sisters. She has not yet discovered the darkness

in my heart or witnessed our bond shrivel into nothing.

Relieved, I grab hold and strain to see her face. Even without it, though, her shame is so tangible and my own fear so overwhelming that I'm able to guess the cause of it all. It's as if the truth has been waiting on the tip of my tongue.

"You were looking at a curse, Kathleen," I whisper, tightening my grip. There can be no doubt as to who she means to perform it on. Kathleen may despise her father, but he isn't the one who shattered her hopes.

She doesn't try to deny my words. "Last night I went to Mr. Alistair, at the boardinghouse, to tell him what was in my heart. And he denied me."

Desperation edges in, dampening the underarms of my nightgown and leaking into my voice. Whatever happened to cause Under's curse, it began in this attic. With Kathleen and me. It's impossible to change the past, but I still try. "Don't do this. Using the magic this way isn't right."

"Isn't right?" she echoes, pulling away. Bereft, I reach into the air. It seems colder than it was a few moments ago. "How can you say that, after everything you've seen? After how much pain he's caused?"

"Oh, Kathleen…" My voice breaks at the end. It's evident we are no longer talking solely about the American.

But she shakes herself and continues. "James Alistair deserves to know how it feels. And, fine, you may be right in that this isn't just about him; I'm doing it to protect us. Once I've learned how, I can do the same spell on Father."

"We'll find another means to hurt him, then!" I insist. She doesn't answer, and my urgency grows until it is a vine that chokes. I dare to crawl closer. She doesn't move.

Horror makes it difficult to speak, and my voice is hoarse as I beg, "Promise me, Kathleen. If our friendship means anything to you, if you trust me at all, make this promise. No curses. We will look for a different way to protect ourselves. Another method to take vengeance."

She hesitates. I stare at her in a wordless plea, and I know she's been silent too long. "I promise," she says finally. But it's weak. She's lying.

Still, resolve hardens in my stomach. I can fix this. Change it. There's still time—

"*Key!* Snap out of it, girl!"

The attic is shaking. A voice drifts through the walls, calling out a name that sounds vaguely familiar. Frowning, I stand and turn away from Kathleen. The knickknacks and crates quiver. What's happening?

"Who's there?" I call. Everything goes still for an instant after I've spoken, and then the voice booms again. The ceiling quakes and the floor trembles. My vision darkens. No! I need to stop Kathleen! Fighting the strange pull, my back presses against something hard. There's a hum in my ears. The world I know disintegrates.

Terrified, I close my eyes, and when I open them again, a haggard face peers down at me. It takes me several seconds to identify the man. Sense returns, sluggishly making its way through the swamp I've been drowning in.

"Tintype? What are you doing here?"

The soldier yanks me to my feet and grips my shoulders again. Were I alive, his fingers would leave bruises. "You've got to run, child," he whispers urgently. His breath is fetid. "Someone has them believing you're the one behind all this. They have moved past speculation.

If you're found, you will be burned. You must leave Under and never come back."

I am slow to respond. My mind is still partially in that attic, making a futile attempt to save all our lives. Tintype makes an impatient sound. His words finally register and a new kind of fear travels down my spine. Who could have convinced everyone of my guilt? And for what purpose?

You know, the beetle hisses.

Confirming this, Kathleen's voice slices through the cloud of terror. *How could you?*

Whoever she is, my adoptive sister must know that I'm close to the truth. Swallowing, I meet Tintype's gaze. He's right. If I don't want to burn, I must run to the safety of the tunnel. "But what about the curse?" I ask faintly. "You—"

"Hang the curse. Go, Leah."

The sound of my name on his lips is startling. Tintype gives me a rough shove. There's so much more to say, but now a different sound echoes through the earth. Shouts. There's fury and hunger in their voices, all of it directed at me.

They're coming.

Without another word to Tintype, I flee. Through the tunnels and the dark, aiming for the safety of the door. The torches cackle with amusement. The doorways watch with detachment. My skirt keeps getting in the way and I pause to gather it up. Suddenly there's movement up ahead. They hold dozens of lights aloft, revealing their rotting skin and hollow eyes. I bolt in the other direction, but they spot me before I can disappear.

"There she is!"

"Catch her!"

"Don't let her escape!"

The thunder of pursuit surrounds me. Overcome with terror, I sob and slip in the dirt. I manage to push myself back up by thinking of the door—I just need to get to it and then I'll be safe.

A leg appears in my path. Before I can check myself, I collide into it and go sprawling. My skirt and petticoats prevent me from jumping up again. A shadow falls over me, and I look up. "Please," I croak.

As an answer, the man places his boot atop my hand and puts all his weight on it. One of the fingers crunches, making it permanently useless. I scream more from shock than pain. The man shifts into the light, and I see it's Eye Patch sneering down. Then the others are here, surrounding me, grabbing what they can reach and moving toward the square. I babble at them wildly, declaring my innocence. No one listens.

The sleeve of my dress tears until it's hanging from the bodice by just a few threads. We burst into the clearing, and I scan the crowd. Ribbon is nowhere in sight, and I know she's probably out looking for me. If my friend were here, none of this would be happening. Where is she? As the bloodthirsty crowd leads me to the front, I silently implore her to hurry.

Using a rope that must be from Henry's collection, they tie me to a thick root jammed into the ground. One tug reveals that the knot is firm. Eye Patch and his followers leave me there. It takes them quite some time, but they manage to find enough kindling to surround me. It would be easier to just put a torch to my dress, but perhaps they see something more humane in this.

The square fills until nearly everyone in Under is present to watch the spectacle. Straining my neck, I spot a familiar face in the throng. "Shilling, please believe me," I beseech, raising my voice to be heard over the chaos. "I couldn't have killed anyone!"

But she averts her eyes, shamefaced. There will be no saviors this time. Losing any last shred of hope, I squeeze my eyes shut and wait.

"Open your eyes, wench!" Eye Patch materializes, a torch in his beefy fist. Perhaps he expects me to beg again. Refusing to give him the satisfaction, I clench my jaw. Eye Patch grins and swings to face the others. "This is for Splinter, Fiddle, Freckles, and Pocket Watch," he roars.

They scream their support and approval. Triumphant, he lowers the flame. The pile is so dry that it ignites instantly, hissing and spitting. I imagine I can feel the heat. Cheering climbs higher than the smoke. I wish I were dying to a better sound. Not Shilling's song, or the stomp of dancing feet, or the hush of snowflakes falling from the sky, though each is striking. Instead, I imagine Smoke's voice, telling me I'm beautiful. Asking me to marry him.

"Key!"

This voice is not part of the illusion, and my eyes snap open. It feels as though my heart quickens at the sight of Smoke and Journal pushing through the horde even as I realize it's too late. They realize it, too, because Journal looks as though he's been punched in the gut and Smoke is arguing with Eye Patch in agonized bursts.

I want the last thing I see in this world to be Smoke, his face, but another memory is creeping over everything. As the blaze consumes me, I close my eyes…and remember.

CHAPTER TWENTY

He waits for me by the gate.

Battling with myself, I halt on the road and watch James pace for a moment. His letter is in my pocket, where it's been safely tucked away for days. The handwriting is very much like the boy himself— beautiful and wild. *Meet me in the cemetery on Thursday night at eleven.* There's no sign of the coach yet, but then, I'm early. I must make a sound, because James spins. He holds a lantern up, which illuminates the curve of his mouth when he spots me. My stomach flutters in response. I hurry toward him, clutching the handle of my carpetbag in both fists.

How is it possible for something to feel so right and yet so wrong at the same time?

"I was worried you'd changed your mind," James whispers, cupping my face in his free hand. Air leaves his mouth in white clouds. They surround me when he bends his head to press his lips to mine. I kiss him back, hard.

Then he's pulling away, urgency in every line of his body. "Our train leaves soon. Maybe we should start walking and try to meet the coach on the road."

I hesitate, staying where I am. In my heart, I know leaving would haunt me forever. The people in my life wouldn't understand. Henry, especially. The best friend who doesn't deserve a faithless, deceitful fiancée, no matter how I feel about our marriage. "James, wait. I—"

Fingers tangle in my hair and yank me back. Shrieking, I lose my footing and fall. Someone kneels behind me. "Get up," a familiar voice commands, putting a sharp object to my back. Even through my coat, I feel it. My gaze flicks up to James, and the expression on his face—a combination of anger, fear, and calculation—helps me find enough composure to obey. Snow clings to my skirt as I rise.

"Kathleen?" I ask unevenly. She doesn't respond, but the wind carries that lavender scent to my nose.

"Release her," James orders.

She laughs. I have never heard her make that sound. Hollow and cold, like someone has yanked her soul out and there's nothing left. "It's not that simple, Mr. Alistair," she says. "I am no longer blind to your flaws, and your words have no effect on me."

Wind howls through the cemetery, stirring the trees. No one speaks. For a few moments it seems as though we are statues ourselves, forever watching and mourning over the deceased. I can see James's mind at work, but he is not Henry. The American's talents lie in adventure and daring, not puzzles and human nature. His hands are helpless fists at his sides.

"What do you want, Kathleen?" I finally ask, feeling the tip of the knife move with each syllable. Her grip on me tightens.

When she remains silent, James dares to take a step closer. "Me," he answers. "You want me."

I sense Kathleen stiffen. "Stay back!" she snarls.

"You won't hurt Leah. She's your best friend."

"Don't presume to tell me what I will or will not do," she counters. James's eyes are back on the knife, and he hesitates again. Silence hovers, none of us knowing what comes next. I try to think of what can mend a broken heart. If there is a spell, we never learned it. And we are past apologies.

As the stalemate continues, doubt spreads through my veins. Kathleen's hand is unnervingly steady. Her voice comes to me, a bitter echo of a long-ago night. *People are capable of anything; it's just a matter of circumstance. Or the right spell.* Wild with fear, I open my mouth to say something—I have no idea what—but James acts on impulse and runs at us. The lantern shatters. With an enraged screech, Kathleen shoves me aside and points the knife to his throat instead. I lose my balance and hit the ground, then instantly roll over to see what's happening. James freezes just in time.

They glare at each other. Darkness seems to coil between them. Kathleen's face is mostly turned away from me, and a thick strand of hair has come loose from her braid to conceal the rest.

"Do it," James says, calling her bluff. *This is not a poker game*, I want to scream. Now Kathleen's hand trembles, causing the knife to touch his tender skin. Blood seeps from a tiny cut. He winces but doesn't move.

Something tiny and wet falls. It lands on Kathleen's arm and leaves a luminescent trail. "I loved you," she whispers.

James just looks at her. As the seconds tick by, I realize that she wants him to say it back. She wants him to lie.

I hold my breath, silently imploring him to do it. An eternity passes in this cold place while we both wait for him to respond. "I can't," James says flatly. Any hope I have fades with those two words. "My heart belongs to another."

With a guttural cry, Kathleen wrenches the blade. For an instant, everything stops.

James's eyes go wide as blood gushes from the open wound. He searches for me. When our gazes meet, he puts his hand out, as though he's close enough to touch. I'm stupid with shock, still sitting on the road. James smiles. Then, slowly, he topples forward and crashes face-first onto the ice.

The *cracking* sound his skull makes is my undoing. *"No!"* I scream, standing on shaky legs. I run to him and fall on my knees so hard there's a shock of pain. A sheen of tears nearly blinds me as I fumble for his wrist, holding it as I've seen physicians do, and whisper a hysterical prayer.

But there's nothing.

Kathleen doesn't give me a chance to mourn him. As if she's forgotten about my presence—she's even turned her back to me—she slices her own palm and tips her head back. The cut gushes and scarlet stains spread through the snow. Still clutching the weapon, she begins to chant, arms outspread. In a daze, I recognize a few of the words from the curse she began in the attic. A new kind of dread takes root, and I stumble back.

Then I run.

It goes against my instincts to flee in the opposite direction of town, but Kathleen blocks the way. So I weave through the graves, heading for the cover of trees, shocked and sobbing. I'm almost to the fence when pain suddenly radiates through me, and I scream again, falling to my knees. I touch my back and discover the handle of the knife jutting out.

Slowly, I tip forward and collapse face-first in the snow. Night closes in around me and I struggle against it. I can't leave Kathleen's curse free to do its bidding. I turn my face, seeking air.

And under my breath I weave a spell of my own. Magic that I pray will work against hers. Leaves and snow crunch beneath Kathleen's boots as she approaches. My eyes flutter shut and James's face fills the darkness.

This time, I let it happen.

By the time Kathleen finds me, my soul is already gone.

Darkness. Shouts. Heat.

I'm walking alone in the oblivion. Part of me knows that I should be worried and terrified. But strangely, this in-between place feels like a haven. It seems familiar, as if I've spent time here before. Out there, my body is heavy, weighed down with the truth of who I am and what I've done. Whatever this place is, it's easy to keep the knowledge at bay. I'm no one. I suspect the person I was everywhere else did things, made choices that caused the muted pain in my chest. So I walk, blind and removed and relieved.

Until something slams into me.

I'm pushed out of the soothing darkness, violently torn from the place where I know I lingered for fifteen years—I was too much of a coward to face what I suspected awaited on the other side. My eyes snap open; I stare at the ceiling of Under and all the open graves, like exposed and festering wounds. There's the sensation of tipping backward with a heavy weight on my chest. The furious faces of the dead swim in my vision, and then I'm hitting the ground, sparks sputtering across the dirt.

I find myself blinking up at Smoke, who's lying on top of me with an unfathomable expression. Slowly, my mind works out where I am. I was at the stake, about to be set on fire by the people of Under. I'm still bound to it; Smoke must've jumped through the fire and his weight made the entire thing uproot. No one else can reach us unless they're willing to do the same—they'll have to go the long way around now. Tintype, too, must've made the leap through heat and flame; while the outraged shouts start, he comes forward to untie the ropes around my ankles and wrists. He helps me up and says curtly, "Run."

But I resist, turning back to Smoke. Everything is happening too fast, and all I can think of now is that last moment between us. When blood gushed from his neck and he just gave me a tender smile. "What about—" I start.

"Just go," he cuts in. "Please. I'm staying here. The hermit is trying to prove your innocence and he'll need *someone* who knows how to use his fists."

There's no time to argue, not if I want to survive long enough to end the curse. Seeing no hope for it, I turn to obey. *No*, everything within me screams. Suddenly I whirl and run to him. Smoke lifts his head, opening his mouth to order me away again. Before he can utter a single syllable, I'm there, wrapping my arms around his neck and kissing him with everything left inside me. He recovers and kisses me back with such need and ferocity that, for a few moments, I'm deaf to the crackling flames and shouting mob. We're both shuddering by the time I manage to pull back.

Then someone bursts through the wall of fire.

I scream, so startled that I stumble back into a wall. Eye Patch lands on his feet, sending up a cloud of dust. His good eye fixes on my face, and Tintype curses, moving in front of me. Smoke does the same, making Eye Patch pause. They would die in my defense, but I don't deserve such devotion.

Without thinking, I bend and pick up a piece of wood from the pyre. The end of it crackles and sparks. My two guardians shift warily, opening a path to Eye Patch. "I am not the one killing these people," I tell him, holding the makeshift torch out.

He leers. "You should have told your lovers to leave well enough alone, girl. Once I'm through with you, burning will seem merciful."

An unexpected sorrow fills my heart at the threat—

I'm just so tired. Tired of all the hatred and death. It must end, which means I'll need Tintype's and Smoke's help after all.

Reluctantly I take a step back, preparing to run. When Eye Patch tries to pursue me, the two other men move to stop him. "You'll soon realize your mistake, Constable Norton," I say sadly. It feels like the knowledge comes through a door in my mind. It's wide open now, and there will be no closing it again. I remember Eye Patch from the life before this, strong and kind. He'd lived in Caulfield, same as the rest of us. Once, I watched him give his horse extra sugar cubes—he noticed me and winked.

I linger long enough to see the shock in Eye Patch's face before slipping away. The sound of his enraged bellow echoes down the alley, but he can't follow because of the two men in his way. I hurry in the direction of the door, holding the torch tight. Brooch hums in the distance. I decide to use her as a guide instead of the fire, since its light exposes me too much. Tossing the wood to the ground, I wrench my skirts up and break into a sprint. This time, the darkness doesn't frighten me. Halfway to the river, I sense movement behind me. I'm surprised to realize it's Tintype, keeping pace despite his limp.

What about Smoke? I want to demand, but we're still too close to the square. The others will be searching for us by now. So I swallow my anxiety and push on.

The gnarled roots loom up ahead. I emerge from the mouth of the passage cautiously, but there are no shouts or footsteps. I glance at Tintype to see if he senses anything. He shakes his head. In unison, we abandon the safety of walls and venture into the open. We are the bats, swift and in shadow. Only once we reach the other side of the river does Tintype speak.

"Do you still have the key?" he asks, hushed. There's a trace of worry in his voice, and I glance down. The chain must have broken during the chaos, but I can feel it against my chest. Turning in an attempt at modesty, I dip my fingers beneath my neckline and pull the key out of my corset.

"It's here."

"Good. Go."

But I grab his hands, knowing that I would be truly dead if it weren't for him. The key is lodged between our palms. "Will you come with me?"

Tintype hesitates, glancing in the direction of the inferno. The orange flames reflect against the ceiling. It feels like nothing has changed between us, and I'm standing in the road, begging him not to ride into the horizon. After a moment, he gently disengages himself. "No. I may be of some assistance yet to Journal and Smoke. If I survive, though, I'll come and find you. I promise."

Reluctant to leave, I bite my lip and study him. His thin hair, that stained uniform, the stern expression. As the precious seconds tick by, I feel a painful sensation in my chest, as though my heart is being tugged every which way. I remember the last time I saw him alive. Even then, I was still hopeful for promises and affection. Instead I just received a few stiff words.

"Thank you," I say, blinking against the memories. "For trying to help me break the curse…Father."

There's a pause. A faint smile touches his lips, making lines deepen and spread from the corners of his eyes.

He takes something out of his pocket and puts it in the center of my palm. It's the only object he fell into Under with, cool and smooth to the touch. Unable to resist, I look down at the image. My mother stares back, her eyes steady and clear. *Be brave,* they seem to say.

Before I can say anything else, someone yells from the maze. It's not a sound of discovery—no one would think to look here, not yet. Quickly I face Tintype again. We both know this may be our final conversation. "What happened to you after my death?" I ask. "How did you know I had a part in the curse?"

Perhaps Tintype realizes that I won't go without an explanation, because he gestures impatiently. "After I fell, I recalled a conversation I had with the Talbot maid. It was just after your funeral. I lingered after everyone else had gone. I opened the casket, kissed your forehead"—a shock goes through me at this, because with that single touch, Tintype set everything into motion and didn't even know it—"and told you how sorry I was. Seeing her chance, Irene sought me out. She was terrified as she told me about overhearing you girls practicing spells. She suspected her mistress was responsible for your death. Since the townspeople began dying after that, and they'd heard rumors of witchcraft in the Talbot household, it was easy for them to assume that dark magic was at work and my daughter was the key."

"Did you believe I was the cause?" I ask, fearful of the answer.

"Not even for a moment." He says it without hesitation.

I smile now, and a strange ache fills me. I'm remembering who we were in the life before this one—ours was a bond made out of obligation and grief. Once Mother died, there was no one to fill the silences between us. On the rare occasion that Father was home, he retreated to his study and emerged only for stilted dinners or required outings. He was as much a stranger then as he is now.

To disguise the direction of my thoughts, I say, "The key belongs to Kathleen Talbot. Whoever she is." There are many girls in Under who could be her. Earring, Bible, Stocking. "I believe she's the one orchestrating these deaths, but someone else is carrying them out for her. The person who attacked me was almost certainly male."

"Indeed." My father sighs. "There have been so many times when I wanted to beg your forgiveness, daughter. If I had been more present, perhaps none of this would have happened. How much do you recall of our life before?"

"You were in the British army and got called away so often that I hardly knew you. The last time, you left me in the care of our friends, the Talbots."

"This you do not know. During my final trip, I was injured and honorably discharged. By the time I returned, you had already died. I wasn't there to protect you. When the cholera spread, I was glad not to be spared." He swallows. "But none of that matters now. We've wasted too much time. The others are looking for you and there are only so many places they will try before coming here. Use the key and—"

"Father," I whisper, staring at a torch in the distance. It's moving toward us, held aloft by a hulking shadow. Terror claws up my throat.

He turns to follow my gaze. Seeing the danger, Tintype

moves in front of me. His expression is alert. I pocket his gift as the newcomer walks to the edge of the wooden river and stops. We watch him climb over the twisted limbs, slow and steady. Then he hops down and faces us.

No one speaks. The fire quivers.

Finally Tintype takes a step forward. His bad leg trembles. "Who's there?" he calls. The light begins to creep closer and closer. Tintype holds his hand out to me wordlessly. I understand and pull the knife from its hiding place. He takes it without looking away from the approaching flame. Weaponless, I press against the wall and seek the keyhole with my fingers.

"Now," Tintype orders out of the corner of his mouth.

Then, before either of us can react, the person holding the torch throws it with an audible grunt. It's meant for me, but Father moves quickly, leaping into its path before I realize what's happening. The flame slams into Father and he is instantly ablaze.

My scream echoes through all of Under.

CHAPTER TWENTY-ONE

Father acts immediately. While I continue to shriek, he drops to the dirt and rolls violently. "Don't let him escape!" he manages to shout. Regaining some of my senses, I kneel and retrieve the knife. I glance at Father to be sure he will recover before turning away.

The river is on fire, and Under is brighter than ever before. Shadows and darkness shrink, revealing the things they have hidden for so long. Our attacker tries to run before I'm able to get a glimpse of his face, but it's too late. My stomach drops. He scrambles over the roots, heat and smoke rising from his clothes, and disappears into the maze.

"Handkerchief?"

In that moment, I remember him. I picture the boy he was before, always lurking and staring at Kathleen. We were both disdainful and wary of the butcher's son, mocking the blood-covered apron he wore in the shop. One Sunday, when Kathleen was upset with how James turned away from her, he offered his handkerchief.

I don't know how the boy hid that scratch from the day he attacked me. Maybe he did what he does best—stood so still and silent, the others forgot about him.

Behind me, Father gets to his feet. "Did you see who it was?" he rasps, adjusting his singed uniform.

I am slow to respond, berating myself for being so blind and disregarding my initial wariness of the boy. "It was Handkerchief," I say faintly. So he's been the one acting as Kathleen's puppet. Apparently even without memories, his devotion never wavered. This means Handkerchief was the attacker in the alley, and he must have caused his own injuries to appear innocent. It was unfortunate we hadn't thought to put on a play in Under; he was meant for the stage.

Father says something else, but I'm not listening. A new danger presents itself—Journal. He trusts Handkerchief, confides in him. I must warn him that his friend is the murderer.

Without another word to Father, I bolt. There's a part of the river that has been completely burned away. I leap over the ashes and scorched remains. On the other side, I begin to head for the square, but my gaze flicks up to Journal's tower out of habit.

There is a silhouette in the window. I stop and frown. Why would he be there? They were just by the pyre, trying to convince the others of my innocence. But it's him, I have no doubt. Changing direction, I break into a run, making sure to keep to unused passageways.

The distance to the tower has never felt so long or the stairs so numerous. When I reach the top, I expect the worst. Journal stepped too close to the fire, or the mob robbed him of an arm, or Handkerchief has already struck. But there he stands, unharmed.

His back is to me and he looks out the window as if there's a moon or stars. There's no sign of the other boy. I release a ragged breath and my knees weaken with relief. I put my hand to the wall. "Journal?" I venture. "Are you all right?" There is something about the set of his shoulders that makes me hesitate in the doorway.

"Fine. The others wouldn't listen to me or Smoke. They left the square to search for you."

He still doesn't turn. And suddenly I know. I know why he came here and why he won't look at me now. "You remember," I breathe.

Journal doesn't answer, but the force he uses to set down a book is all the answer I need. It *thud*s against the floor. I swallow. Now I recall the letter I left him before going to meet James, written in haste and pain. *Forgive me. I'm honored that you asked Father for my hand, and I will always adore you. But this isn't what I want.*

How it must have wounded him, when Journal heard of my body being found in the cemetery…with James Alistair. There is nothing I can say that will possibly ease the pain my actions have caused him. Caused everyone.

In the end, all I can manage is, "I never meant to hurt you."

Journal jerks around to face me, his nostrils flaring and his eyes bright. "Hurt me? You've destroyed me!"

In the life before this, if he had been arguing with the girl before the fall, I might have stayed silent. But I have been struck and deceived and terrified. I have fought and run and sought the truth. I am that girl no longer. "And what of your part in all this?" I demand incredulously. "You were my *friend*, Journal, but you didn't even offer the courtesy of a discussion before choosing the path my life would take. It's little wonder I struggled in staying true to it."

"You're right. *I'm* the one who's behaved badly here." The corner of his mouth lifts in a small, bitter smile. "Please, Key, just leave."

His tone is so final, so broken. Relenting, I turn and take a step toward the door. But then I pause. There's the soft sound of shuffling papers, a sound I once knew better than any other. It was my lullaby, my harbor, my heartbeat.

I glance back at him and murmur, "I did love you, Henry Wisely."

He looks up. There's such longing in his expression that something sparks within me. Then the light in his eyes dies and he turns back to his distractions. "Not enough."

I nod. It was a silly hope, really. After all, there is no reviving something that is dead. Not even magic can do that.

Just as I reach the threshold, though, I remember why I came here in the first place. I say over my shoulder, "You should know that Handkerchief is the killer. And he isn't working alone. I'd guess that it's whoever convinced the others of my guilt."

The boy goes still but doesn't look at me.

Tracing his bent head with my eyes, memorizing the outline of his noble features, I slowly retreat. "Goodbye, Journal."

And I leave his tower for the last time.

I sit on my headstone and wait.

The graveyard is strangely beautiful tonight, perhaps because I know this may be the last time I see it. Frost glitters on stone and a cold wind whistles over the snow. Sitting there, making a valiant effort to keep terror at bay, I remember the object still hidden in my pocket. I take the round, golden piece out and open it. The faded image shows a woman. She wasn't beautiful, but she had a kind face. Her hair was brown and curled, her features pale and soft. We have the same eyes.

I smile faintly and touch my mother's cheek. In that moment, I remember being told she died having me. I never had the opportunity to know her, but once, when he'd had a bit of drink, Father mentioned that she snorted when she laughed.

The piece closes again with a *click*. I tuck it away and tilt my head back to enjoy the light spreading through the expanse above me. Morning comes this way, slowly, and I pray I'll be able to see it. In the distance, a bird calls. Spring is also on its way, it seems.

"Hello, Leah."

At the sound of Ribbon's voice, something inside me breaks.

I close my eyes and try to memorize the sounds of a season I will never see. "Hello, Kathleen."

Her feet crunch in the snow. I tense, but I know she won't hurt me. Not yet.

"So you remember everything, do you?" she questions lightly, moving to perch on the grave opposite me. Even though her face is hard with cruelty, she is beautiful. I study my friend, and all the shadows in my memories shift until her face is in every one. Smiling, sobbing, screaming. A lump forms in my throat.

It's clear that the girl I once knew is truly dead. It's no wonder I didn't recognize her.

She is still waiting for me to answer. "For the most part," I say bleakly. "I even know the reasons for your actions in Under. The murders and the fire at Mrs. Room's."

Ribbon raises her eyebrows with interest. "Do tell."

The wind strengthens. I make a vague gesture, ignoring the hair blowing across my face. "Around the time of your death, I imagine there were rumors. People whispered the word 'witch' and spoke of dark magic. When you fell, it was vital that no one remember any of it, else they would burn you. Handkerchief was still loyal, poor soul. So you ordered him to watch my betrothed. You thought that if anyone would find the truth first, it would be Henry."

I take a breath. Thank heavens she only met my distant father once, else she would have remembered Tintype's true identity and harmed him, too.

"Every time someone began to regain memories, you told Handkerchief to silence them. With every death, you fanned the flames of suspicion. That's why they're now so convinced I'm the killer."

For a few moments, the air winding through the trees and stones is my only response. Even the bird has gone silent. I force myself to meet Ribbon's gaze. She's… smiling. "Well done," the girl says. "Truly. I shouldn't be surprised, though. You were always so clever."

Her words remind me of a detail that's been standing out in my mind like a loose string. "You could've killed me as soon as I arrived in Under. Why did you stay your hand?"

At this, her nostrils flare. "Because Smoke was your valiant protector from nearly the moment you fell. Every time Handkerchief or I drew near, there he was, obsessing over you like a lovesick fool. Apparently even death doesn't change some things."

Danger, the beetle whispers. Fear burns in my veins. I hide it and lift my chin. "I understand why you cursed James and me. You were angry and betrayed. But why all the rest, Kathleen? Why did you make everyone pay the price for our mistakes?"

She purses her lips and squints, as if in deep thought. The leaden sky casts patches of light over her skin. After a few moments, Ribbon focuses. "It was a clumsy curse." She sighs, running her hand over one of the headstones. "I didn't realize the extent of my power. And I hadn't quite learned how to translate the language in the book. I *think* I shouted, 'May you succumb to a slow death. May you lose everything that was once dear to you. May you never find peace.'

"But you and James died by my own hand, and nothing seemed to come of the curse," she adds. "After the night I created it, I had no idea the power lingered inside me. Over the next few weeks, everyone I touched fell down dead in one way or another. Muriel, Irene, Mayor Young, Constable Norton. Then my father was infected with cholera, and that spread, essentially eliminating over half the village. Even I contracted it eventually. And because of the wording in my curse, people lost their memories and awoke in their graves."

My scalp prickles at the sound of her giggle. Until this instant, I hadn't truly seen it. The glint of madness in her eyes.

Then, before I can blink, she sobers. "But nature finds a balance in everything. Under was the result, and I believe it was an opportunity to counteract the curse, if I so wished. The key to Mother's chest was in my pocket when I fell," she concludes.

I'm struggling to find a safe response when our conversation is interrupted. "Our blood sealed the magic," a voice says from behind. I begin to whirl in surprise, but my instincts go against putting my back to Ribbon. So I dig my fingers into the headstone beneath me and watch her, instead.

At the sight of the man she once loved—still loves, considering how affected she is by him—her lip curls into a semblance of a smile.

"Oh, good," Ribbon purrs. "You found us. I left the door open especially for you."

"Our blood sealed the magic," Smoke repeats, more forcefully this time. He stops, so close that our thighs nearly brush, but his attention is not on me. His face is turned toward the road, toward the place where he died. He's holding a torch. "I felt it happening."

He's trying to tell me something. Any other person might mistake the razor edge in his tone as bitterness, but I know him. His anger is more potent. No, this is the voice of someone making a discovery. If he felt the spell sealing, could it be he was still alive when I ran from the cemetery that night? Why should the blood be so important?

A gasp catches in my throat. All at once, I understand his meaning.

Another memory flashes of Kathleen cutting her hand during the incantation. I think of the knife jutting out of my back and red stains in the snow. "The blood would undo it," I whisper. It would only take a drop from each of our veins, regardless of its vitality. So many things end the same way they began, particularly with magic.

Smoke looks down at me and the lines in his face have deepened, making him look older. I have a terrible feeling that history is about to repeat itself.

Thankfully, Ribbon doesn't hear me. She stands, brushing her hands off in a brisk manner. "Before we begin, *I* have some inquiries for *you*," she announces. "Now, I can guess how you got your hands on my key. Tintype couldn't have 'found' so many trinkets if he weren't journeying to the outside world—in fact, if he weren't so skilled at staying hidden, I would've eliminated him long ago. But what I don't understand is how you and everyone you came into contact with seemed to be regaining memories."

Sorrow curves around my heart like a cold finger. "You forget, I learned the magic alongside you," I say, though it feels like so many lifetimes ago. "Before I died that night, I had just long enough to do a spell of my own. I spoke words that would counter yours, preserving both my body and my mind. Magic that would do everything opposite yours. If you were a key, I was a door. If you were death, I was life. I had no way of knowing if it would work, but thankfully, it did. The only flaw was how long it took me to waken."

She tilts her head, hair swinging unbound over her shoulder. "Once again I commend your intelligence. But it won't save you, sister."

Dread, which has been a knot inside me, begins unraveling at these words. Smoke's fists clench in my peripheral vision. He'll fight at my side, despite the price he's already paid. Still, I can't help attempting to reach her one last time. "Hasn't enough blood been spilled?" I implore her, standing. "Let's end this, Kathleen. Forgive each other and finally let the dead sleep."

"Never," she spits, her guise dropping. Gone is Ribbon, the sweet girl who instills calmness and acceptance into the corpses trapped beneath the ground. The person seething in front of me is wild and full of such wrath that it's a tangible taste in my mouth, like gunpowder and dirt.

She buries her nails into her right palm, digging for blood. Even cold and lifeless, it's the only ingredient necessary to awaken the magic.

In response, I let go of my own facades. I am not content to hide behind books or rules of society, and I'm tired of allowing fear to control me. My spine becomes steel, and I meet her churning gaze head-on. "I was more powerful than you," I say evenly. A warning, though I have no idea if I can do the magic now. "Don't force my hand."

"Prove it."

We dive at each other. Smoke shouts my name, but Ribbon throws her arm out and directs a guttural word at him. He freezes. The moment of impact is jarring, and the pain is so unexpected that she gains the upper hand. We roll through the snow, hitting and shrieking. It's as though her skin is alive with embers. I try spells of my own, but the power isn't even a flicker inside me. Then Ribbon is on top of me and I'm sinking. I struggle to regain my freedom, but she is unnaturally strong and holds me down with one hand while I buck and claw.

"Bring the torch to me," she instructs Smoke.

"No, Smoke, don't!"

But his expression is slack and vacant. On graceless, plodding feet, he approaches. Ribbon snatches the torch from him and lowers it so that the flame is right beside my cheek. The crackling beast begins eating my skin. Apparently we're not immune to pain when it comes to fire; agony tears through me. Ribbon laughs when I scream. There is no glimpse of my old friend, no shred left of the girl who taught me magic, hid me from monsters, kept me from loneliness.

"I'm glad Handkerchief didn't succeed in killing you," she hisses, leaning so close that I can smell the rot I never noticed before. In that moment, I know the end is near. "It would have deprived me of this moment."

Just as she begins to lower the flames toward my face again, a new voice shatters the frozen air. "Miss Talbot, if you don't release my best friend, I'm afraid there's going to be trouble between us."

Ribbon is so startled that she pulls back. The torch slips from her fingers and falls into the snow, extinguishing with a wet hiss. Steam rises and I cough, pushing myself up. My vision clears. Ribbon evidently doesn't view me as a threat; she releases her hold and takes a step toward Journal, menace emanating from every part of her.

Words of power flow from my lips like old friends, and this time I feel them. Living things that seek to do my bidding, drawing their reserve from the blood exposed in my burns. Perhaps the magic answers because I'm desperate to save them, or it's been there all along and I was the one keeping it at bay. All that matters is how Ribbon turns scarlet, like an engulfed log just before it crumbles in the fire.

She whips back toward me and stares. "It can't be. It's impossible."

There's no time for Ribbon to form a counter spell; in the time it takes to gather a breath, she bursts into flames.

My gut heaves, but I don't stop. I keep at the string of words as we listen to her scream over and over, a shrill sound that I know will haunt me until I am truly dead. Nausea grips my stomach—this time, it has nothing to do with a memory—and I take no pleasure in watching the girl burn. She tries to put the flames out by throwing herself into a snow bank, but it's too late. Finally she goes still, a black and sizzling husk of what she used to be. Only then do I fall silent.

Blood spreads through the snow like a deadly flower in full bloom, and I feel the tingle of old magic; Ribbon's curse has started to unravel. All it needs now is Smoke's blood.

As soon as her soul slips free from its tether, finding peace at last, Smoke gasps. He lurches and dazedly takes in the aftermath of our battle. The stench of burnt flesh fills my nostrils; I turn away, fighting the urge to gag. Journal is there, his mouth a thin line. As though we are once again the boy and girl arguing in that study, he opens his arms.

I don't hesitate to walk into them. He smells like old

books and rich earth, and it pushes the scent of Ribbon away. Instead of looking at her remains in the snow, I squeeze my eyes shut. "She always fueled her power with hatred. She never learned that love is infinitely stronger," I murmur. Journal's only response is to hold me tighter.

When I find the strength to face the world again, I pull away from Journal and swipe at my cheeks without thinking. But of course, there are no tears to dry. The two of them watch me as I square my shoulders. "Thank you," I say, finally ending the silence between us. "I owe both of you my life and a great deal more."

Journal shakes his head. "You owe me nothing. In fact, I hope the score between us can be considered settled."

"Score?"

"Perhaps I should... I think I see something over there," Smoke mumbles. Avoiding my eyes, he leaves us, taking long-legged strides through the snow. He ascends a hill and stops beneath a great tree, a lean shadow against the horizon.

Frowning, I turn back to Journal and try to prepare myself for more harsh words. "You were right," he says, raising his gaze to meet mine. To my surprise, there's shame hidden within those depths.

I raise my eyebrows. "Oh?"

He nods, a jerky movement that's unlike his usual grace. "I did take your choice away," my friend says bluntly. "And in doing so, I drove you into his arms. Perhaps if I hadn't been such a fool, you wouldn't have been in the graveyard that night, and none of this—"

"Stop." I touch Journal's arm and give him a sad smile. I decide not to address the bit about Smoke; we probably won't ever agree on that particular topic. "It seems everyone is determined to blame themselves for all this. The truth is, it doesn't matter. Not anymore. Don't you agree?"

Journal doesn't smile back, but there's a tender light in his eyes, and it warms me more than any fire could. "Quite."

I glance toward Smoke again. He's fiddling with that cigar of his—the one I gave him in life and he cherished enough to keep in death—and looking toward the brightening sky. I refocus on Journal, and my stomach quails as I gather the nerve to ask, "So are you saying... you forgive me?"

"Only if you forgive me."

There's no hesitation in his reply. With those simple words, any lingering guilt leaves my body like smoke from a dying candle. The wind snatches it up and carries it away to a place where it can't harm anyone else again.

I let out a long, long sigh, and now Journal smiles. He strokes the side of my face with the tip of his finger, then turns toward the mausoleum. In doing so, his gaze collides with Smoke's. For a moment, they just stare at each other. Then, slowly, Journal nods.

Smoke hesitates a moment before he nods back. They will never be friends, but finally, at the very least, they can respect each other.

I'm about to go to Smoke when Journal stops at the door and faces us again, one hand on the wall, elegant fingers splayed over the stones. "Will I see you below?" he calls.

There's an unspoken question within the words. He's wondering if I plan to return or if I'll take my chances in the land of the living. But my time here was finished long ago, and now that my search for answers has come to an end, as well, I feel ready to start something new. "Yes, you will," I say firmly. "Be down soon; there's one more thing I'd like to do."

Journal disappears into the darkness beyond, bound for Under.

Once he's gone, I heave my skirts up and climb the hill. Smoke stays silent as I reach his side. Something seems amiss, but our ordeal with Ribbon is so fresh that I don't want to force him to reveal anything. For a time, we remain like that. Silent and touching. Together and apart. "We never had the chance to do this," I say suddenly.

At last, Smoke looks at me. His expression is carefully blank. "Do what?"

"Wait a moment. You'll see."

For some reason, my words seem to upset him; Smoke purses his lips and looks away again. The beginnings of dawn tint his skin the color of newly harvested wheat. I shift closer to him, thinking to take his hand. "I suppose you're relieved; the hermit finally knows the truth," Smoke says abruptly. That telltale muscle ticks in his jaw. "It appears all is well."

He's jealous, I realize. Smoke thinks Journal and I have reconciled romantically.

Stifling a giddy laugh, I grab his shirt and yank him to me. Smoke is so startled that it takes him a moment to react. Then he makes a sound deep in his throat and buries his fist in my hair, pulling me even closer.

This kiss is different from all the rest—it's free of urgency, uncertainty, guilt. I never want it to end.

Alas, I feel the weight of obligation pressing in on me. There are souls, far below our feet, who still don't know that the danger has passed and there is nothing more to fear. I put my hand on Smoke's chest, a wordless request.

His grip loosens and he pulls back with obvious reluctance. Just as he did in life, he presses his forehead to mine. He takes a deep breath, contentment in the sound, as though he's finally come home after a long journey. "Yes, I *am* relieved," I tell Smoke, thankful yet again that we don't need to breathe. Mine would be a bit uneven, were it so. "He's finally accepted that friendship is all there will be between us. And that my affections lie elsewhere."

His eyes gleam with understanding. He tucks a strand of hair behind my ear and I automatically lean into the touch. "Well, this is a bit awkward, then," Smoke says. "I'm afraid I told Spoon I'd marry her."

I make a sound halfway between laughter and indignation. I try to pull away, but he won't let me, his arms tightening in response. Luckily for Smoke, the sun peeks over the edge of the world, like a child hauling itself up by the fingertips. It sets the snow on fire in brilliant hues of orange, yellow, and pink. I go still.

"Look," I whisper, nodding over his shoulder.

Smoke follows my gaze. His silence says more than words.

A few minutes go by, sunlight and colors pouring over everything like spilled paint. *We never had the chance to do this*, I'd told him. This was the moment I had meant. Standing in the daylight together. Simple, perhaps, but everything.

As the moment stretches into minutes, Smoke

rummages in his pocket and takes that cigar out. I watch him cast about for something to light it with, but the torch died with Ribbon. He swears quietly.

An idea blooms. I wrap my hands around Smoke's arm for support, put all my attention on the end of his cigar and, under my breath, utter a lilting word.

The magic responds quicker this time, as though it's been hovering nearby, just waiting for an opportunity. The cigar lights with a tiny spurt of sound, sending a rush of exhilaration through me. A thin tendril of smoke rises into the air. The thing is so dry and old that it instantly crumbles, but still, Smoke inhales as if the experience is euphoric.

His eyes close, and as I admire him, I forget the sun. He has never been more beautiful to me.

Regret threatens to creep in—we had so little time together—but I banish the feeling by tucking myself against Smoke's side. "I love you."

Careful to keep the crumbling cigar away, he puts his arms around me. His voice is soft as he replies, "I love you, too."

There's nothing else to say, really. Though there's work to be done, neither of us moves. Not yet. We stand at the top of the hill and watch the sun crest that distant horizon. After so long, we are unafraid. We are together.

And we are so, so alive.

CHAPTER TWENTY-TWO

I lead them to the door.

Their whispers of wonder and trepidation bounce off the passageway walls. Smoke walks close behind, his presence a comfort after all that's happened.

With Ribbon gone, the time for secrets is over. The people of Under now know the truth. About the choices, the curse, the murders. There are some who resent me, resent Ribbon, which I can understand. They were innocent in all this; their deaths should not have been so premature or their afterlives so bleak. Most of them, however, are just…relieved.

To avoid being seen, we wait for night to fall before making the journey. They follow me to the surface willingly when the time comes. A sense of anticipation builds, a pressure on the air that makes my still pulse want to race.

There is one from our party who's missing. After the confrontation in the graveyard, the citizens of Under went in search of Handkerchief. We soon found his body—or what was left of it—in Ribbon's room. His last words were etched on the wall above him:

I em sry. I luvd hr.

My thoughts linger on the butcher's son the rest of the way to the door. Once we emerge into the night, though, I think of nothing but the stars. Jaws drop in shock and disbelief. They've existed so long in the darkness, they had begun to believe there was no light anywhere else. One woman puts her arms out and spins, around and around, laughing at the moon. Others join her, looking like children in a game. While they revel in the sensation of fresh air and open space, the rest get to work. The ground is still frozen, so we build fires on top of the graves and wait for them to thaw. It takes hours.

By the time our shovels—conveniently found in the mausoleum—*thump* against the top of the caskets, another morning is nearly upon us. It would not do to be discovered by anyone living, so I call to those who've wandered away. "It's time," I say. No one argues.

"Can you imagine the townspeople's reactions when they find us like this? Graves unearthed and wide open?" says a girl whose name I never learned. She giggles with wicked delight.

"Not to mention the fact that our corpses should've been past decomposed by now," someone adds. Brooch, who is cradled carefully in the crook of Eye Patch's single arm, hums a happy note.

It strikes me, then, that I got exactly what I wanted. At the start of all this, I longed for more than death. More than a single object and a fatal wound. I wanted to stand in the land above and have a head full of memories.

It's a strange sensation, contentment. But it also feels right.

While everyone gathers to say their farewells, I drift away. Snow falls gently from the sky, covering everything in a glowing blanket of white. It helps me to find the grave I'm seeking.

KATHLEEN TALBOT. A brittle vine twines around the edge of her headstone. Kneeling, I whisper one last apology to the girl who I once thought of as a sister. She knew such pain and anger. Like me, she made the wrong choice. She turned to magic and revenge instead of hope and love.

Perhaps she is waiting for us, wherever that is. And ready to make peace.

I begin to stand, but a thought that has been lurking in the back of my mind pushes forward. Pausing, I succumb to the urge and lean over, writing words in the snow.

Someone says my name. I lift my head and see Muriel throwing her spoon aside. I wave at her, and she winks and lowers herself out of sight. Next I find Emily, who we used to buy flowers from on the street. She plays with that toy in her final moments. She feels my gaze on her and gives me a shy smile, that one eyeball bobbing with the enthusiasm of her movements. There's Irene, singing to herself as she straightens the bedding in her casket. Lastly I locate my father. His expression is one of unconcealed, unadulterated relief. So many things end the same way they begin, yes, but there are instances when they are vastly different. Like this. In life I did not know these people. In death, I loved them.

Thinking of love, I turn again. Henry looks at me, and I look at him. Neither of us says a word. The corners of his mouth tip in a bittersweet smile.

"Are you ready?" James asks. I tear my gaze away from Henry. I know that he will find peace with the rest of us.

"Almost." I step back and survey the message embedded in the snow. *My name is Leah.* Maybe, just maybe, it'll last long enough for someone else to see. Someone else to notice and carry back to Caulfield, where a woman called Mary will hear about it. Well, she did say she loves a good story.

Finished, I go to James. We clasp hands and step onto the soft velvet of his resting place. "It's fortunate that you were buried in a rather large casket," I murmur.

He kisses my nose in agreement, then asks, "Are you ready for another adventure?"

Fear is suddenly a bitter taste in my mouth. Facing the unknown is always unnerving, no matter how badly we want to see it. "I think so."

"See you above," James whispers. And just like that, my anxiety fades. I tuck myself into his side and wait. I know it will be beautiful.

Though I don't watch it happening, we all sense the moment James cuts his hand and presses his palm to the ground. A sound escapes me, a sort of half gasp as I feel my soul lifting. James's grip loosens. Everything becomes bright and glowing. I am weightless.

Together, we ascend into the next chapter of our afterlives.

ACKNOWLEDGMENTS

The first individuals I need to acknowledge in the making of this book are my family. Dean, Mariana, Mayis, Jeremy, Josh, Chris, Jay, and Michelle. You were so patient and understanding every time I left early, every time I didn't make an appearance, and every time I brought my work along with me. I'm so lucky to have a supportive family like you.

Next I want to express undying gratitude to my agent and my editor, Beth Miller and Stacy Abrams. You both read the manuscript countless times during revisions, sent so much encouragement when I needed it, and exercised endless patience and grace with each missed deadline. Thank you for being the best readers and cheerleaders an author could ask for. *Smoke and Key* wouldn't be what it is without you.

To the rest of my team at Entangled. My production editor Curtis Svehlak, formatter and designer Heather Howland, publicists Deb Shapiro and Heather Riccio, copy editor Lisa Knapp, QA reader Hannah Lindsey, and cover designers Stefanie Saw and Bree Archer. Thank you also to Judi Lauren for her editorial input. This story would be a mess were it not for all your dedication.

I would be remiss if I didn't thank Stephanie Kuehn, who read a very, very early draft of this novel. Thank you for reading so quickly and being one of the first people to tell me this book had something special.

My love and appreciation also to Amber Hart, who was another person to read an early draft. When the rejections started coming in, you kept urging me to pursue this story. You sang its praises whenever I had doubt. It was exactly what I needed. You are such a wonderful friend and I'm quite certain I would go insane without you to listen and support.

Last but not least, eternal gratitude goes to my partner, Jordan. You are my rock and my inspiration. Thanks for all that you do, babe. I love you. It's my turn to make dinner now.

EXCERPT FROM
ANALIESE RISING
BY BRENDA DRAKE

I bump Dalton's shoulder with mine and smile up at him. "I saw the mail. Congratulations. First place, huh? Your sculptures are going to make us millions one day."

He pulls on the back of his neck. "Yeah, if I live through high school. That mythology final is going to kill my GPA."

"If you let me out of the dishes tonight, I'll help you study for it." I live and breathe mythology. Our dad was a history professor, and that was our thing. I know the obscure gods and goddesses, not just the ones made popular by comic books and movies.

"Deal." Now he bumps my shoulder, but it has his weight behind it and makes me stumble a little. He chuckles. "Graceful."

The streets are crowded with rush-hour commuters. Across the way, some old man wearing a black newsboy cap and a camel-colored overcoat stands in front of the coffee shop we're heading for. His eyes follow our approach, causing a shiver to prickle up my spine. I keep my eyes on where my feet are landing to avoid catching the man's gaze.

The scent of freshly ground coffee beans fills my nose. We spent many Saturdays in this shop after our hikes with Dad. Back then, we were only allowed to drink hot chocolate while he sipped an Americano.

A crash sounds behind Dalton and me, and we spin around. An SUV and a small red car are mangled together. The tires of a black sedan squeal as it speeds in our direction.

It's as though it all happens in slow motion. The sedan jumps the curb, and someone shoves me out of the way and into Dalton. We land hard on the sidewalk. One tire of the car rides the curb until coming off to join the other on the road. The driver weaves around a few cars before disappearing around a corner.

I scramble to my feet and glance back. The old man in the newsboy cap lies on the sidewalk. Blood trickles down the side of his face.

"Call 911," I tell Dalton and drop to my knees beside the man. The gash in his head is deep. I search the crowd now forming around us. "Someone get a towel or something. I need to compress his wound."

A woman removes her scarf and hands it to me. I take it, and I'm about to press it against the gash in the man's head when his gloved hand catches my arm.

"Don't touch me," he says. "I'm dying."

I push my eyebrows together. "You're not going to die. The ambulance is coming."

"My bag," he says weakly. A worn-out leather satchel lays on the sidewalk a few feet from him.

I snatch it up and lift it for him to see. "This one?"

He nods, his lids half closed over soft blue eyes. His

face scrunches up in pain. "That's it." He keeps his voice low. "Take it to my grandson. Don't let anyone see you have it. You're in danger, Analiese. Run. Don't stop."

My heart drops like a stone in my chest, and the case falls from my hands, slapping against the concrete. "How do you know my name?"

A fire truck and an ambulance pull up to the curb.

"Wh—" His eyes close, mouth slackens. I don't know why I believe the man, but I do. I slip the strap to his bag over my shoulder, stand, and back away into the crowd beside Dalton. So many faces stare down at the man. Unknown faces. And one could belong to whoever this man feared.

Paramedics rush a stretcher and medical bags over to the old man. A woman places an oxygen mask on his face while another assesses his injuries.

"What are you doing with his bag?" Dalton asks.

"He wants me to give it to his grandson. Maybe his number or address is in it." The man saying I was in danger made me nervous. I search the faces in the crowd again. No one looks menacing or suspicious. "Come on. Let's get out of here." I sprint-walk down the street and away from the accident.

Dalton keeps step with me. "That's stealing. Taking the bag."

"No, it isn't. He gave it to me."

"What's in it?" he asks.

I dart glances at the people and cars passing us. We have to get off the street. I spot an ice cream parlor and dash inside with Dalton close behind me.

My gaze goes to the window. Sitting behind the large

panes of glass making up the front of the store is like being in a fishbowl—trapped and exposed.

"Get us each a scoop," I say, nodding to a table in a back corner. "I'm going to sit over there."

The chair screeches across the tiled floor as I drag it away from the table. I sit, and it wobbles a little on its legs. The tiny buckles on the straps of the old man's satchel are challenging to undo. The smell of leather oil clings to the bag.

The man's injuries looked fatal. The driver who caused the accident never stopped. Had to be some drunk afraid to face the police.

You're in danger, Analiese. Run. Don't stop, the man told me, his sad eyes haunting.

How did he know my name?

I'm worrying too much. No one from the street can see me in my seat in the back corner of the parlor. And there probably isn't anyone following me. The old man had to be delusional.

The accident was real, though. I'm still shaken up from it, because my hands are trembling as I remove items from the bag. My stomach's doing that dip-and-fall thing it does while riding the monster roller coaster at the amusement park.

There are many objects in the bag, along with a tattered notebook—a ring, envelopes, keys, and other various things. I pick up the ring and spin the wheel with letters of the alphabet etched into the round steel. There're two other wheels. One with numbers and the other with symbols.

A decoder ring? I pause a moment, wondering why

the man would have one, before returning it to the bag. The envelopes have what I believe is the old man's name and address on them.

Adam Conte. "He lives in Lancaster," I say out loud, which causes the girl at the next table to look at me. I give her an awkward smile and tuck the envelopes back into the bag. Avoiding eye contact with her, I flip open the cover to the notebook. The first four pages hold a list of names. Many of the names are crossed out. I run my finger down the column.

Dalton returns from the counter, holding two cups with a mound of Oreo ice cream in each.

On the third page, I stop at a name with a line drawn through it — Alea Bove Jordan — my mother. Beside her name, written at an angle in pencil, is Jake Jordan, my father. He's like an afterthought. A line runs across his name, too. Underneath them is my uncle, Eli Bove. His name is also marked off. I turn the page and gasp. Halfway down the list, written in thick black ink strokes, is *Analiese Jordan.*

D alton's tiny red-with-rust-spots Civic sputters down the I-76 highway toward Lancaster. An hour and a half there and back and I'll be home before Jane ever knows I ditched school. It's almost Spring Break, anyway. I've turned in most of my work, I reason with myself.

Besides, Jane won't care. She's barely around to notice. The hospital is more her home than our house.

I'm not even sure she'll be there on Sunday morning to see Dalton and me off to that bereavement camp for kids she insists we go to over the break.

The gas light flashes on.

"Crap. *Dalton*," I seethe under my breath. He's always running out of gas. I'm approaching the next exit and turn on the blinker.

The Turkey Hill Minit Market isn't as busy as I thought it'd be during morning rush hour. I pull up to the pump right beside a black Audi sedan with a front license plate that reads *My God Carries a Hammer*.

"Nice." I snicker and pop open the gas tank cover.

I fill up the Civic and rush inside to get a horrible gas station coffee. The lanky guy behind the counter straightens. His wide-set eyes follow me the entire way to the coffee bar. A man, way over six feet tall, with red hair that's short on the sides and fades up to a dovetail on top, has one of the refrigerator doors open. With his stare on the contents inside, he rubs his neatly cut beard.

The Styrofoam coffee cup plunks from the holder when I tug it out. I pour a premade cappuccino from the fountain.

The man steps back and looks over, his hand still holding open the door.

The air between the man and me feels off—tense. It's probably just me, and the fact I'm practically alone with a suspicious man in a gas station. I secure a lid over my cup and turn to leave.

"Which one do you suggest?" he asks, stopping me. There's a slight accent to his voice, but I can't place it. Possibly Scottish?

I glance around, and my eyes stop on him. "Are you talking to me?"

"There's no one else about." His smile is off. Like he has to remember how to create one or something.

"I don't drink the stuff, but my brother likes the one with the gold star." I want to look away, but something in his eyes captures me. They're like a kaleidoscope of fall leaves—orange, yellow, and brown. Their focus on me causes the tiny hairs at the nape of my neck to stand straight up.

He picks up a can of the drink I suggested and lets go of the refrigerator door, his eyes never leaving me.

Now he's freaking me out.

I pretend to search the pastries near the coffee bar.

"A young girl such as yourself should not be traveling alone," he says. "You should be in school."

The pastries blur out of focus, the display stands are closing in on me, and the coffee cup shakes in my hand. Great. The creeper knows I'm alone. I have to lie. Tell him Dalton is in the back seat, sleeping.

I glance over at him. "I'm not alone—"

He's gone. I search over the display cases, but he isn't anywhere in the market. The guy behind the counter watches me intently while taking my cash for the coffee. It's as if he's never seen a dollar bill before. Probably hasn't, with everyone paying with debit or credit cards.

"You okay?" he asks.

"I'm fine." I force a smile to back up my statement. "Thank you."

"Have a nice day." His eyes have left me to watch two younger guys shuffling around the display cases.

The front door slides shut behind me. A brisk wind whips dark strands of hair around my face. I wrap my arms around me and dart for the Civic. The black Audi is gone, and I wonder if the man who strangely disappeared owns it. He did look like someone who would have a Thor license plate.

I'm nervous during the rest of the ride to Lancaster, glancing through the rearview window, checking and rechecking that no one's following me. That the black Audi isn't there.

"*In 1.5 miles, turn left*," the female voice on my phone's GPS directs.

Lancaster is a pretty cool town, with nearby farmlands and Amish country. When Dad was alive, we'd take weekend trips here and do touristy things like buggy rides and hikes. He loved checking out the architecture.

"*In five hundred feet, your destination is on the left*," the GPS says.

I've never been in this neighborhood before. The houses are older, and the area is quaint. I pull the Civic up to the curb and stare at the home. It's a two-and-a-half-story stone house and resembles a French countryside chateau with its bay windows, dormers, steepled gables, and cone-shaped roofs.

Dalton and I went to the hospital the night of the accident to see how the old man was doing, but he hadn't made it, dying only minutes after arriving in the ER. His family left before I could give the bag to his grandson.

I would've come sooner, but I figured the family needed space to mourn. His obit said they were having a memorial and reception for family and friends. So here

I am. At his house. Two weeks after the accident. Feels like a lifetime.

It's almost nine in the morning. He probably would've been at his kitchen table, drinking coffee and reading the paper, as old people do. His day might've been spent tending to the beautiful and colorful flowers in the beds surrounding the lawn.

For all I know, the house might be deserted. His grandson could live somewhere else.

After grabbing the man's bag, I pop open the Civic's door and slide out. The sidewalk is uneven and broken in spots. Because I'm superstitious, I avoid stepping on the cracks. The scent of freshly cut grass lingers over the lawn. The door has several locks and a peephole at eye level. I count them.

Seriously? Five? The door is metal, too. Above my head is a security camera.

Someone's expecting the apocalypse.

I press the doorbell and wait.

And wait.

I press it again.

When no one answers, I turn to leave but then pause. A faint bass comes from around the corner of the house. The stone pavers on the lawn lead me to the front of the garage.

The doors are open, and a guy about my age works a tattered punching bag hanging by a chain attached to the ceiling. He's shirtless, and his shorts are slung low on his hips. Tall, with dark, wavy hair, the boy isn't bad to look at.

With each throw of his fist or kick, his muscles flex then go slack. The way he's hitting the bag, he's definitely letting off steam. Maybe I should come back later when he's calmer.

This is a bad idea. I could just leave the bag at the front door. But then I won't find out why my name is on that list. Or why the man crossed my parents off that same list. The guy needs some cooling down. I can go find a coffee shop somewhere and come back when he's less angry and more dressed.

His music is so loud, he hasn't noticed my approach, so I ease around and head back the way I came.

"Hey," he shouts.

Crap. He spotted me. I turn back around.

He's walking my way. His bare chest rises and falls with heavy breaths. A nautical star medallion with a silver chain rests just below his collarbone. "You need something?"

"Um." *Don't look at his abdomen.* My eyes betray me and go there. His half nakedness distracts me, and I forget what I was going to say. "Um…"

His lips twist into a smirk, amusement igniting in his eyes, so dark they're almost black. He places his fist on his hip. It's obvious he's doing that to flex his bicep.

The corners of his mouth lower, and his fist drops away from his waist. "Where'd you get that bag?"

My hand instantly goes to the satchel's strap. "He gave it to me."

His eyes fix on mine. "My grandfather would never let it out of his sight."

"I was there. Um. At the accident." I sound insensitive. "I'm sorry for your loss. My name is Ana. Analiese Jordan."

"Thank you. I'm Marek Conte." He grabs the back of

his neck, and I look everywhere else but at him. The boys at my school don't look like him. He must work out a lot.

"Nice to meet you," I say.

"Why would he give it to you?" he asks, nodding at the satchel against my hip. "His bag?"

"I'm not sure, but he told me to return it to you." I remove the strap from my shoulder, step closer to him, and give him the bag. Our hands touch, and a rush of adrenaline surges through my body. It's a strange-encounter kind of day. First the Thor worshipper, and now Marek in all his bare-chested glory.

Marek stares at the bag for several beats before walking off while saying, "Again, thanks."

Is that it? I didn't drive all this way to not get any answers.

"Wait," I say.

He looks over his shoulder at me. "What? Is there something more?"

"Yes, as a matter of fact." I level him with my best *"it doesn't faze me that you don't have a shirt on"* look. "There's a list in that bag. It has my name on it. More importantly, it has my parents' names, too, and theirs are crossed off. Do you know why he put us on it?"

A confused look passes over his face, and his eyes drop to the bag. "I don't know. Come inside, and we'll check it out."

"Inside?" *With you?* No matter how hot the guy is, being alone with him is probably not a good idea. Some serial killers aren't bad looking. That's how they trick their prey.

"Yes," he says. "Don't worry. I won't bite. Plus, my gram

just made apple bread. Do you drink coffee?"

"That's like asking if I breathe."

He laughs. It's not genuine, but more like the laugh you do when you've heard a joke too many times before. "Good. We have something in common. Come on."

I trail him to the front and up the porch. The house has a small foyer, decorated in warm browns and shocks of red. Paintings crowd the walls. Aging flowers arranged in cut-glass vases sit on a long entryway table with sympathy cards stacked to the side. Probably from the funeral. My heart sinks at the thought.

He drops the bag on a bench by the door, grabs a T-shirt hanging off the edge, and pulls it over his head. I try not to watch the soft blue material slowly cover his extremely fit torso, but can't help it. His eyes meet mine just as I catch the last glimpse of his tanned skin above the waist of his shorts. The smile on his lips widens, and I quickly look away, pretending to study one of the paintings on the wall.

"My gramps's work." He smiles at the one my eyes are fixed on—a boy and his dog playing fetch with a red ball. "That's Bandit and me. I'm six there."

"He was really talented." And I'm not lying, like you do when someone is proud of their kid's work and it's horrible. The paintings are beautiful. "I bet they'd sell well—"

My words jam in my throat when my gaze lands on a painting of a young girl with dark hair, cradling a doll, a death's-head hawkmoth sitting on her arm.

"That girl is me."

Marek pours coffee from a French press into two mugs. He failed to mention that his grandmother had left with one of the loaves of apple bread. Says she's at her bridge group. I'm not sure it's a good idea to be alone with Marek. I don't know the guy. He could be dangerous. Well, his muscles are, anyway.

"That painting has to be a coincidence," he says. "How do you even know it is you?"

"The jean jacket. It has the same patches as mine. A unicorn and stars. I still have it. Of course, I don't wear it. It's too small." I'm rambling, trying to string my jumbled thoughts together. "Since I made it, it's one of a kind."

"So what are you saying? That my grandfather was stalking you? He has better things to do. *Had.* He *had* better…" He trails off, staring at the steam rising from the press as he pours coffee into his mug.

It looks like he isn't going to stop pouring.

"Watch it," I clip.

He blinks and places the press on the table. "Maybe he just so happened to be there painting when he saw you. He spent a lot of time in Fishtown. By the river. You were his inspiration or something like that."

"Maybe." I sound doubtful. "So then why was he watching me the day of the accident? And he knew my name."

He passes me a sugar bowl. "He said your name?"

I spoon the white granules into my mug. "Yes. He told me to run and that I was in danger. And my name's on that list with my parents."

"Right, yeah. That is strange." He lowers his head and studies the intricate lace in the tablecloth, then glances out the window. "But he was a bit eccentric."

"Yeah, I'd say." I have the feeling he isn't telling me something. There are times when a warning blares through my mind like the one that announces class is over at my school. And I know not to ignore it. I did that once while riding my bike and ended up at the bottom of a ditch. Long story.

The warning goes off, and it makes me uneasy, right when Marek turns his eyes away from me and stares out the bay window. There isn't anything out there to see but the lush green garden just past the rock-paved patio. And I'm pretty sure he's seen it many times before and wouldn't give it another glance on most other days. Other days than today. When he wants to hide something from me. Hide the fact that he knows more than he's letting on.

I shift in my seat.

Marek tears his gaze away from the window, a serious look on his face, so serious it makes me recoil.

"You should go," he says, the legs of his chair screeching across the tiles as he stands.

I shoot to my feet. "But…but what about that bag? You know something, don't you? You know why I'm on that list with my parents. Tell me why."

He lowers his head to avoid my pleading glare. "I know nothing."

I let out an exasperated breath and stomp my way to the door to show him my frustration. Before I reach the entry, he stops me.

"Wait," he says. "I don't know anything about that list

or what my grandfather was up to. This isn't my home. I live with my parents in Baltimore. I was just here for the… for my grams."

For the funeral, I'm sure he was going to say. "I'm sorry, that has to be tough."

"It is," he says. "Grams is having a difficult time. I practically had to force her to go to her bridge club. Anyway, my gramps was a secretive man. I wasn't blowing you off. Just thinking. Or, more like trying to decide if I should break into the basement."

I lift my eyebrows. "Break into the basement? Why would you have to do that?"

"My grandfather spent most of his time down there," he says. "It was off-limits. Not even my grams could go in. We haven't found the key to the door. She wanted to sort through his things and clean it up after the funeral. But it's lost."

I brighten. "Keys. There's a ring of them in the bag."

He glances around as if he's forgotten where he put the bag. I don't have to search for it. Ever since we entered the house and he placed the satchel on the bench by the door, it's been a leather beacon calling me.

"It's over here." I gather the bag and hand it to him.

He digs through the contents and retrieves the keys. Sadness crosses his face as he flips through them. The metal ring's tarnished by age. He stops on a skeleton key that strangely looks newer than the other ones that are modern.

"This is it," he says.

The light coming in from the windows beside the door glints across the silver key. On the tip of it are two tiny red bulbs. "That's unusual," I say, pointing them out.

He starts down the hall. "Come on. Let's see if it works."

Everything in the house is old. The solid wood doors are tall and thin.

The front of the house is bright and cheery, painted in yellows and creams. This part is dark and decorated in warm browns. We pass what looks to be the family room. Antique furniture and delicate figurines and vases with lace doilies under them sit on the tables between the chairs. There's a black onyx sculpture of a cat wearing one gold hoop earring and a thick necklace with hieroglyphs on it. Bastet. She's the Egyptian goddess of protection. It looks heavy and entirely out of place with all the other stuff.

There're more decaying floral arrangements placed throughout the house. I want to remove them. The drooping petals are like sad reminders of their recent loss.

Marek stops at the door near the back of the house, inserts the key, and tries to turn it in the lock. "It doesn't work—"

A bright red glow illuminates the keyhole. Metal sliding against metal sounds from the other side. A series of clicks go off, and the light goes out.

"That's interesting." Marek turns the knob and opens the door.

"More like creepy," I say.

He searches the wall for a switch and flips it up. The lights below flicker on, and I follow Marek down the steps.

It isn't your typical basement. This one has a stone staircase and wooden beams on the ceiling. The smell of cigar or pipe smoke attacks my nose. Marek reaches the bottom, and four computers on a long cherry wood desk hum to life.

"They must be connected to a sensor." He crosses the polished concrete floor to the desk.

"Wow, this is nice," I say, scoping the place. There're built-in bookcases on one wall and a seating area in front of it with expensive-looking leather couches. "Talk about a man cave."

Embedded in the wall above the desk are rows of security monitors—six down, six across. Marek clicks on the master power switch, and the screens blink to life. Each one is a live shot of a house or an apartment building.

"Was your grandfather in the CIA or something?" *Or worse, a voyeur.* I keep that to myself because the dude just lost the old man, after all.

"No." His eyes scan the images. "At least, I don't think so. He owns a butcher shop. Owned. Sold it. He's retired. Those two," he says, pointing at a pair of monitors on the top right. "That's the front and back of this house."

I try to keep my mind from going there, but there's no stopping it. A butcher? A great profession for a serial killer.

One of the screens catches my attention. My stomach drops. I recognize the red brick structure with the blue shutters. "That's my house. Why was he watching us?"

"I don't know." He searches around the desk and then kneels to inspect the floor. "There isn't a recorder. He must've just been monitoring people."

"Okay," I say. "I'm completely *freaked out.*"

Marek straightens. "Me, too. There've got to be answers in here somewhere. I'm going to check the drawers. You see if there's anything in that cabinet."

The cabinet has four doors. Behind the first two are office supplies. On the middle shelf is a stack of passports. I snatch one from the top and open it. The photograph is of Adam Conte, Marek's grandfather, but the name on the passport is Martin Cleary.

I check another one. Same picture, different name— Ted Johnson.

They all have his photo with an alias.

My finger bounces on the spine of each one as I count them. "There are fourteen."

Marek glances up from the drawer he's searching. "What's that?"

"Passports." I hold one up. "All with your grandfather's picture but different names. Why would he need these? I'll tell you. He was a spy, that's why."

He hurries over and flips through the passports. The look on his face changes from confusion to anger. He throws the stack across the room. "Who was he? What else was he hiding?"

I back up against the cabinet. This isn't really happening. Some old man was stalking me, and probably many others. The thing is, I didn't even know I was being followed or monitored. It's as if bony fingers scratch up my back and over my skull. I've never felt so vulnerable before. Then a new thought comes to me. One that rips my heart completely out.

Did he kill my parents and my uncle?

"The list." My voice sounds shaky, and my legs wobble

a little. "He was watching us. Why was he watching us?"

Marek grabs the back of his neck, and his eyes flick in my direction. "I don't know, but we're going to find out. Let's keep searching. The answers have to be here."

I should run. Go to the police. Tell them some crazy— maybe perverted—old man was stalking me. But he's dead now, and I need answers. Why would my family be so important to this man?

And how had he hidden his secret life from his family?

IF YOU ENJOYED THIS EXCERPT, PICK UP
ANALIESE RISING
WHEREVER BOOKS AND EBOOKS ARE SOLD.

LOST MEETS *THE MAZE RUNNER* IN THIS
IRRESISTIBLE YA THRILLER.

ECHOES

by Alice Reed

They wake on a deserted island. Fiona and Miles, high school
enemies now stranded together. No memory of how they got
there. No plan to follow, no hope to hold on to.

Each step forward reveals the mystery behind the forces
that brought them here. And soon, the most chilling discovery:
something else is on the island with them.

Something that won't let them leave alive.

THRILLING NEW SERIES FROM
NEW YORK TIMES BEST-SELLING AUTHOR
SARA WOLF

BRING ME THEIR HEARTS

Zera is a Heartless—the immortal, unaging soldier of a witch. Bound to the witch Nightsinger, Zera longs for freedom from the woods they hide in. With her heart in a jar under Nightsinger's control, she serves the witch unquestioningly.

Until Nightsinger asks Zera for a prince's heart in exchange for her own, with one addendum: if she's discovered infiltrating the court, Nightsinger will destroy Zera's heart rather than see her tortured by the witch-hating nobles.

Crown Prince Lucien d'Malvane hates the royal court as much as it loves him—every tutor too afraid to correct him and every girl jockeying for a place at his darkly handsome side. No one can challenge him—until the arrival of Lady Zera. She's inelegant, smart-mouthed, carefree, and out for his blood. The prince's honor has him quickly aiming for her throat.

So begins a game of cat and mouse between a girl with nothing to lose and a boy who has it all.

Winner takes the loser's heart.

Literally.

THE BOURNE IDENTITY MEETS *BOY NOBODY*
IN THIS YA ASSASSIN THRILLER.

PROJECT
PANDORA

by Aden Polydoros

Tyler Bennett trusts no one. Just another foster kid bounced from home to home, he's learned that lesson the hard way. Cue world's tiniest violin. But when strange things start happening—waking up with bloody knuckles and no memory of the night before or the burner phone he can't let out of his sight—Tyler starts to wonder if he can even trust himself.

Even stranger, the girl he's falling for has a burner phone just like his. Finding out what's really happening only leads to more questions…questions that could get them both killed. It's not like someone's kidnapping teens lost in the system and brainwashing them to be assassins or anything, right? And what happens to rogue assets who defy control?

In a race against the clock, they'll have to uncover the truth behind Project Pandora and take it down—before they're reactivated. Good thing the program spent millions training them to kick ass...

entangled teen

an imprint of Entangled Publishing LLC